From Third to Home

Companion Publications

COMPANION **P**UBLICATIONS LLC

To my late father, Morris C. Paynter: Thank you for instilling in me the love of The Game. This one's for you, Dad.

From Third to Home

Companion Publications

by
Chris Paynter

This is a work of fiction. All characters, locales and events are either products of the author's imagination or are used fictitiously.

FROM THIRD TO HOME

Cover design by Ann Phillips
Editor: Nann Dunne

A Companion Publications Book
Published by Companion Publications LLC

www.ckpaynter.com

ISBN: 978-1-942204-12-1

First edition: April, 2016

Printed in the United States of America and in the United Kingdom.

Acknowledgements

This series was born in June 2009 with Blue Feather Books' publication of *Playing for First*. In May 2011, the series continued with *Two for the Show*. Once again, I'd like to thank Blue Feather publishers Emily Reed and Jane Vollbrecht for their faith in the story and in my writing. Em and Jane, I hope you like Companion Publications' continuation of the series.

In my opinion, Nann Dunne is one of the best editors in this business. I thank her again for her work with me on this book. She was meticulous as we traveled through the many, many… many passes of the manuscript. Each pass refined the book even more. I tease her about being a rabid Philadelphia Phillies fan since my loyalties lie with the Reds. It's fun simply to be a fan, though, and to stick with our teams through thick and thin. After all, that's the true definition of a fan.

A special thank-you to my beta reader, Erin Saluta. She offered invaluable suggestions and helped polish the book even further. You're the best, Erin! And a huge thank-you to ebook formatter extraordinaire, Toni Whitaker. You rock!

I especially would like to thank the fans of the series. You've been so patient as you waited for the publication of this book. I'm sure it didn't help when you'd see "Coming Soon! *From Third to Home*!" in the front pages of my last couple of releases. I'd like to explain the delay.

My father was diagnosed with Stage IV lung cancer in January 2012. After battling the disease for sixteen months, he passed away April 3, 2013. Although I was relieved he was no longer suffering, it was still a blow when he left this world. My dad taught me the love of The Game. We bonded over watching the Reds, as well as IU basketball and Indianapolis Colts football games. He loved the *Playing for First* series, because we thought a woman could make it to the major leagues. And since I connected the series to him, it was hard for me to write this book. In a way, I thought I would be letting him go if I finished it.

Then my wonderful wife, Phyllis, told me that I wouldn't be letting him go. Instead, I would be honoring him and his memory in the continuation of the series. It's been a hard road to walk, writing this book. In September 2015, I attended Lori L. Lake's Autumn Women's Writing Retreat in Rockaway Beach, Oregon, and pushed myself to write 23,000 words in five days. With that impetus, I finished the first draft when I returned home. In the months since my return, I still struggled with my grief. Grief is a fickle thing. You don't simply say, "Okay, I'm sad. Now let's move on." It hits you at different times.

Thank God for Phyllis. I mean that in every sense of the word. She's my heartbeat and has been since the day we met in December 2001. She inspires me and offers support when I'm at my lowest. We've had many conversations about my father and shared laughs over things he said or did. None of the books I've published would've been possible without the love we share. Thank you, Phyllis. I love you.

To my dad… I felt you urging me to write this book, even when I was reluctant to do so. In the midst of struggling with the writing, someone would send me an email or post on my Facebook page, saying how much they enjoyed my books. I know that was you, encouraging me to keep at it. You joked that I could write a seventeen-page dedication to you in this one. Well, it ended up being the entire book. So, thank you for everything. I hope you enjoy the story, Dad.

And to my readers… I hope you enjoy the story, too!

Chapter 1

"Ohmygodohmygodohmygod! I can't believe I'm standing here getting Amy Perry's autograph again. It's like it's not real, you know? Me and my best friend decided at the last minute to make a trip to Arizona for spring training because we just love you."

Amy waited for the petite blonde with the butch haircut to take a breath, but she wasn't finished yet.

"We, like, traveled to Phoenix two years ago to watch you play in the Arizona Fall League when the Reds signed you with the Mesa Solar Sox. Does that help your memory? We had you autograph the back of our T-shirts."

"No, I'm sor—"

"You're sure you don't remember us?" The woman, probably in her early twenties, motioned to her dark-haired companion. "What about when you were in Double-A Chattanooga? We drove down to a couple of your games. But we're not, like, stalkers or anything. Right, Candy?"

"Naw. We just like watching you play."

"Then last year, when you came up in May from Triple-A Indianapolis and were with the Reds for the season, how many games did we go to?" the blonde asked her friend.

"Wow. I dunno. Twenty?"

"That's a lot of games—" Amy started to say.

The blonde cut Amy off again. "We wanted to go to a lot more, but we have to work. Sorry about that loss at the end of the season. I bet that double play you hit into at the end of the tiebreaker game against the Rockies still haunts you, huh?"

By now, Amy wanted to smack the woman over the head. She'd had nightmares in the off-season over that play that had ended any chance for the Reds to make the playoffs.

"Amy! Amy! Can I have your autograph?" a little boy yelled, hopping up and down beside the blonde.

Thank God, Amy thought. A reprieve. "I need to sign some more," she told the two women. "Thanks for your support." She managed to give them a tight smile before signing the boy's baseball and two more that kids thrust in her face. She took the program someone offered to her, not raising her head.

"Could you make that out to 'the love of my life'?"

Amy's mouth pulled into a grin before she looked into the dark eyes of her wife, Stacy.

"I don't think so, ma'am. I'm taken," Amy said.

Stacy's face lit up and her dimples became more pronounced. She leaned over the railing and kissed Amy on the cheek. "Right answer, babe. Frankie asked if we wanted to go out to dinner tonight with her and Lisa. Is that okay?"

Amy spotted the reporters who hung out on the field at the Reds' Goodyear, Arizona, spring training camp. Lisa Collins was talking with another sportswriter, Sarah Swift. Amy caught Lisa's eye and waved. Lisa waved back.

"Sure. The guys told me about a great Mexican restaurant. Would that be okay?" she asked Stacy.

"Sounds good."

"Quit talking to your wife, Perry. We've got some loosening up to do."

Amy half-waved toward her friend, third baseman Nick Sanders. "Keep your uni on, Sandy. I'm almost done."

"The next voice you hear won't be mine." He trotted off into the outfield.

Max Murphy, the manager, stood in the infield with his hands on his hips. He jabbed a thumb toward the outfield.

"Guess I'd better let you go, huh?" Stacy said with a teasing lilt. "Don't want to get your boss upset on your first day in camp."

Amy squeezed her hand and jogged out to right field to join Nick.

Lying on the ground, Nick stretched out his legs and grabbed his toes. Amy plopped down beside him and did the same.

"How are you and Stacy doing? Ryan and I didn't see you much the past couple months."

Amy and Stacy had married in the off-season in late October in Provincetown. It had been a simple wedding, presided over by a local minister. The press hadn't been informed about it until afterward. Lisa and Frankie witnessed for them. They'd kept it low key, but Nick and Ryan had flown out to be there, too.

"Come to think of it, haven't seen much of you since you and Stacy went on your honeymoon, although we understood the need to have some alone time." He shifted his right leg to the side to stretch his hamstring, and Amy mimicked him.

They stood up and continued stretching out their quads, grabbing one leg and lifting it behind them, then the other.

"We're great."

"Any more talk about a baby?"

"We're still thinking about the timing. I want to be there for the birth, so if we try, it'll be during the season. We just don't know when yet."

"Yeah, Ryan and I aren't sure when we'll adopt, either."

"It may not be until next year—" Amy stopped and whipped her head around. "What did you say?"

Amy could tell Nick was trying to maintain a straight face, but then he broke into a huge grin. "We're hoping to adopt after I retire this year. We've already made some phone calls and plan to start the legal paperwork soon."

She grabbed him in a bear hug and pounded him on the back. "That's fantastic! You both will be wonderful parents. Ryan's such a supportive partner to you."

Nick blew out a breath. "I don't know. It's a lot of responsibility."

Murphy walked by, accompanied by his coaches. "Warm-ups is where you warm up, not stand around and chat."

"Sorry, Skip." Amy started her wind sprints, and Nick trotted beside her.

They didn't talk until they turned. "Ryan was so happy for you and Stacy. We'd thought about the surrogate route, but I don't want anyone changing their mind. That'd be heartbreaking."

They switched to crossovers. Geesh, Amy thought. Sometimes it seems we do more warming up than playing. After another thirty minutes or so of exercises, Nick punched Amy lightly on the arm.

"Come on. Murph wants us to get going."

* * *

"What do you think, Collins?" Sarah Swift stood behind the batting cage with Lisa.

"You mean about their chances?"

"No. What about the weather? Think it'll rain?" Sarah rolled her eyes. "Yes, about their chances this year."

"I swear, Swift, you're such a smart-ass."

"But you love me."

"Whatever."

Donny Crews, the Reds hitting coach, smacked a ball to Nick at third, who fired it to second baseman, Tim Rawls. Rawls did a quick pivot and relayed it to Amy. "I think they'll have a fire burning in their bellies. Not only because of the way they ended the season last year but also because of Nick's retirement."

Nick dove for a line drive and snatched it out of the air. "Lord," Sarah muttered, "the man plays hard the first day of spring training. Ever hear any reason for his retirement?"

"I'm thinking he's tired of being banged up. That hamstring hit him hard last year. I spoke with Murph. He said it's all healed."

Amy jumped high for a ball headed into right field and caught it in the webbing of her glove.

"How's Amy doing with the way the year ended?" Sarah asked.

"She took it hard the first few weeks or so, but her relationship with Stacy helped smooth all that out."

"And they're good? It was rough with Amy's mother's passing last year."

"They worked through all that and are better than ever."

Sarah nodded. "Glad to hear it."

Stacy was snapping pictures of Amy. When she pulled the camera down, she spotted Lisa and waved.

"Damn, she's cute," Sarah said, following Lisa's line of sight.

"And very, very taken."

"Hell, I know that, goofus. Doesn't mean I can't look, does it?" Lisa laughed.

"How's Frankie?" Sarah asked as Amy flubbed a catch.

"Watch it into your glove, Perry!" Murphy shouted.

"Man, he's wound a little tight this early, don't you think,

Collins?"

"Like I said, fire in the belly. Frankie's doing great. I told her to sleep in this morning."

"God, don't tell me, all right? You two can be sickeningly sweet. And for single me, it's a little hard to take."

"Do you need me to set you up with someone?"

Sarah glared at her.

Lisa held her hand up in defense. "Kidding."

They watched the infield practice until the team broke off into groups. Donny went with the outfielders. Amy was with the group ready to begin situational batting with Wally, the bullpen coach. First up was bunting.

They kept quiet as each player took their turn. Nick laid down a bunt in front of the plate, followed by one to the third base side and one to the first base side. After fifteen minutes of bunting practice, batting practice began.

The day passed quickly, but not fast enough for Lisa. She was hot as hell. She and Sarah got in a few quotes from the players. Lisa's articles were mostly feature articles in the spring, just as they'd been with the Indianapolis Indians when she was covering them for Minor League.com.

She walked with Sarah toward the lot where the reporters parked.

"Any plans tonight, Sarah?" Lisa keyed open her car door.

"Just me and a couple of beers in front of the TV." Sarah put her satchel in the backseat of her rental car.

"You're welcome to join us. Frankie and I are meeting up with Amy and Stacy for dinner. I'm not sure where we're headed, but we can always swing by and pick you up on our way."

Sarah tapped the top of her car and cocked her head. "Having dinner with you four sounds much more exciting than watching ESPN. What time?"

"About 6:30? I think Frankie was asking for dinner at 7:00."

"Casual?"

"Well, yeah. Would we do anything else?"

"How the hell should I know? You and Frankie seem to enjoy those fancy places sometimes."

"T-shirt and shorts. How does that sound?"

"Sounds like I'll definitely be coming." Sarah got into her car and drove away.

Lisa was about to do the same but stopped when she heard Amy shouting her name. Stacy was right behind her.

"Hey, Lisa. The guys mentioned Macayo's. It's about a mile up the road. Supposed to be great, authentic Mexican food."

"Sounds perfect. Do you mind if Sarah tags along?" Lisa asked.

"As long as you both don't decide to ambush me for an interview."

Lisa scrunched up her face as if thinking about it. "That's not a bad idea."

Amy pointed at her. "Now, stop."

"I'm joking. How do you get to this place?"

Amy gave her directions, and she and Stacy walked over to their SUV.

"Decided to bring your Equinox for spring training this time?" Lisa called.

"Yeah, it felt more comfortable than renting something that both of us would have been unfamiliar with for the time we're here."

"Makes sense."

Amy motioned to Lisa's sedan. "How's that working for you?"

"I'm missing my Sebring, but it'll do. We'll see you around 7:00?"

"Yup."

* * *

"Frankie, I'm home!"

Frankie came out of the bathroom dressed comfortably in shorts and an old T-shirt with the logo from her bar in Indianapolis, the Watering Hole, stitched on the upper left. Her short, salt-and-pepper hair was still wet from her shower.

Lisa's heart did a little flip as it always did when she saw Frankie. She walked over and gave her a long kiss.

"Good to see you, too, Leese." Frankie leaned in for another quick kiss then smacked her on the butt. "Now, off with you, woman. Grab that shower so we can get going."

Lisa brushed past her. "I thought we weren't meeting up with everyone until 7:00?"

"I saw a shop I'd like to hit before we go to the restaurant."

Lisa stripped down and stepped into the shower. "You don't mind if Sarah joins us, do you?" she shouted over the sound of the water.

"Why would I mind?"

Frankie's voice sounded closer. Lisa pulled the stall door slightly open. Frankie stood in front of the mirror, brushing her fingers through her hair.

"I don't know. I wasn't sure if maybe you wanted it to just be the four of us," Lisa said as she scrubbed up her washcloth.

"I like Sarah. It'll be fun."

Lisa finished showering and dressed in shorts and a T-shirt. She called Sarah to see if she'd like to join them shopping. After Sarah quit laughing, Lisa figured she'd prefer to be picked up later. Frankie and Lisa drove to the shop that sold Native American artifacts and spent an hour shopping. They pulled up in front of Sarah's hotel at 6:45 and made it to Macayo's on time.

Amy, dressed in a red polo and jeans, and Stacy, in khaki shorts and a tank top, sat in a booth in the back. Amy waved at them.

When they got closer, Amy and Stacy stood and hugged Lisa and Frankie. Amy shook Sarah's hand and motioned to Stacy.

"Sarah, this is my wife, Stacy. Stacy, this is Sarah Swift. She's a reporter for *Baseball Weekly*."

"Nice to meet you," Sarah murmured.

Lisa cut her a look. She'd never seen this side of Sarah before. Almost… blushing.

They took their seats, and the server came for their drink order.

"How's it feel getting back at it, Amy?" Sarah asked.

"Great, actually. Can't wait for camp to end already and get started on the season."

"Is Murphy still having you bat third?" Sarah asked. "And how's Nick Sanders handling the start of his last spring training camp?"

Amy shot Lisa a glance across the table.

"Yo, Swift," Lisa said. "How about we focus on these fantastic chips and awesome salsa instead of grilling Amy? We're not here to interview her, remember?"

Sarah had the common sense to look sheepish. "I'm sorry, Amy. I didn't mean to make you uncomfortable. I'm not used to social outings as Lisa can attest to. Right, Lisa?"

"Yes. I can back up that statement one hundred percent."

"I'll answer your questions, Sarah," Amy said. "Yes, I'll still be batting third. Nick seems fine. I think he's looking forward to retirement."

An almost imperceptible smile creased Amy's lips, but Lisa knew her well enough to catch it. Hell, now *she* was curious. But she curbed the reporter side of her personality and focused on being there with a friend.

Talk drifted to other topics besides baseball and into more personal matters. Like Amy and Stacy's decision to have a child. They just didn't know when.

Amy grabbed a chip, dipped it into the salsa, and crunched into it. She finished chewing. "We're not sure if it'll be this year or next. There are times when we're absolutely certain it'll be this year, and then we think, no, let's give ourselves another year together."

"You'll know when the time's right, Aim." She caught Stacy's eye. "Both of you. And you'll make great moms."

Amy put her arm around Stacy. "Stacy will be fantastic."

Stacy leaned her head on Amy's shoulder. "You will be, too."

Watching them together, Lisa couldn't help but remember how closeted Amy had been when Amy and she had first met. The mildest show of affection—even touching—had, well, freaked her out. Once, Lisa reached over to wipe some ketchup off Amy's chin and Amy pulled away like a scared bird.

Amy nodded slightly, as if she knew exactly what Lisa had been thinking.

Lisa put her arm around Frankie. "I'm not sure we'd ever have kids, right, Frankie?"

Frankie had been sipping on her Coke and started sputtering. Lisa tapped her lightly on her back.

"It's not *that* far-fetched is it, hon?" she asked with a crooked grin.

"God, Leese, quit trying to give me a heart attack."

Lisa ruffled Frankie's hair. "I'm messing with you. I think with all your nieces and nephews, we're covered as far as kids go."

"You can always babysit for Amy and Stacy, sweetheart," Frankie said with a smirk.

It was Lisa's turn to choke on her drink. She finally caught her breath enough to speak. "Um… despite how much I love you two, I'm not sure I'm the go-to-gal for babysitting. I've never changed a diaper in my life."

They all chimed in with "you're kidding," and "you've got to be shitting me."

Lisa held up her hand. "Nope, and it's my life's goal to *never* change one."

"Oh, it's not that bad, Lisa," Sarah said as the waiter delivered their food.

"Speak for yourself, Sarah," Frankie said. "I've changed some of my nieces' and nephews' diapers. At times, it resembled toxic waste."

"But you love them all." Lisa bumped shoulders with her.

"I absolutely love them all… but not their dirty diapers."

"Okay," Amy said, "I don't know about everybody else, but I think we need to get off this subject with the food in front of us." She took a bite of her chimichaunga.

They all murmured their agreement and dug into their food. After an hour of eating and chatting, it was time to call it a night. Frankie, Lisa, and Sarah said good night to Amy and Stacy as they reached their cars.

"See you tomorrow at the park, Aim." Lisa slid in behind the wheel of her car.

"Bright and early." Amy opened Stacy's door for her. "I would say with rings on my fingers and bells on my toes, but you know me better than that."

"Uh, yeah." Lisa powered up her window, gave them a wave, and drove away.

Chapter 2

"Jesus, Sandy, you don't have to rip my glove off this early in camp," Amy shouted. She wasn't exaggerating either. Her hand still stung from Nick's throw.

"Buck up, Perry!"

Amy flipped her glove off and shook her hand out with her middle finger pointed toward Nick.

"Perry, quit goofing off!" Murphy yelled. He glared at her from where he stood with Lisa and the other reporters.

"Damn, Murph," Amy muttered under her breath.

Max Murphy cupped his hand over his ear. "What's that, Perry?"

Amy tossed the ball across the diamond without responding. Nick grinned when he threw the ball back. Amy pointed her glove at him, as if to say "wait." He shook his head and kept smiling.

A little over a week had passed since the position players had reported to Goodyear, and they were about to play their first spring training game against the Cleveland Indians. Even though it was only a spring training game, Amy had butterflies as she settled into her position for the first batter.

Roberto Sanchez, the Reds right-hander, hurled a fastball that the umpire called a strike. The crowd cheered, and the game was underway.

The next pitch was a curve on the inside part of the plate to the left-handed batter. He screamed a liner right at Amy. It got to her so fast, she didn't have time to react. She felt the ball hit her nose with a loud crack. Everything went black. The next thing she knew, Nick was standing over her with Murphy beside him.

"Amy, Amy, you with us?" Nick asked.

If the worry on his face was any indication, Amy didn't look so great. She raised her hand to her face. She felt the warm stickiness of blood and stared at her hand. She tried to sit up. Maybe that wasn't such a good idea as everything started spinning.

Tom, the head trainer, and Barry, one of his assistants, came into view. Tom held a towel to Amy's nose.

"Take it easy, Perry." He lowered the towel and pressed his thumbs against the bridge of her nose. She flinched. "Yeah, I think it's broken. Can you sit up now?"

"I… I think so." She slowly sat up.

"Damn, Perry, you're already getting shiners," Nick said.

Tom and Barry helped her stand up and held onto her elbows as she swayed a little.

"God, I hate that Stacy is here for this," she said as she allowed them to lead her to the dugout. A ripple of polite applause spread around Goodyear Ballpark. She ventured a peek into the stands and caught Stacy's worried expression. Amy waved at her and mouthed, "I'm okay."

Once they got into the dugout, she asked Tom about the damage.

"Definitely broken. I could feel the cartilage moving around in there. I think you may need stitches too to bring that cut back together. We'll get you to the emergency room."

Amy thought of her trip to the emergency room right before the playoff game at the end of last season. It wasn't a pleasant memory. She still had nightmares about that damn needle.

"You're sure it needs stitches?" Amy couldn't believe she'd been injured on the first play of the game. Not just a game—a spring training game.

Murphy leaned over and peered at her.

"I've seen my fair share of cuts, Perry. That definitely needs to be sewn up."

Amy sighed.

"You're not a baby about injuries, so let's get you to the hospital."

Amy took one last look at first base where her replacement, Brett Colston, had taken over. She followed Tom down the steps into the tunnel that led to the clubhouse. It didn't surprise her that Stacy was already there, pacing. The worry and concern etched on her face tugged at Amy's heart.

"I'm okay, Stace. Just a broken nose and a cut that needs stitching." Amy's voice sounded funny as she kept the towel pressed to her nose.

Stacy reached a tentative, shaking hand to Amy's curls. She brushed them off Amy's forehead.

"What are we going to do with you?" Stacy asked. "Let me see." She gently lifted the towel away from Amy's nose. Her brow furrowed in concern. "Oh, babe."

"That bad, huh?"

"I hate to say it, but, yeah. I'll go with you. Is that okay?" Stacy asked Tom.

"Sure. I don't think an ambulance is needed."

"You're kidding, right?" Amy caught the playful glint in his eyes. "I'm glad everyone's having fun with this. I'm never going to hear the end of it from the guys."

"Come on, Perry. Let's get Barry to take you to the hospital before you mess up any more of the clubhouse floor."

* * *

Two hours later, Amy was lying on the hotel bed with an ice pack on her nose.

"Look at it this way, it'll add character to your face," Stacy said from the kitchenette. "The stitches make you sexier. Besides, the doctor said you passed the concussion protocol."

The bed shifted as Stacy sat down beside her. Amy felt Stacy's fingers sift through her hair. She fluttered her eyes open.

"There's always that." Amy grabbed her hand and held her palm to her cheek. "Have I told you lately how much I love you?"

"Yes. This morning as a matter of fact, but I never grow tired of hearing it." Stacy leaned over and placed her lips to Amy's. The kiss was soft and as familiar as warm sunlight on a summer morning.

"Remember our talk at dinner the other night?" Amy asked.

Stacy raised her eyebrows. "Yeah?"

"I've been thinking…"

"Well, don't think too hard." Stacy smoothed her fingertips over Amy's creased brow. "You'll hurt yourself."

"I'm serious, Stace. Why not this summer?"

"Why not this summer for…"

"The baby."

"Oh, Amy—"

"No, wait. We said we'd think about it, but I don't see why we can't—"

Stacy put her fingers against Amy's lips and nodded, tears in her eyes. "Yes."

Amy sat up and pulled Stacy into her arms. "I was thinking that a little to the left or a little to the right and that line drive would have been in my eye. And who knows where I'd be? Or if I could play. At the end of last season, I realized when I saw you standing there, waiting on me after the loss—you're what matters in my life. Baseball is great. I love the game." She squeezed Stacy's shoulders. "But I love you, so, so, much more."

Stacy sniffed. "I can think of nothing better than starting a family with you."

"I want more than one. Can we do that?"

Stacy gave her a big smile. "I don't see why not."

Amy shook her head slightly. "I have no idea how you go about doing this, though."

"Don't worry. I've got it covered."

"Oh, you do, do you?"

"I've been talking to Lainie. Remember? She and Roselle have Teresa?"

"They're perfect to talk to. I can't believe I didn't think of it."

"Well, you do have other things on your mind. Like, oh, I don't know, staying focused on your game, getting ready for spring training, being prepared for the season and what you want to accomplish. Should I go on?"

"Still…"

Stacy leaned on her elbow and caressed Amy's cheek. "Still nothing. You're perfect, Amy Perry."

Amy thought back to the night she felt she'd lost Stacy. She herself had felt so lost since her mother's passing that she'd almost left a bar with another woman.

Stacy interrupted her painful memory. "What's wrong?"

"Hmm?"

"You were thinking of something serious."

Yes, it was definitely serious. She brushed her lips to Stacy's.

"It's okay now. Why don't we give Lainie a call?"

* * *

"Skip, I'm fine. Even the doctor said I didn't have a concussion." Amy was having a hard time convincing Murphy that she was good to go for the game the next day.

Nick grabbed his glove and snorted as he passed by Amy on his way to the field.

"It's not funny, Nick!" She turned back to Murphy who was still shaking his head. "I can see the ball, Murph. I'll be—"

Murphy held up his hand. "Need I remind you we're only in spring training? And need I remind you that today's only the second game? I talked it over with Tom. A couple days to get the swelling down isn't going to hurt."

"But—"

"No. That's final. Sit next to Donny and try to learn more about hitting. Not that you need that much more help, but it's still a good idea. Just don't sit next to me and whine the entire game, all right?"

Amy sighed. "Fine."

"You sound like my wife when I've pissed her off." Murphy stepped up the stairs to take the lineup card to the home plate umpire.

"Shit."

"Hey, what am I? Chopped liver?" Donny asked her.

"No."

"Good. Then why don't we watch and learn? We need you to work on pulling the ball even more this season, Amy. You're a great hitter, but you have more power than you give yourself credit for. Turn on that inside fastball and send it where it belongs. Either up against the left field wall or into the bleachers."

So, that's what Amy did. Sat next to Donny Crews, the Reds hitting coach, and discussed hitting for the duration of the game. The Reds beat the Indians 3-2. Amy grabbed her unused glove and equipment and clattered down the stairs to the clubhouse with the rest of her teammates. She quickly changed into street clothes. No reason to shower.

Lisa was interviewing Nick next to Amy. Before she had a

chance to leave, Lisa finished with her interview and asked how she was doing.

"Damn, Aim. That looks painful."

Amy gingerly touched her nose. "It's not exactly pain-free."

"And those shiners of yours…" Lisa's lips twitched.

"Go ahead. It's okay to make fun of me."

"Nah. I'm just giving you a hard time. When do you think you'll be back out there?"

"Probably Thursday against the Rockies. Hey, when you're done here, want to get a beer?"

"Sure, anything bothering you?"

"No, just wanted to talk to my friend."

"Give me about fifteen more minutes, and we can head out of here."

* * *

"So, what's up?" Lisa popped some peanuts in her mouth and took a swig of her Michelob. She met Amy's gaze but was glad to see nothing seemed out of order.

"It's Stacy and me…"

Then again… Lisa's heart did a little skip. "You're not having trouble, are you?"

"Oh, no, no. Nothing like that. I told her I thought we could start on the baby thing this summer."

"You're shitting me. That's fantastic." Lisa clapped her on the back.

Amy picked at the label of her bottle. "Yeah."

"Don't act so excited about it," Lisa teased. Then she noticed Amy's serious expression. "Hey, I'm kidding."

"It's not that. You're fine. I'm a little worried about being a mom. I mean I'm the one who suggested we try now. That freak play yesterday made me think how fast everything could be over."

"What? You mean life?"

"No, I mean my career. I want to do this now while I still have a good income."

Lisa nudged her shoulder. "You're not thinking of retiring, are you?"

"Baseball's something I really can't see me doing much longer if we have a kid. And I really, really want us to have kids."

"Aim, there are a lot of ballplayers with families. They make it work."

"But I'm not them. I'd want to be there as much as possible. This summer, we'd still have my income from playing to pay for the pregnancy. We talked about it last night. It isn't cheap. I knew that, but damn."

Lisa tried to imagine the day when she wouldn't see Amy out on the field. It was hard.

"Hey, didn't mean to go all serious on you there, Lisa."

"What? Oh, no. I get what you're saying. How much longer would you play, you think?"

"This season for sure. Maybe next. Hell, if we won the Series this year, that'd be a great way to go out on top, right?"

"Stacy's okay with this?"

Again, Amy went back to picking the bottle label.

"Aim?"

"I haven't told her yet."

"I take it you think she won't be happy?"

Amy took a sip of beer. "No. It's not that. I think she'd feel I'd regret it." She shook her head. "But I wouldn't, Lisa. I've lived my dream. I got to the bigs. Made it to the show. But having a family with Stacy? That would be the ultimate dream."

Lisa put her arm around Amy's shoulders and squeezed. "If this is what makes you happy, then I'm happy for you, my friend. There's just one thing."

"Yeah?"

"Remember. I don't do diapers."

* * *

Lisa held Frankie in her arms and stroked her shoulder. They were home again in Cincinnati and had spent the afternoon making love. Tomorrow would be the beginning of six months of craziness for Lisa. While they'd still share times like these, it would be a lot more hectic. When Lisa traveled with the team, there'd be days, if not more than a week, in between seeing one another.

Frankie pulled out of her arms and lay back. "Come here, you, and let me hold you for a while."

"No argument from me," Lisa murmured. She cuddled against Frankie's right shoulder. She lightly trailed her fingers along the mastectomy scar. Without thinking, she leaned over and brushed her lips against the slightly raised skin.

Frankie tilted Lisa's chin up. "You take my breath away some times."

Lisa moved to capture Frankie's lips in a deep, languorous kiss. Desire throbbed through her body, and she lowered her hand down to Frankie's wetness.

"God, you feel good." She focused on Frankie's eyes as she thumbed Frankie's clit and dipped her fingers into her opening. "Come for me again, Frankie." She steadily pushed into her until Frankie gasped and tensed. After the throbbing had subsided around her fingers, Lisa slowly eased out.

Lisa kissed Frankie again and fell back into her arms.

"You trying to wreck me, woman?" Frankie said in a teasing voice.

"That's my intention. How am I doing?"

"Do you hear me complaining?"

Lisa chuckled. "No."

They lay in comfortable silence as the shadows engulfed their room.

Frankie finally spoke. "I hate I won't be here for opening day tomorrow, but we have the state health inspector coming in bright and early. I especially hate I have to leave you in a couple of hours."

Lisa's heart sank. It had already begun. She loved her job, and she was proud of Frankie's ownership of the Watering Hole. But sometimes, damn it, she wanted to hide away for weeks on end. Especially after getting used to being together all the time in the off-season. She refused to let those thoughts ruin what they were sharing now.

"Touch me again, Frankie," she whispered and moved onto her back, pulling Frankie with her.

"Gladly, Leese. Gladly…"

* * *

Monday, April 4, dawned bright and sunny with the cool crispness of an early spring day in southwestern Ohio. The parade through downtown had proceeded without a hitch. Lisa already had some pre-game quotes. Now it was time for the first pitch.

She settled into her seat next to Sarah.

"Hey, Lisa. You're awfully cheery. Need I ask why?" Sarah said low enough for no one else to hear them. The press box hadn't filled up yet, but a few reporters sat close enough to possibly overhear their conversation.

"No, you needn't." Lisa plugged in her laptop.

"Damn, woman. You're a tad touchy."

"Sorry. Frankie left late last night for Indy, and I'm missing her. Sometimes…"

Sarah made a motion with her hand. "Sometimes?"

"I get tired of being without her. It's the start of the season, and it hits me harder. I'm sure once I get into the rhythm of covering the games, it'll be okay." Lisa shook her head. "Who am I kidding? I don't think I'll ever get used to it."

"Didn't we have this discussion last year?"

"Yeah, yeah, yeah," Lisa muttered. "Doesn't mean it changes how I feel *this* year."

She waited for Sarah to say something. She looked over. The color had drained from Sarah's tanned face. Sarah was staring at something or someone below them. Lisa followed her gaze. "What?"

"It's her," Sarah whispered.

Lisa finally noticed the woman below. She was attractive, of average build, but she carried herself like she was sure of her place. What Lisa had thought was sandy blonde hair was really gray sprinkled liberally throughout her short cut. Lisa glanced back at Sarah.

"Her?" It suddenly dawned on Lisa. Only one woman could cause this kind of reaction from her friend. She leaned closer. "Is that Mary?"

Sarah nodded.

Sarah had talked last season about Mary, her ex, and how she'd been the love of her life. Lisa could only imagine what was going through her mind. She didn't think it was possible for her friend to get any paler, but she did, and her eyes widened and seemed to follow the woman's steady progression. Before Lisa knew it, Mary was in their row, standing beside Sarah.

"I thought that was you," Mary said in a soft voice, tinged with a slight southern drawl. "How have you been, Sarah?" Lisa thought she had a touch of sadness in her tone.

"I've been…" Sarah cleared her throat. "I've been well, Mary. How are you?"

"I'm well. I'm here covering 'Opening Day in America.'" Mary framed the words with air quotes. "The *Seattle Times* thought it'd be fun to have a spread on it this year. We have reporters in various cities. Cincinnati, of course, since it's such a holiday here." Mary tilted her head at Lisa.

"Oh, I'm sorry," Sarah said. "This is Lisa Collins. She covers the Reds for Major League.com. Lisa, this is Mary Jacobson. She's a reporter for the *Times*."

Lisa held out her hand. "Nice to meet you. Sarah has said great things about you." Lisa felt Sarah's stare but ignored it. Damn it, there was something still there between them, and if Sarah wasn't going to do anything about it, Lisa could maybe help it along.

A genuine smile creased Mary's lips. "She has?"

Sarah's pale face now couldn't be any redder.

Mary stood there a few seconds as if hesitant to leave. She met Lisa's gaze again. "Well, it's nice to meet you, Lisa. Good to see you again, Sarah."

She started back down the stairs to her seat. Sarah finally spoke. "Mary?"

Mary turned back.

"You look great."

Mary's face lit up. "Thank you, Sarah. You do, too."

Before she got farther away, Lisa asked, "Would you like to join us after the game? We usually head to Tim's Place for a beer. We'd love to have you come with us."

"Well…"

"Please, Mary. I'd love to catch up," Sarah said.

"All right. Where do you want me to meet you?"

"Are you doing any interviews in the clubhouse?" Sarah asked.

Mary nodded.

"I'll see you there, but how about we all meet up here in the press box after we finish our stories?"

"Perfect." Mary gave them a little wave before heading back downstairs.

When she was well out of earshot, Sarah glared at Lisa. "I've said great things about her?"

"You did, you big goof. I don't know if you're aware of it, but you most definitely used 'the one' or 'the love of my life' on more than one occasion when talking about Mary. Don't give me any shit over this, Swift. You needed a nudge, and, well, I provided it. So there."

Sarah's scowl quickly disappeared. "Thanks, Lisa."

"You can thank me by buying me a Mich."

"Done."

The mayor of Cincinnati threw out the first pitch, a local singer finished with the National Anthem, and the Reds took the field against the Milwaukee Brewers. Most sportswriters picked the Brewers and the Cardinals to compete for the National League Central Division title and chose the Reds for an outside shot at a Wild Card spot. Lisa thought the division would come down between the Brewers and the Reds and wrote as much in an article with her predictions for baseball's six divisions.

She might be overly optimistic, but she had the Reds playing the Braves in the National League Championship Series with the Reds moving on to the World Series. The Reds had made some key trades over the winter. Josh Taylor, the brash young right-hander on the mound today, would be counted on to provide some extra wins this season.

He finished his warm-up tosses, raised his cap, and brushed his forehead with his forearm. He bounced the rosin bag on his pitching hand before settling on the rubber. After he peered in for the signs, he reared back with a high leg kick and threw a ninety-five-mile-per-hour fastball over the inner half of the plate for a strike.

Taylor quickly got into trouble. Two straight singles brought up the power-hitting left fielder, Quinn Strong, with runners on the corners and no outs. Taylor jumped ahead 0-2. After five straight foul balls, Strong hit a ball deep to left, a long sacrifice fly, to score the runner from third. Taylor got the next batter to ground into a 4-6-3 double play to end the top half.

The score remained 1-0 until the fifth inning. Amy strode to the plate with the speedy Rawls on second after a two-out double. She gave a cursory glance at Pete Servace, the third base coach, and stepped into the batter's box.

She fouled the first pitch straight back, a high fastball. Rudy Green, the Brewers ace, then threw her two of his patented slow curves. Amy swung ahead on both of them and lined them well foul down the third baseline.

She leveled her bat, waiting for his next pitch. Green tried to sneak a fastball by her on the outer part of the plate, but Amy lifted it over the second baseman's head for a solid single. Rawls easily scored from second. Amy slapped her hands together and leaned in to talk with Tom Jeffries, the first base coach, before taking her lead off first.

Nick Sanders lumbered to the plate. He was 0-2 for the game, striking out both times and looking bad with each plate appearance. Barely managing to foul off two fastballs in the mid-nineties, he quickly fell behind against Green. He adjusted his batting helmet and settled into the batter's box.

"Sometimes I wonder if he's lost some on his swing, don't you?" Sarah asked.

Lisa didn't answer but continued to watch the action below.

The next pitch was a fastball that painted the outside black of the plate. Nick connected and sent the ball four rows up in the right field bleachers.

Lisa tapped on her keyboard. "You were saying?"

"Oh, shut up," Sarah muttered.

Lisa glanced over and caught her bemused expression.

The game ended with the Reds closer, Danny Lopez, striking out the would-be tying run at the plate to seal a 3-1 victory.

Lisa and Sarah filed behind the other reporters down to the Reds clubhouse: the *Cincinnati Enquirer* beat writer, the reporters who covered the Brewers, and a smattering of national baseball writers rounded out the group.

Lisa talked to Nick about the pitch he hit for a home run in the fifth, to Josh Taylor about settling down after a shaky first inning, and she scribbled down a couple of quotes from Amy. She then followed other reporters to Murphy's office.

She left his office after her interview and saw Sarah talking with Mary. She slowed her steps to give them a little privacy before joining them to get on the elevator that would take them back to the press box. Once there, Lisa concentrated on her story and filed it in twenty minutes.

Sarah tapped the table beside her in a rapid staccato as Lisa slid her laptop into her case. She zipped it up and glared at Sarah.

"What?" Sarah asked.

"Nervous?"

Sarah immediately stopped the tapping. "No. What gave you that idea?"

"Right. Here comes the object of your non-nervousness now."

Sarah jerked around as Mary approached them.

"Ready?" Mary asked. "I have no idea where we're going. Can I ride with one of you?"

"I'm sure Sarah would be happy to oblige, Mary. I'll meet you over there." Lisa tried not to snicker at the panicked expression on Sarah's face. As she brushed past her, she whispered in Sarah's ear, "Five blocks, Swift. You can handle it."

As she took the elevator to the garage, the last sound she heard was Mary's soft laugh.

* * *

Lisa entered Tim's Place and found an empty booth toward the front. Mary and Sarah showed up about ten minutes later. Sarah still seemed like a nervous wreck but was having a conversation with Mary when Lisa waved them over.

Lisa scooted to the middle of her seat so it would force Sarah to slide into the booth with Mary. The server quickly breezed over to get their drink orders. A silence settled between them. *Hell if I'm going to let this happen.*

"Mary, Sarah told me you're an award-winning journalist. How long have you been in the business?"

"I got my start right out of college with a small newspaper in Georgia, which is where I'm from. I eventually moved west and worked my way up over the years to the *Times* in Seattle." She scrunched her face. "I believe twenty-six years. Yeah, that sounds about right."

"Do you enjoy it?"

"Oh, absolutely. It's just that…"

When she didn't finish, Lisa said, "Yes?"

"Sometimes it's hard on relationships. The odd hours. There's really no set nine-to-five to it at all, but I'm sure I'm telling you something you already know."

Lisa instantly thought of Frankie. "Yeah. I know what you mean."

The server set the drinks in front of them. None of them was hungry for dinner, so they ordered a plate of appetizers to share.

"Getting back to what you said, Mary, I think you work at it until you reach a balance," Lisa added. "You'll find it with the right partner." As soon as the words left her mouth, she received a hard kick on her shin. She tried to act like nothing had happened, but she scowled at Sarah across the table.

Sarah kept her focus on her Budweiser bottle.

"I think you're right, Lisa. Balance is key. I gave up much too easily in the past." Mary took a sip of her gin and tonic.

"You… you did?" Sarah asked in a tentative voice.

Mary held her gaze for several seconds. "Yes."

Sarah took a deep breath and slowly let it out. "If we're being honest here, I gave up too easily, too, Mary. Way, way too easily. And… and I've never gotten the chance to apologize to you for that shitty thing I said."

Mary didn't help her out but kept staring at her drink.

Lisa decided to repay the favor and kicked Sarah in the shin. Sarah glowered at her. "Come on," Lisa mouthed.

Sarah's attention returned to Mary. "It was so wrong of me to throw it in your face about me making more money and that you should quit your job. That was wrong on so many levels, and I can't tell you how many times I've regretted those words over the years."

"Thank you for that, Sarah." Mary grinned. "I think I have you beat on the salary now, though."

"Oh, you do, do you?"

"Besides that, it doesn't matter, and it never did." Mary

grabbed Sarah's hand. "How about we get reacquainted, hmm?"

Lisa made a show of glancing at her watch. "Wow. Look at the time." She got out her wallet and threw some money on the table. "This should cover everything." She slid out of her seat.

"Hey, Collins, I said I'd buy you a Mich, and you sure as hell don't need to pay for everything."

"Seeing the two of you together is payment enough, Sarah. Mary, nice meeting you. Hope we can get together again, but I have a feeling you're probably heading back to Seattle soon."

A flash of disappointment skittered across Mary's face. "I'll be leaving day after tomorrow."

Sarah's shoulders slumped.

"But I've got a few days off. Once I cover this one story in Seattle, I can fly wherever the Reds are playing. Would that be okay?"

It was the happiest Lisa had ever seen Sarah get.

"It would be perfect," Sarah said.

Lisa tucked her wallet into her back pocket. "In the meantime, you two enjoy the rest of the evening and the off-day tomorrow. Sarah, I'll catch up with you at the game on Wednesday."

Sarah didn't pay Lisa much attention but managed a weak "sure," as Lisa passed by the table on her way out of the bar.

Lisa walked to her car. After she settled into the driver's seat and switched on the engine, she connected her phone to the car's Bluetooth system and punched in Frankie's number.

"Hey, Leese. I see the Reds won the first game of the season."

Lisa let the welcome voice of the woman she loved flow over her like a mist from a waterfall. "Yeah. I think it'll be a great year." She pulled out into traffic. "But it'll be an even better night if you tell me you're on your way to Cincy."

"Oh, I can do one better than that. I'm waiting on you at home."

Lisa's heart rate picked up. "On my way."

Chapter 3

On Tuesday, an off-day for the Reds, Amy sat holding hands with Stacy outside Dr. Penelope Rodriguez's office. They had talked to Lainie and Roselle, whose doctor recommended Dr. Rodriguez in Cincinnati.

"Nervous?" Stacy squeezed Amy's hand.

"A little. Aren't you? Well, especially you."

Stacy brought Amy's hand to her lips and planted a light kiss. "Anything I do with you will be perfect."

Amy was about to reply when the nurse opened the door and called them back.

"I'm Kim, Dr. Rodriguez's nurse," the petite blonde said. Rather than lead them to an exam room, she took them to a room with Dr. Rodriguez's nameplate on the door. She motioned to the two plush chairs in front of a large oak desk.

"Would you like some juice or water while you wait?" she asked.

"No thank you," Amy said. "Stace?"

"No, but thank you."

"Dr. Rodriguez is finishing with a patient, but she'll be in shortly." With that, Kim left and the door shut with a quiet click.

Amy took in the décor of the room, and the warmth set her at ease. One of the framed photos behind the desk caught her eye. A beautiful woman with dark hair to her shoulders had her arm draped around a redhead with shining green eyes. Amy recognized the brunette as Dr. Rodriguez from her online picture. She wondered if the other woman might be her partner. As she allowed her mind to wander, the door opened. They rose to their feet.

The white lab coat emblazoned with "Penelope Rodriguez, M.D." in red stitching wasn't needed. The dark-haired beauty obviously matched the woman in the photo. She flashed them a wide smile.

"I'm Dr. Rodriguez. You must be Stacy," she said as she took

Stacy's hand. "I recognize Amy, of course. She's kind of hard not to recognize. Great game yesterday afternoon."

"Hi, Dr. Rodriguez. Yes, I'm Stacy and this is my wife, Amy." Stacy motioned to Amy and did a double-take, no doubt noticing Amy's full blush. Stacy's eyes sparkled with amusement. "Amy gets a little embarrassed when someone compliments her," she said in a stage whisper.

Amy shook the doctor's hand. "Nice to meet you."

Dr. Rodriguez motioned them to their chairs and took a seat behind her desk. "Ann Monroe in Indianapolis told me you two want to have a baby."

"Yes, Dr. Monroe is our friends' doctor," Amy said. "It's Stacy, not me, who'll be having the baby," she added hurriedly.

"I understand completely."

"Could you explain how this works?" Amy asked. "I mean, Lainie and Roselle explained some and obviously it worked out for them, but..."

Dr. Rodriguez leaned her elbows on the desk and intertwined her fingers. "Do you have a donor in mind?"

"No," Stacy said.

They thought of talking to Nick and Ryan, but Amy figured the men would have enough on their hands with planning for an adoption.

"We can connect you with the cryobank we use for sperm donors. They have many candidates who would work for you and can try to match coloring, ethnicity, educational background—if that's important to you. They run extensive health scans on all donors." Dr. Rodriguez leaned back in her chair. "One of the other matters we need to discuss is if Amy would like for her eggs to be fertilized as well as yours, Stacy. We can do that through in vitro. There's a greater expense. I don't know if that's an issue for you."

Amy glanced at Stacy. "Actually, we discussed it. We're both happy with using Stacy's eggs." Amy reached for Stacy's hand. "If our baby turns out to look anything like her, I'll feel blessed, believe me."

Tears sprang to Stacy's eyes as they stared at each other for a long moment.

"All right. The other decision is whether to do intracervical or intrauterine insemination and whether Stacy wants to do this naturally or to also take ovulation-enhancing medication."

Stacy answered. "I'd rather try this first on my own without the medication. What's the difference between intracervical or intrauterine insemination?"

"Intrauterine has a slightly higher success rate and is also a little costlier. We use washed sperm that's injected directly into the uterus using a thin catheter. There can be some mild cramping with the procedure as well. With intracervical insemination, the sperm is inserted into the cervix and more closely replicates natural conception."

"Intrauterine?" Stacy asked Amy.

"Yes. The cost doesn't matter."

"All right, then," Dr. Rodriguez said. She pulled open a drawer and slipped out a sheet of paper and a brochure. She passed them across the desk to Stacy. "Here's a chart to track your ovulation and a brochure from the cryobank. We'll run some tests on you, including a pelvic along with the blood tests, and we'll connect you with the cryobank so you can start looking at prospective donors. When you come in for insemination, we'd like you to return the next day to repeat the procedure. We've found there is sometimes a higher success rate with two inseminations per cycle. But that's ultimately your decision."

Amy turned to Stacy. "Honey?"

Stacy nodded. "I'll come back the next day."

Amy almost blurted out to Stacy that she loved her, but judging from the expression on Stacy's face, Amy thought her own feelings must be obvious.

* * *

Amy leaned over with her hands on her knees, catching her breath after hustling around the bases for a triple. In the second series of the season, this was the second game of three against the Cardinals and FOX Sports's late-Saturday-afternoon "Game of the Week." The thermometer had hit an unseasonably warm eighty-three degrees. Sweat stung Amy's eyes, and she used her uniform sleeve to wipe it away.

Servace leaned close to Amy and whispered "jackrabbit" into her ear. Amy kept her expression neutral even though he'd told her they were about to attempt a suicide squeeze. With the Reds down 5-4 in the bottom of the eighth, and the heavy-hitting Nick Sanders at the plate, Murphy was gambling the Cardinals wouldn't be anticipating it.

Amy edged off the bag. She glanced back every few seconds to make sure the third baseman wasn't sneaking in behind her. As Richards, the Cardinals reliever, started his motion toward the plate, Amy charged for home. The catcher jumped out of his crouch as soon as Sanders squared to bunt. Richards sprinted in after Sanders made contact. The ball dribbled along the first baseline. Rather than attempt a throw to the plate, Richards and Torres, the catcher, hovered over the ball as it wobbled along the line. They obviously hoped it would roll foul. When it clearly stayed fair, Torres picked it up and threw it to first in time to nip Sanders. Amy had scored easily.

She took the congratulatory hand slap from Roberts, the on-deck batter, and trotted to the dugout. Murphy gave her a fist bump. She slapped hands with everyone in the dugout, ending up in front of the Gatorade container. She filled a cup and drank it down in three big gulps. Nick motioned her over to sit beside him on the dugout bench.

"Nice job on the bunt, Nick."

"Thanks. What are your plans after the game tonight?"

"To sit in front of our new, big-screen, high-definition TV and watch a DVD."

"Why don't you and Stacy come over for some drinks?"

Amy noticed Nick didn't mention Ryan being there, too, but she understood his caution. Their teammates surrounded them, and Nick had no intention of coming out of the closet until he retired at the end of the season.

"Let me talk with Stacy. I'm sure she'd love to visit."

"Let's win this game first, though, huh?"

Nick grabbed his glove after the last out. Amy joined him on the field.

Unfortunately, the Reds lost the game in ten innings. Amy had made an error in the top of the tenth to allow the go-ahead runner to get aboard. As she stood in front of her locker and talked with Lisa, she debated about telling Nick she and Stacy couldn't make it. She wasn't in the mood.

When Lisa finished with her interview, Amy sat down on the chair in front of her locker and stared straight ahead.

"Waiting on your clothes to levitate?" Nick asked as he quickly stripped down and wrapped a towel around his waist.

Amy opened her mouth to speak, but he cut her off. "Not taking no for an answer about tonight unless Stacy isn't feeling well or something. Your error didn't cost us the game, Perry. I came up with the bases loaded in the bottom of the ninth and struck out. I could be sitting there pouting, too, but I'm not. I've been in this game too long to dwell on this shit."

Amy immediately felt stupid and decided to lighten the mood. "All right, Sandy. You've given me your lecture for the day. Off with you to the showers so I can clean up and go home to my wife."

"That's better."

Amy stripped down to her sliding shorts and red T-shirt she wore under her uniform and waited for her turn in the shower.

* * *

Amy gave Stacy a call on the way home to see if she felt up to going over to Nick and Ryan's place.

"Sure. I'll jump in the shower and be ready by the time you get home. When do we need to be there?"

Amy glanced at the dashboard clock. "Around nine. He said he knows it's late, but apparently Ryan missed seeing us over the winter."

"I've missed them, too. I'll see you when you get here."

It took Amy another twenty minutes of fighting through traffic to make it to their condo on the Ohio River. They'd finally decided to purchase one after renting an apartment the year before. In those twenty minutes, she thought about how much she'd miss Stacy. The Reds were flying out tomorrow after the game for a nine-game road trip. They'd talked about it. With Amy's frequent traveling, they knew she wouldn't always be there as Stacy went through fertility treatment.

Amy unlocked the door and tossed her bag on the floor. Suddenly, she had an overwhelming desire to hold Stacy in her arms. She heard Stacy humming from the bedroom and followed the sound down the hall.

Stacy was tugging a scoop-necked T-shirt over her head. Amy admired her ass as she bent over to retrieve her sneakers.

"Getting a good view back there?" Stacy asked before turning around.

Amy put her arms around Stacy for a long hug.

"Hey, hey, what's this about, babe?" Stacy whispered in her ear.

"I've missed you," Amy said as she held Stacy tighter.

Stacy pulled back and looked long into her eyes. "You saw me at ten before you left for the ballpark. What's this really about?"

"Nothing," Amy mumbled. She went to the bed and flopped back on the mattress.

Stacy quickly joined her and straddled her waist. She leaned over and gave Amy a kiss. "Now, let's try this again. Why don't you tell me what's bothering you?"

Amy tried to look away, but Stacy gently touched her cheek.

"It's that… it's…" Amy sighed. "I'm going to miss you."

"I always miss you when you're not here, Amy. I hope you know that."

"Yeah, but I hate that I won't be with you on your first visit to Dr. Rodriguez's office."

"Ah." Stacy nodded, knowingly.

"Ah, what?"

"Ah, I thought you'd have trouble with this. Sweetheart, I told you we can wait until off-season to try for the baby. It's okay."

"But if we do that, I won't be home with you in the first months after she's born."

Stacy cocked a dark eyebrow. "She?"

Amy grinned. "Yeah. I can teach her how to play baseball."

Stacy returned her smile. "You can teach our *son* to play ball, too."

"Girls are more fun."

Stacy laughed and draped her body over Amy's. This time, her kiss was deeper and left Amy breathless.

"Remember. This exam involves a full physical, plus the blood tests. You're not missing out on the actual procedure. But back to having a boy or a girl... I think"—Stacy nibbled on Amy's ear—"that regardless of whether it's a girl or a boy, they're going to love you showing them how to play the game."

"God, it turns me on when you do that," Amy said in a hoarse voice.

"Yeah?"

Amy quickly flipped Stacy onto her back and covered her with her body. "Yes, it most certainly turns me on. Like you didn't know."

Stacy's expression sobered. "Are you going to be okay with this? I don't want anything to come between us. We've worked hard this past year to always talk things through, and I don't want to—"

Amy placed her finger against Stacy's lips. "Shh. Every time I think about not being here as you go to these appointments, I'll think about the months ahead when the two of us will be holding our baby."

Stacy's eyes shimmered. "Our baby," she said softly.

Amy leaned over and kissed her, delving her tongue inside and lingering. She caressed Stacy's cheek. "I love you so much, Stace."

"Love you, too. Now, how about we go visit with our friends?"

* * *

"How are you and Stacy doing?" Nick took a sip of his beer and peered at Amy over the bottle. Stacy and Ryan were engaged in a friendly, but spirited, game of darts in the den while Nick and Amy sat out on the deck.

"Great. In fact, so great we've decided to start on the baby-making trek during the season."

Nick seemed surprised. "You had mentioned you weren't sure if it'd be this season or next. Guess you both made up your minds, huh? You okay being away from her during the season? I imagine she'll be going to some doctor's appointments without you."

Amy took a swig of her beer. "It's funny. We had a talk before coming over."

"And?"

"We're good. I want to be there not only for the birth, Nick, but for the first months of our baby's life. I can't do the 'run to the hospital, take a week off, and go back to playing' routine that a lot of the players do. That's why we're hoping this takes right away. It would mean she gives birth in the off-season."

"I understand. I told you, that's why Ryan and I are waiting until after I retire to start the adoption proceedings." He grinned. "So?"

"So, what?"

"Boy or girl. And please don't give me that line that you only hope for a healthy baby. Every parent hopes for a healthy baby."

"Girl, but—"

"Yeah, yeah. But as long as the baby is healthy, that's all that matters."

They laughed.

Ryan and Stacy met them out on the deck.

"What's so funny?" Ryan asked before giving Nick a peck on the cheek.

"Amy didn't want to admit it, but she's hoping for a girl."

Stacy sat down beside Amy and scooped up a handful of chips. "She wants a mini-me running around."

"Hey." Amy nudged her shoulder.

"It's true. Don't try to deny it, Perry," Stacy said.

Ryan put his arm around Nick. "We just want a healthy child, girl or boy. Don't we, sweetie?"

Amy hid her smile by taking another drink of beer. She met Nick's eyes that crinkled in bemusement.

"That's right, Ryan," Nick said and winked at her.

Chapter 4

"Gonna miss you, Frankie." Lisa gave Frankie a kiss at the door.

"I'll miss you, too, Leese. When does your plane land in Philadelphia?"

"Nine."

"Give me a call when you have time, will you?"

Lisa leaned in for another kiss. "Absolutely." She picked up her bag and gave Frankie one last look before leaving.

"Call me when you get to Philadelphia," Stacy said, caressing Amy's cheek.

God, Amy thought, I could stay lost in her eyes forever. "Still wish I could be here tomorrow for you."

Stacy brushed her lips. "You're here even when you aren't. Besides, only the preliminary tests are tomorrow, remember? We'll make sure you're there for the first try in Dr. Rodriguez's office."

Amy kissed her again, lingered for a long moment, and reluctantly pulled away. "I'll call you when we get there."

* * *

Amy checked Pete Servace for the signs. She scuffed her front foot into the batter's box and settled in for the pitch.

In the first game of a three-game series, the Reds were behind 3-2 in the top of the sixth with a runner at first and one out. Servace had given her the sign to sacrifice. Murphy's getting a little conservative here, Amy thought.

Tim Fairchild, the Phillies ace, glared in for the sign. He held his glove up to his face so that his eyes were barely visible over the top of the webbing.

She squared around to bunt when Fairchild released a fastball that came screaming in at Amy's chin. It was the second pitch of the game that had nearly hit her. She backpedaled out of the way of the ball. If it hadn't been a fastball, hell, she would've taken one for the team. But Fairchild's fastballs hit the high nineties at times.

Thinking it had simply been a pitch to get her to pop up the bunt, Amy settled back in and quickly squared. Again, it was a fastball, and it was coming toward her head. She ducked and landed on her back in an effort to get out of the way.

The crowd cheered. Of course. Only in Philadelphia, Amy thought. She glanced out at the mound. Fairchild picked up the rosin bag behind the mound, bounced it on his pitching hand, and flung it hard into the dirt. He stared at Amy and stepped back on the rubber.

Amy stared back. Fine. She could see how this was going.

She dug in again. When the pitch came in this time, she twisted and let it hit her in the back.

Fuck, fuck, fuck. She dropped her bat and hesitated going to first. The home plate umpire stayed beside her as she started down the line and kept pace with each step.

"Let it go," he told her in a low voice.

She wanted to say, "You didn't fucking get hit by a ninety-seven-mile-an-hour fastball, did you, asshole?" Instead, she kept going with Fairchild still glaring at her when she reached the bag.

Tom Jeffries, the first base coach, put his arm around her shoulder.

"You all right?" he asked.

"Yes," she said through gritted teeth. She stripped off her batting gloves and shoved them into her back pockets. Hit the damn ball out of here, Nick, she thought as she took her lead.

Nick took the first two breaking balls for strikes. Fairchild checked the runners and fired in a knee-high fastball. Nick connected and launched it into the second deck of the left field bleachers.

Amy tried to suppress a grin as she rounded the bases. She heard Fairchild's loud "fuck me" when she made the turn at second. She waited for Nick at the plate.

"Yes, big man," she exclaimed and slapped him on the batting helmet. "Make 'em pay."

Nick most decidedly was not holding back a smile. "That was my intention," he said as they headed for the dugout.

The game ended with the Reds on top 5-3. Amy gathered her equipment and made her way into the clubhouse. The reporters quickly gathered around Nick to ask him questions about the pitch he hit out in the sixth. After they finished, they scattered in the clubhouse. Lisa approached Amy's locker.

"Hey, Aim. How's your back?"

Amy stretched and grimaced. "A little sore." She gingerly removed her jersey, pulled up her T-shirt, and craned her neck to try to get a glimpse of the bruising. "How's it look?"

Lisa flinched. "Going to need some ice."

"That bad, huh?"

Sarah Swift walked up to them, and she didn't seem too happy.

"What?" Lisa asked.

"Just came from the Phillies clubhouse. Fairchild's over there saying he intentionally hit you in the sixth, Amy."

Amy snorted. "I could have told you that."

"He didn't stop there. He said a woman has no place in the majors and"—Sarah flipped the pages of her notebook—"'she needs to go back to softball or whatever it is that girls do.' End of quote. Care to comment?"

Amy wanted to say he could kiss her ass, but she refrained. She couldn't recall another time when any player had been so blatant in their protest about her playing the game. Of course, she'd encountered brush-backs and snide remarks on the bases from time to time, but nothing where a player had said exactly what he was thinking.

Her jaws tightened. "No comment."

"You sure?" Sarah asked.

"How about this. He's entitled to his opinion, but I don't share it."

Both Lisa and Sarah wrote down the quote.

"Thanks," Sarah said. She motioned to Amy's back. "You really do need to get some ice on that." She headed for Murphy's office.

Amy started for the training room. Lisa kept pace beside her.

"You sure you're okay?" Lisa asked.

"Yeah. Tom will ice it up, and I'll be fine. Bruised but fine."

"No, I mean with what Fairchild said."

Amy stuttered to a stop. "Are you asking as my friend or as a reporter?"

Hurt flitted across Lisa's face, and Amy immediately regretted her words.

"You know me better than that, Amy. At least I hope you do."

Amy rubbed her face in frustration. "Yeah, I do, Lisa. I'm sorry. It's that this shit hasn't happened in a while. Down in Chattanooga, yes. And there have been times where they threw at me or where I caught some snide remark out on the bases. But nothing where the guy flat out says he was trying to hit me, hell, hurt me, because he didn't like the fact I'm a woman playing *his* game. It's bullshit."

"He'll be fined for that, maybe even suspended."

"I hope the league does suspend him."

Tom waved her into the training room. "Take your T-shirt off, and let me see your back."

She took off her T-shirt so that she only wore her sports bra and uniform pants. She started to hop up on the table but winced at the move.

Lisa held out her hand for Amy to grab while she situated herself on the table. "Damn, Amy. It looks like it's bruised even more in the past few minutes."

"Great," Amy muttered. She flinched when Tom probed her back.

"Sorry. It's a bruise. The ball hit you high enough that it didn't affect your ribs. Why don't you get your shower now? I think the guys are out of there. Come back in here when you're done, and I'll get you set with some ice and an Ace bandage. Keep icing it during the night."

Lisa helped her down.

"Just how I wanted to spend the evening," Amy said. "Thanks, Tom."

"Don't mention it."

"I was being sarcastic."

Tom chuckled. "You didn't have to tell me, Perry."

Lisa and Amy headed back to the locker area. The other players had cleared out of the shower.

"Well, I need to go upstairs to get my story in. You going to be okay?"

"I will be. Thanks, Lisa."

Amy undressed, wincing as she bent over to take off her uniform pants, socks, and cleats. She wrapped herself in a towel and made her way to the showers.

* * *

"I'm really all right, Stace. Honest." Amy bit her lip as pain shot to her back when she shifted in bed. The icepack was annoying, but she knew she needed it. No way was she missing any game time over it. She'd already told Murphy she was fine, and she would be. She wouldn't give Fairchild the satisfaction of knowing he'd knocked her out of some games.

"I watched the replay three times tonight. He didn't hit you with a breaking pitch. It was a hard fastball."

"Damn, woman, it didn't take you long to pick up on the lingo."

"I'm not joking, Amy."

Amy heard the fear in Stacy's voice. "I'm really okay, and since you understand baseball, you know these things have a way of evening out. Don't be surprised to see one of their top hitters get plunked in the series."

"Serves them right, damn it."

Amy could picture her pacing in the living room with that fierce expression on her face that she wore when she was angry.

"There's the Irish in you I love."

"It's not funny."

"I'm teasing. Let's talk about something else. You went to your appointment today. How'd it go?"

Amy stood up and got a bottle of water out of the small refrigerator hotel rooms provided. She gingerly settled back on the bed.

"Dr. Rodriguez did a full physical and took some blood. We should get those results by Wednesday. She said she could see no reason why we couldn't have a baby."

Amy hadn't realized she'd been tense until she heard those words. She immediately relaxed. "Good, sweetheart."

"Oh, I didn't know how late it was. Almost midnight. I'd better let you go. I love you, Amy."

"I love you too, sweetheart. I'll talk to you tomorrow."

"Okay. Now kick some ass in the game tomorrow night."

"Will do."

* * *

Payback didn't come until Wednesday night, the last game of the series. In the bottom of the seventh, the Reds were up 6-2. They'd lost 5-1 the night before. A win would take the series.

Felipe Rosales, hitting third for the Phillies, settled into the batter's box. Bob Davidson, one of the Reds late-inning relievers, didn't even wait until deep into the count. He promptly plunked Rosales in the back with a low-nineties fastball.

Rosales made a move toward the mound, and Davidson waved him on. The home plate umpire quickly stepped in front of Rosales before he had a chance to go any farther. The umpire pointed at both dugouts and up at the press box to let everyone know the benches had been warned. He walked Rosales all the way to first with Rosales jawing at Davidson the whole time. The second base umpire kept Davidson occupied, and soon everyone was back in their positions and play resumed.

Amy stood with her back foot in front of the first base bag. Davidson tossed the ball to her to keep Rosales close. When Amy cocked her arm to throw the ball back, she pointed her glove at Davidson in a silent "thank-you."

* * *

"On to New York, right, Leese?" Frankie asked.

Lisa muted the hotel TV. "We leave bright and early tomorrow, but it's an off-day before the game on Friday with the Mets."

There was a beat of silence. "I probably shouldn't bring this up…"

"You can't leave a statement like that hanging, Frankie."

"You got an envelope in the mail. It's pretty thick."

Lisa tried to think who'd be sending her snail mail. The only corresponding she did was through email and texting.

"What's the return address?"

"Steubenville, Ohio."

"Huh. Doesn't ring a bell. You can open it."

"No, Lisa. Since the envelope is thick, to me it means that whatever is in it is important. It can wait until you get home."

"That won't be for another week. Damn, Frankie. I don't think I can wait that long."

"Like I said, I probably shouldn't have brought it up. I didn't know if you knew anyone from Steubenville and figured it would ring a bell right away if you did."

Lisa wracked her brain for any clues again. "Nope."

"It'll be here when you get home. It wasn't sent registered mail or anything. While it might be important, it can't be too pressing."

"Okay. I'll read it when I get back. That's, of course, after I thoroughly take advantage of you in the most pleasant ways possible."

"But of course," Frankie said with enthusiasm.

Chapter 5

Amy gazed out the airplane window and marveled at the beautiful sunrise.

"Nice, huh?" Nick said beside her.

She nodded.

"How's your back feeling," he asked.

"Much better. Iced it again last night in my room."

Nick returned his attention to his book. An honest-to-God book, too, not an e-reader. She got a peek at the title. A biography on *Ulysses S. Grant*.

"Kind of deep, isn't it?" she asked in a playful voice.

"Shut up, Perry. Not all of us are *Sports Illustrated* fiends." He pointed at her open magazine.

"Hey, it's research. I'm catching up on where they picked us this year."

"And?"

"You mean you don't keep up on this?"

He shook his head. "Nope. Doesn't affect the way I play, either." He marked his book and closed it. "What are you doing tonight?"

"I don't know. Hadn't thought about it. Why?"

"Ariana Montegue called me since she knew we're coming into town. Wanted to know if I could join her for dinner. You're welcome to come."

Amy glanced around them and kept her voice down. "If it's supposed to be a date, shouldn't you be going alone?"

"We can still pull off the 'we're dating thing.' We just need to be seen together. It won't be a problem with you there. Trust me. In fact, she asked to meet you."

"Me?"

"Uh, yeah." He leaned in close and lowered his voice even more. "In case you forgot, you're a hero to the lesbian community, goofus."

"Oh, gee, how could I forget?" She thought of something. "Wait. She knows I'm with Stacy, right?"

"She's not going to jump your bones, Perry. I hate to disappoint you there."

"Oh, shut the fuck up, Sandy."

* * *

Amy ran gel through her hair and checked out her reflection. She grabbed her black leather belt and tugged it through the loops of her slacks. She thought she'd dress up a little. Wherever they were going had to be chic. Especially since the whole purpose of Nick and Ariana going out was so the photographers could take shots of the supposedly happily dating straight couple. She knew it was hard on Nick, despite how nonchalant he was about the whole thing. But it was the game he played to stay in the closet.

She thought back to how she'd been so scared about anyone knowing her sexuality. Once she and Stacy had started dating, though, she knew there was no way she could introduce Stacy as her "friend" or "roommate." It felt wrong. Hell, it was wrong… at least to her.

She checked herself in the mirror one last time and hoped that her black slacks, blue silk blouse, and black suit jacket passed the test.

She walked down to the elevator. Before she got on, she gave Stacy another call. She'd already called her from her room as soon as she realized what they were doing for the night. Even though she gave Stacy no cause to doubt her, it didn't feel right being seen with Ariana without Stacy getting a heads-up. A second call wouldn't hurt.

"I told you. It's fine, Amy," Stacy said as Amy asked her again.

"You'd tell me otherwise, right?"

"Didn't we decide to be completely honest with each other and talk things through? And don't you think that's what we're doing?"

"Yes. It's just that… I don't know…" Amy closed her eyes as she thought back to last season and her drunken escapade at a lesbian bar in Atlanta. Yes, she was grieving her mother, but getting drunk and allowing a woman not named Stacy to drape her body all over her was downright stupid.

As if Stacy could read her mind, she said softly, "That's in the past."

Amy felt the tension leave her body. "Right."

"Now, go have fun with Nick. Give him my love."

Amy ended the call and got on the elevator. When she entered the lobby, she spotted Nick by the front doors. He looked great in a dark-blue, pinstriped suit.

"Shit, Nick. You clean up good," she said as she approached him. "Armani?"

He smoothed the lapels. "Nobody else." He waved his hand in the air in front of her. "You're pretty damn sharp yourself, Perry."

She glanced down at her clothes. "Thanks. Hope this is okay."

"It's fine." He turned his attention back to the hotel doors. "Here's Ariana."

A black limousine eased to a stop in front of the hotel. Amy and Nick went outside, and the hotel attendant quickly moved to open the limo door for them.

Amy slid onto the seat across from Ariana. Nick moved in next to Ariana and gave her a quick kiss on the cheek.

"Beautiful as always, my dear," he said.

Her dark hair was almost raven-black and hung loosely on her shoulders. She wore a black cocktail dress that seemed tailored for her sleek body. There was a hint of cleavage, but the rest of the dress showed off the expanse of her long, shapely legs.

Jesus, Amy thought. I knew she was a beautiful fashion model, but seeing her in photos and seeing her in the flesh are two different things entirely.

"So, Nick, where are your manners? Introduce me to your teammate." Ariana flashed Amy a brilliant smile.

Amy noticed a slight accent. "Nick" sounded like "Neek." Although Ariana's last name was Montegue, Amy had read somewhere that her mother was Italian.

"Sure. Amy Perry, my very good friend, Ariana Montegue."

Ariana gently squeezed Amy's outstretched hand. "Pleased to finally meet you, Amy. I've been on Nick for months for this chance."

"Nice to meet you, too, Ariana."

"Need I say you're an inspiration to us all?" Ariana asked and quirked a dark eyebrow.

Amy felt the heat rise to her cheeks. Oh my God, I'm blushing, she thought.

Nick smirked. "Don't let it go to your head, Perry."

She glared at him. "Shut the fu…" Amy stopped herself. "Shut up, Nick."

"Oh, please, Amy. I tell him to shut the fuck up all the time."

They all laughed, and any unease Amy felt instantly dissipated.

"So where are we going, Ariana?" Nick asked.

"A new restaurant, On the Town, opened two weeks ago. The waiting list is a mile long to get in there, but I have my ways."

"And what are those ways?"

Ariana patted Nick's leg. "Let's just say that the head chef and I are on very good terms."

"I bet you are."

Their limousine pulled to a stop behind two other limos. The restaurant attendants practically sprinted to open the doors. Amy reached for the door handle and held back a gasp when it was yanked from her hand.

"Good evening and welcome to On the Town," a twenty-something, tuxedo-clad attendant said. "Ah, Ms. Montegue. So good to see you. Maria said to watch for you. And Mr. Sanders, hello."

"This is Amy Perry," Nick said.

"Of course. Good evening to you, too, Ms. Perry."

He hustled in front to open the door to the restaurant. The hostess immediately met them and escorted them to a table. At first, Amy wondered why they hadn't been seated in a more discreet area of the restaurant, but then she remembered one of the purposes of their visit—to be seen.

The hostess handed out the menus. "Roni is your server this evening. She'll be with you shortly. In the meantime, may I take drink orders?"

"I'll have a glass of your house wine," Ariana said and studied her menu.

Nick gave Amy a look that screamed "do not order a beer."

"A glass of your house wine sounds perfect," Amy said. She resisted the urge to kick Nick under the table.

"And I'll have a vodka collins."

The hostess left them.

"What was that look for, Nick? You don't think I'm capable of being couth?"

"Oh, I never question your couthness, Perry."

Ariana chuckled and shook her head.

"It's that I remember the time we went car shopping," Nick said. "Ariana, let me ask you this. If you had a choice between an Audi or a Malibu, what would you choose?"

"You know the answer to that. You've seen my fleet of cars, and an Audi is part of it."

"See?" he asked Amy.

"Nick, I'm getting pretty tired of you bringing up this car shopping thing anytime you think I'm doing something that doesn't jibe with your supposed hipness."

"What do you mean 'supposed'?"

Amy didn't have the chance to play-argue with him any further because the hostess returned with their drink order, followed closely by their server.

"Good evening," Roni said. "Are you ready to order? Or do you need more time?"

"Actually, they're having a spat," Ariana said. "But you can tell us your house specials."

"Certainly. Tonight we're featuring salmon with a sweet soy glaze accompanied with our chef's special recipe of black rice pilaf. Our lamb chops are also featured tonight."

Ariana pointed at her menu. "Your vegetable mélange looks wonderful."

"Excellent choice. It comes with white bean puree, mushrooms, and slow roasted tomatoes."

Amy perused her menu. Jesus, the price of the entrees was enough to feed a small country.

"It's on me tonight, Amy." Nick seemed to be reading her mind.

"Nick, you don't have to—"

"You're our guest for the night," he said.

Hell, she wasn't going to argue. "I'll have your London Broil, medium well, a baked potato, and a house salad, please."

"Good choice. And you, sir?"

"A filet, medium, and your lobster sound perfect. I'll have the baked potato as well. No salad."

Roni collected their menus. When Amy handed over hers, Roni took a few seconds longer to make eye contact.

After she walked away, Ariana smiled. "Seems you caught Roni's eye."

"Well, she can look somewhere else," Amy said.

Soon, Amy sat back and enjoyed the stories that Nick and Ariana shared of their time "together." Nick touched Ariana's hand on occasion and eventually settled next to her with his arm draped over the back of her chair. Anyone watching would assume that they were intimate.

It didn't take long for photographers to spot them. They were in strategic locations and didn't use flash, so they weren't intrusive.

Roni brought Amy's salad to her and asked if anyone needed refills on their drinks. Amy decided to go with water after her glass of wine. Ariana ordered another glass, but Nick followed Amy's lead and settled on water.

"You two are entirely too boring," Ariana said and winked. "So, tell me about your wife, Amy."

"Stacy. Wow. What can I say? We met two years ago while I was still playing in Double A. My friend Lisa Collins—she's a reporter for Major League.com—introduced us, and my heart hasn't been the same since. In fact…"

"Yes?" Ariana tilted her head in question.

"We're keeping it pretty quiet until it actually happens, but we're trying for a baby."

"You?" Ariana's beautiful face registered shock.

Nick stifled a laugh.

Amy glared at him. "Why is it everyone has such a hard time seeing me pregnant?" Amy heard herself and stopped. Even she couldn't see it. "Okay. I get your point."

This time, Nick couldn't hold back with his laughter. "Good. I didn't want to have to list the many, many ways that's so implausible."

"Whatever."

"I am happy for you, Amy," Ariana said. "You're lucky to have found someone you want to share your life with and start a family." She raised her wineglass. "To you and your Stacy. I wish you many years of happiness."

Amy noticed a touch of sadness in Ariana's dark-brown eyes. She wanted to ask Ariana about her plans for the future but felt it really was none of her business. They'd only just met.

Roni appeared at that moment, carrying a large tray with their dinners. Trailing behind her was a brunette in a white chef jacket.

"Maria," Ariana said warmly. She stood and kissed Maria on both cheeks. "Thank you for gracing us with your presence."

Maria held Ariana's gaze before turning to Nick and Amy. "It's my pleasure."

"Nick Sanders and Amy Perry, Maria Alvarez. The best executive chef in New York City." Ariana took her seat again.

Maria shook her head slightly. "As always, Ariana is much too kind in her praise. I do hope you enjoy your meals tonight." She gave Ariana an almost imperceptible nod.

Ariana returned the gesture.

After Maria left the table, Nick leaned over and said, "Is that lesbian code or something?"

A sly grin tugged at Ariana's lips. "You are so observant, Nick. I'm impressed."

"Well, us dumb jocks do have some smarts, huh, Perry?"

Ariana slapped his arm playfully. "You are not dumb." She shifted closer. "After all, you were smart enough to fall in love with Ryan, hmm?"

Nick's face flushed an adorable red.

"Oh my God. Nick Sanders is blushing," Amy teased.

"Shut up, Perry," he mumbled as he cut into his steak.

Amy took a bite of her own steak. She was enjoying herself. The only thing that would have made the evening better was if Stacy could have been here. Three games here and another three in Atlanta, she thought. She couldn't get home soon enough.

* * *

The cursor blinked on Lisa's blank computer screen. She'd planned on working on a feature about Jody Harrelson. He was replacing Nick Sanders in the starting lineup for today's afternoon game that would end the Reds road trip. Murphy had said he intended to rest Nick as often as possible on day games following night games. This was the first game where he implemented his policy.

Lisa had already questioned Sanders about it after last night's game. Sanders had gone 3-4 with a double and two RBIs. The Reds had lost the game but not because of his play. Not surprisingly, Nick was on board with Murphy's plan for the season. He was, as always, the consummate professional. Nick said he understood his role coming into his final season and told Lisa he looked forward to tutoring Harrelson in the finer aspects of the game. She'd already noticed Harrelson sat next to Sanders in the dugout as often as possible.

Lisa had interviewed Harrelson in the preseason and again last night about his first start of the season. She had the quotes scribbled down in her notebook, but she sat staring at the laptop screen. She couldn't get her mind to work. It was about 500 miles away in Indianapolis. The more she thought about the letter waiting on her at home, the more uncomfortable she became. When Lisa again asked Frankie to open it, Frankie told her no, she could wait.

"They're fascinating aren't they? You think you've seen it all, and they up and invent this new-fangled contraption."

Lisa turned at the sound of a familiar voice.

"So despite how happy you appear now, you're still sarcastic to the core, huh, Swift?"

Sarah sat down next to her. "You're right. I'm very happy. You, on the other hand, seem to be wound a little tight."

Lisa thought of keeping it to herself but decided she needed to talk about it. Maybe it would help her refocus on the feature. It was 11:00. She'd like to get the story halfway finished before the game time of 12:35.

"Frankie called me a few days ago to tell me I have a letter, make that a thick letter, waiting for me when I get home."

"And you didn't ask her to open it?"

"I did, but she didn't want to. She said whatever it is might be important enough for me to wait."

"Now you're wondering why the hell you went along with that?"

"You know me too well."

"Any idea what it is?"

Lisa shrugged. "I have an uneasy feeling about it. Maybe it's just as well I'm waiting. I can concentrate on the game today and read it when I get home tonight."

"You have a good point." Sarah gazed down at the field and seemed lost in thought.

"How are you and Mary?"

At the mention of Mary's name, Sarah transformed into a new person.

"That good, huh?" Lisa said.

"That good."

"Back to sharing a condo, two dogs, and aquarium yet?" Lisa couldn't help but tease.

"We're getting there. I never thought I'd get this chance again, Lisa. Never. Now that it's here, I'm not letting it slip away. I'm not letting her slip away. There might be an opening at the Seattle Times by the end of the season. Something I might go for. We'll see." Sarah waved at the computer screen. "What are you working on?"

"Feature on Jody Harrelson."

"Good choice. I haven't gotten Nick's take on it yet, but he seems to be okay."

"He is. He's a veteran. What do you think of the game today?"

Sarah powered up her laptop. "They need this one to avoid the sweep."

After taking two out of three against the Phillies, the Reds had lost the series 2-1 in New York. What had started as a promising road trip had now deteriorated into a possible 3-6 record before heading home. A loss would put them three games behind the Cardinals in the young season.

Ninety minutes later, Lisa had the feature almost finished before the first pitch. The Reds scored first in the third inning on Mark Roberts's solo homerun. The Braves tied it up in the bottom of the fifth on a homerun by Chad Walters, their power-hitting first baseman.

Going into the top of the ninth, the game was still 1-1. Amy strode to the plate with two on and two out. She crouched in her stance, ready for the first pitch. Marino, the Braves closer, threw her a slow curve for a strike that appeared to be low. Amy shook her head slightly, adjusted her batting gloves, and stepped back into the box. Marino tossed her another slow curve. Amy held back and hammered the ball into the left field gap for a stand-up double. Both runners scored. Amy smacked her hands together. Sanders flied out to deep left for the final out.

Danny Lopez, assisted by a diving catch by Amy, worked a 1-2-3 bottom of the ninth to preserve the win.

Lisa and Sarah spilled into the clubhouse with the other reporters. Lisa talked with Amy about the hit that broke the tie and her diving stop that prevented a double and would have brought the tying run to the plate.

"The hit was nice, but like I've told you before, I still love making a defensive stop. Nothing like getting your uniform dirty and feeling good when you come to your feet with the ball in your glove." Amy unbuttoned her jersey. "Wish we could've had a better road trip, but it's early. I have no doubt we can turn it around. It'll be good to get home."

"Yes it will. Thanks, Aim." Lisa left for Murphy's office and passed other reporters heading the other way. Murphy was flipping through some paperwork when she tapped on the door jamb.

"Oh, hey, Lisa." He motioned her into a seat in front of his desk.

"What do you think so far, Murph?"

He ruffled his red hair in obvious frustration. "That I hope we start hitting in the clutch soon."

Lisa echoed Amy's words. "It's early."

"Need I remind you about last year? Every win counts."

"How do you like your rotation so far? Especially the addition of Josh Taylor?"

Max's face lit up when she said the name. "That kid has an arm and a half. He's going to be a horse for us this year. The rest of the starting five I think will be fine. Still a little young. They need to learn that throwing hard stuff down the middle of the plate doesn't work up here as much as it did in the minors. Paul has been pushing the breaking stuff. Got some hardheads, but eventually they'll come around."

Lisa stood up. "Thanks, Murph."

"Anytime, Lisa."

On her trip through the clubhouse, Lisa watched absentmindedly as the players gathered their equipment. Her thoughts returned to home. It would be good to see Frankie and hold her in her arms. They'd face whatever was ahead together.

Chapter 6

Stacy closed the trunk to the Equinox after Amy had placed her bags inside. She slid into the driver's seat and buckled her seatbelt.

"Hungry?" she asked Amy.

"Not really. We had a meal on the plane that wasn't half bad." Amy twisted in the seat to face Stacy. "God, it's good to see you."

"You, too. Let's get you home."

When they arrived at the condo complex and got out of the car, Amy grabbed her bags and reached for Stacy's hand. A familiar, comfortable feeling settled over her like it always did when she came home to Stacy.

They entered the condo. Amy carried her bags to the bedroom, but she didn't let go of Stacy's hand. She dropped the bags beside the bed and spun Stacy into her arms. Bending down, she pressed her lips to Stacy's and pushed her tongue inside. Stacy moaned and grabbed the back of Amy's neck in a tight grip.

Amy lifted off Stacy's T-shirt off and kissed her down to the top of Stacy's bra. Stacy gripped Amy's hair in a rhythmic motion that kept time with the thrusting of her hips against Amy's thigh. Stacy stepped back and unclasped her bra.

Amy started to unbutton Stacy's shorts, but Stacy stilled her hands.

"Let me." Stacy unbuttoned the shorts and tugged them off her hips in tantalizing slowness.

Amy's mind went into a foggy haze as she stared at Stacy's hardened nipples and let her gaze fall to Stacy's lacy panties.

"Let's get you undressed, hmm?" Stacy whispered. She unbuttoned Amy's cotton shirt and pulled it down Amy's broad shoulders. "God, you make my mouth water every time I see you." Stacy rubbed Amy's nipples through her bra, making Amy instantly wet.

Stacy unclasped Amy's belt and quickly shucked off her khaki pants.

"You are one fine-looking woman, Amy Perry."

Amy couldn't take it anymore. She tore off the rest of her underwear and tugged down Stacy's panties. She sucked on Stacy's neck and felt the beating of her pulse against her lips. Trailing kisses down her body, she fell to her knees and placed a soft kiss on Stacy's mound. Stacy gripped her shoulders hard.

"Amy, please..."

Amy rose to her feet, scooped Stacy into her arms, and laid her gently onto the bed. She still couldn't believe that this beautiful woman loved her. She felt the tears well in her eyes and didn't try to hold them back.

"Hey..." Stacy softly caressed her cheek. "You all right?"

"I love you," Amy choked out.

"Oh, God, I love you, too."

Amy draped her body over Stacy's and bit her lip at the exquisite feeling of their nipples pressed together. She pushed Stacy's legs farther apart and gasped when she encountered the wetness there.

"Touch me," Stacy said.

Amy ran her fingers through Stacy's dripping folds, already finding Stacy's clit hard. She kept her thumb there as she lowered two fingers to Stacy's opening. She slowly inched inside. Stacy's hips rose off the bed and her nails bit into Amy's back as Amy began to thrust deep inside her. Amy took a nipple in her mouth, nibbled at first, and then sucked hard. Stacy tightened around her fingers, and Amy knew it was time. She rose on an elbow. Stacy threw her head back against the pillow, and the veins in her neck bulged.

"Come for me, Stace," Amy whispered against Stacy's mouth. Then she plunged her tongue inside, almost coming herself when Stacy's entire body tensed as she climaxed. Amy didn't stop moving her tongue or her fingers until Stacy loosened her grip of her shoulders and sagged back against the mattress.

Amy slipped her fingers from inside and gathered Stacy into her arms. Eventually, Stacy's breathing slowed. She cupped Amy's breast and, in a quick move, straddled Amy's hips.

Amy grinned. "I didn't wipe you out?"

Stacy sucked Amy's nipple into her mouth and tugged hard.

Amy arched off the bed. "I take that as a no," she rasped out.

She didn't try to speak anymore as she surrendered to the sensations bombarding her body.

* * *

Frankie greeted Lisa with a warm hug. She started to pull away, but Lisa tightened her arms.

Frankie kissed her neck. "Good to see you, too, Leese."

Grabbing Lisa's bags, Frankie walked to the bedroom as Lisa followed her.

"I thought we'd order a pizza a little later." Frankie set the bags on the bed. "Sound good to you?"

"Sure." Lisa unzipped one of her bags and tugged out the clothes. "I'll get started on the laundry." Now that she was home, she wasn't looking forward to opening the letter. At all.

Frankie touched her arm. "How about before you do that, you come into the living room and sit beside me on the couch while I hold you. Then you can tell me about your trip. After that..."

Lisa sighed. "Yeah, I know. After that, I open the letter."

"Remember, I'm right here, Leese. Whatever it is, good or bad, we'll face it together."

Lisa followed her into the living room and sat beside her. Frankie held her close and petted Lisa's shortly cropped hair.

"Tell me how the trip went." Frankie kept running her fingers through Lisa's hair as Lisa told her about the trip and gave her the highlights of some of the games.

With each brush of Frankie's fingers, Lisa felt the muscles uncoil in her neck. She gave into the sensation. The sensation of being surrounded by love... and safety. She stared at the thick envelope on the coffee table in front of them.

No time like the present. Lisa straightened and reached for the envelope. She felt the thickness and studied the writing. It appeared to have taken great effort for whoever had written it to scribble out the address.

Lisa didn't realize how long she sat there unmoving until Frankie spoke.

"Go ahead, Leese."

Without another thought, Lisa ran her thumb under the flap of the envelope and tore it open. She pulled out the sheets of paper and began to read. Lisa leaned into Frankie, drawing from the strength she knew and could depend on.

> *Dear Lisa,*
>
> *I've wanted to contact you these past several years, but I never had the courage. After your mother died, I was sure I'd be the last person you'd want to talk to. But now I feel compelled to write to you. Whatever you think of me or have thought of me, I'm still your father.*

Lisa jumped to her feet. Her grip tightened on the pages, and her knuckles whitened.

Frankie stood quickly and came to her side. "What is it?"

"It's my… my father." She raised her head. "It's my father. He abandoned my mom when she was pregnant with me. I've not heard from him in all my thirty-seven years. I didn't even know he was still alive. I don't think I can read this. Hell, I don't want to read it." She thrust the pages into Frankie's hands.

Frankie took the letter, sat down again, and began reading.

Lisa paced back and forth and occasionally glanced at Frankie to gauge her reaction. Frankie finished the last page and set the letter down on the table. She rose, walked to Lisa, and embraced her.

"I don't want to know, Frankie. What can he tell me now that he couldn't have said years ago? Why now?"

Frankie held her tighter. "He's not well, Leese."

Lisa's eyes slammed shut, and she tensed in Frankie's arms. She was shocked when tears trickled down her cheeks. Then, as quickly as she felt sympathy for a man she'd never met, she felt a surge of anger. She jerked away and stomped to the balcony, yanked the sliding glass door open, and stepped up to the railing. She gripped the cool metal as tight as she could, like it was her anchor to reality. Because right now she was surely in a dream. No, not a dream. A nightmare.

She heard Frankie shut the sliding glass door and walk across the deck to stand beside her. She waited for Frankie to speak, but they stood there in silence for a long time. The lights from a riverboat winked at them from the Ohio River, and Lisa heard sprinkles of laughter from the people on board. She wished she were there with them, living another life, not facing what she was facing. Then she gazed at Frankie's profile in the shadows. Who was she kidding? She wouldn't trade her life for anyone else's if it meant she couldn't have Frankie's love.

"You should read the rest of the letter," Frankie said in a soft voice.

She was about to object, but Frankie was right. "I need a few minutes." Lisa gave her a weak smile.

Frankie kissed her lightly on the cheek. "Of course. I'll order the pizza. You come inside when you're ready."

Lisa turned back to the black water below her. The Ohio River flowed strong and sure. She only wished she felt the same.

She shook free of her thoughts and entered the apartment. Frankie hung up from ordering the pizza. Lisa approached the coffee table and the letter. She hesitated one last time before she picked it up. She stood as she read the weak script.

Her dad said he had no excuses for not being there for her over the years. He had left before her mom had even given birth with no contact throughout Lisa's life. Until today. He had followed her reporting career and searched for her address on the Internet. He said he had many regrets, the first was how he treated her mother. And he regretted the years he'd lost with Lisa.

Lisa stopped when she came to the next words.

Congestive heart failure. Could he see her soon?

Lisa slowly folded up the letter, slid it back in the envelope, and set it on the table. She heard Frankie in the kitchen dropping ice cubes into glasses. She'd been so caught up in her father's words, she hadn't noticed until now that the pizza had been delivered. She joined Frankie, leaned against the counter, and folded her arms.

"Coke okay?" Frankie asked.

Lisa didn't answer at first. She still thought about the letter.

"Leese?"

"Hmm? Oh yeah, Coke is fine." Lisa helped carry the drinks and plates to the table, and they sat down. Lisa poured her Coke into her glass and watched as the bubbles rose to the top and fizzed.

"Do you want to talk about it?" Frankie asked in a gentle voice.

Lisa shook her head slightly to clear it and sat back in her chair. "There's not much to say. He's old. He has regrets. And he's not well. I don't mean to be bitter, but damn, I'm thirty-seven-years old. The only reason I see that he's contacting me now is to clear his conscience. I don't know if I can do that."

"You mean you don't know if you can see him?"

"I think about all the years of living with my mom. How hard she worked. How she never took anyone's help. I asked her once why she had never remarried, and she told me my dad was the only man for her." Lisa blew out a breath. "That even pisses me off. She gave up her life for him, and when she died, I was the one at her bedside." She pounded her chest as the painful memory flashed into her mind. "Me." Tears rolled down her cheeks, and she swiped them away.

Frankie moved around the table. She took Lisa into her arms and pressed her head under her chin. "I know, Leese, I know."

Lisa couldn't speak as sobs wracked her body. Frankie kept stroking her back until, eventually, Lisa's sobs became sniffles. Frankie took Lisa's unused napkin and dabbed at her cheeks. Lisa almost started crying again at Frankie's compassionate expression.

"This is a shock," Frankie said. "You don't have to make up your mind now." Lisa started to speak, but Frankie stopped her with a touch to her cheek. "Because right now, I think I know what your answer is. Give it time. He said he wouldn't contact you again, that he'd wait for you to make the next move, and if he didn't hear from you, he'd understand. So how about we eat our pizza and then sit on the balcony for a while. It's beautiful out tonight."

"I'm not very hungry now."

"You still need to eat. Try at least."

In answer, Lisa lifted a piece from the box and put it on her plate. Frankie sat back down and reached for a piece. Lisa stopped her hand and squeezed it gently.

"Thank you," Lisa said.

"You don't need to thank me. I love you."

"Love you, too, Frankie."

Chapter 7

Amy sat next to Stacy in Dr. Rodriguez's office. She tapped her finger against the arm of the chair. Taptaptap. Taptaptap.

Stacy grabbed her hand. "Honey, it's okay." She intertwined their fingers. "This is the next step, and remember it might take several tries."

The door had opened quietly. "That's right, Amy." Dr. Rodriguez moved behind her desk, set down the chart she held, and patted it. "But Stacy's blood work has all come back normal. My exam shows she's in excellent physical health. And she's a prime candidate for a pregnancy. We just have to get one of those little guys to swim the right way into the egg, and we go from there."

Stacy squeezed Amy's hand and held her gaze. "You ready for this?"

"Yes."

Dr. Rodriguez stood. "Good. Let's get at it then."

They followed her to the door of an exam room. "Step in here and get undressed, Stacy. There's a gown on the table. I'll be right back."

Amy accompanied Stacy into the room. She helped her out of her clothes and into the gown and then up on the table. "You're beautiful, sweetheart." She leaned in and placed a gentle kiss on Stacy's lips. "And you'll make a beautiful mother."

The door opened and Dr. Rodriguez entered. Her nurse, Kim, trailed behind. "Are we ready?"

Amy kept her eyes on Stacy. "Yes, we're very ready."

Dr. Rodriguez had Stacy lay back and put her feet in the stirrups. Amy stood at Stacy's side, holding her hand and rubbing her shoulder.

"Now I need you to relax as much as possible," Dr. Rodriguez said. Kim handed her a thin catheter. "Okay, Amy. Help Stacy think of pleasant things."

"Do you remember when we first met, sweetheart?" Amy

asked Stacy.

"At the Watering Hole. You kept beating me at pool." As she spoke, Stacy flinched slightly.

Amy flinched right along with her. "Okay?"

Stacy gave her a tentative smile. "Yes."

Dr. Rodriguez glanced up over the tenting of the sheet that covered Stacy's legs. "Almost there, Stacy."

"And we met again down in Nashville and shared our first night together," Amy said in a soft voice.

"How could I forget?" Stacy whispered.

Amy lifted Stacy's hands to her lips and murmured more words of encouragement until Dr. Rodriguez completed the procedure.

She handed the instrument to Kim. "We've found that lying in this position for about fifteen minutes increases your chances for conception."

Stacy gave her an incredulous look.

"It's not the most pleasant thing in the world, but believe me, I only want what's best for you. Any cramping?"

"A little," Stacy said.

"That should lessen in a few minutes. I'll leave you two alone and come back shortly. When I return, we'll get your appointment scheduled for tomorrow."

Dr. Rodriguez and Kim left the room.

Amy brushed her fingers through Stacy's dark strands. "How are you really?

"Like Dr. Rodriguez said, considering this isn't the most pleasant position to be in, I'm okay."

Amy leaned over and kissed her.

"What if this doesn't work?" Stacy's brow furrowed with worry.

"Then we try again."

"But—"

Amy rubbed her thumb over Stacy's forehead. "Please don't worry. Let's take this one step at a time. We'll face everything together."

"Together?"

"Always."

Stacy tugged her closer. "Kiss me again," she whispered.

* * *

At practice, Amy leveled her bat and waited for the pitch from Wally. She lined it to right center.

"Gonna throw you some inside. Work on pulling, too, Perry," he yelled out to her.

He threw one so close, she had to back away from the plate.

"Jesus, Wally!"

"Wanted to make sure you were paying attention. You seem a little distracted."

You have no idea, she thought, as she smacked his next pitch down the left field foul line.

"Better, Perry."

Amy worked up a sweat after fifteen minutes of hitting. She stepped out of the box and snatched the towel out of the air that Nick tossed to her.

"Everything okay?" he asked. "Wally's right. You do seem a little off."

"Got a minute?" Amy walked toward the dugout.

"Yeah." Nick waved Tim Rawls into the batter's box. "I'll come back in a bit, Rawlsy."

They clomped down the stairs and moved to the far end of the dugout to sit down.

"What's up?" Nick said.

Amy finished wiping down her face. "Stacy had her first treatment."

"Hey, that's great." Nick clasped her shoulder. He frowned. "Isn't it?"

"It's great. It really is."

"But…"

"But it scares the shit out of me. It's a lot of responsibility. And…"

Nick waited on her to finish her thought.

"And now that we're doing this, and it's real, I'm not sure I can handle being away for weeks at a time."

Nick gazed out at the field. Then he snapped his head toward her. "Wait. Are you thinking of quitting the game?"

"I don't know, Nick. I've lived my dream. I could play on for probably another ten years if I wanted and if I stayed healthy. But then our kid will be ten and I will have missed out on so much."

"Have you talked to Stacy about it?"

Amy shook her head. "No. I don't want her thinking about me giving up the game. I'm afraid I'll scare her."

He gave her a look.

"What?" she asked.

"Last year, you got into deep shit by not communicating."

She twisted the towel in her hands. "I'm still working on it, okay?"

He squeezed her shoulder. "Keep working on it, Amy. She deserves to know what you're thinking."

"Your turn, Sanders, if you can break away from your little heart-to-heart with Perry," Wally yelled. He scowled at Nick from the front of the mound.

"Coming!" He jumped to his feet, started up the dugout steps, and stopped. "Have you talked to Lisa?"

"Yeah."

"Okay"—he drew out the word—"you've talked to me and you've talked to your best friend. It's time to talk with your wife. In case you forgot her… the one having the baby?"

Amy threw the towel at him. "All right already. Go hit before Wally drags you out there."

Nick bounded up the steps and took his place in the batter's box. As he sprayed balls all over the field, she thought about how she'd approach her talk with Stacy.

"Hell, Amy," she muttered to herself, "just freaking tell her."

* * *

"What?" Stacy looked up from her place on the couch where she was reading a book. She stared at Amy in shock and blindly set the book aside on the end table. "You're thinking of what?"

Amy sat down next to Stacy and grabbed her hand. She needed the connection. She had taken another shower when she got home from the game. When she was showering, she realized she was only stalling. Afterward, she'd thrown on her tank top and boxers and joined Stacy in the living room.

"Retiring after this season."

Stacy squeezed Amy's hand. "We didn't talk about this before."

"No, we didn't. I didn't think about it until taking steps to have a baby became a reality. Even if this first one doesn't take, we're going to keep trying. I have to believe that by the end of the season, you'll be pregnant."

"Amy, I'd never ask you to give up the game. Something I know you love."

"Come here." Amy held open her arms and Stacy cuddled into them. "I know I've told you this already when we talked about you having the baby, but it doesn't hurt to repeat it. When we lost that game at the end of the season last year, I hurt like hell. Like I had my gut kicked in." Amy's voice caught. "You're the one who keeps me going, Stace. You're the one I come home to and hold in my arms. You're—"

Stacy silenced any further talk by kissing her long and hard. She held Amy's face in her hands. "I love you. You don't have to do this for me."

"I'm doing it for me," Amy said. "And for you and the baby. For all of us."

"Do me a favor, sweetie," Stacy said and kissed her again gently on the lips. "Don't decide now. We've got some time before we need to be making a decision. Let's wait, and we'll talk about it again. A lot of young women look up to you. I'd hate to see you leave the game and regret it later."

Amy started to speak, but Stacy put a finger over her lips. "Trust me on this. We'll be able to sit down and take all the time needed to talk seriously about it. But after the season, okay? I think it's too soon to make a final decision."

Amy kissed Stacy's finger before taking it into her mouth and sucking gently.

Stacy squirmed. "God you know how much I love it when you do that."

"Yeah? You've never told me." Amy grinned and pushed her back onto the couch. "Let's find out what else I do to you that you love."

Chapter 8

By the third week of the season, the Reds had fallen farther behind in the standings and trailed the Cardinals by five games. They were on their first West Coast swing in San Francisco. The Giants, who won the World Series last season, were again on top of their game with their young arms dominating hitters.

Lisa stood on the field with the pool of reporters gathered around Giants manager Bobby Buchanan.

"Your staff is already strong," Lisa said. "But I understand you have another big arm ready to come up from the minors."

Buchanan smiled. "You're talking about Terry Poland?"

"I read where he's clocked in the high nineties, plus he has two more pitches to back up the heat."

"We're excited about him. You're right about that, but we're not going to rush him. We don't need to. The staff we have now is doing fine. It's a luxury that we can wait. He'll be up at some point this season. Don't know when yet. Paul will make that decision after we discuss it."

Paul Hollingsworth, the Giants young GM, had been named Executive of the Year, one of many postseason awards for the Giants team.

Lisa wrote down some more quotes, then she went to Nick Sanders and got his take on the series. She walked to the nearly empty dugout and sat down at the end by herself. The players shagged fly balls while the Reds hitters took batting practice. Her thoughts drifted to her father.

Lisa didn't know how long she sat there. She returned to the present when a shadow blocked the sun. Amy's six-foot frame stood in front of her.

"Lisa? You okay?"

"Hey, Amy. I'm okay. Thanks, though."

Amy sat down next to her. "All right. How about you tell me the truth?"

"Guess I'm pretty transparent to you, huh?"

"Is that a bad thing?"

"No." Lisa thought back to last season. "Why is it we always have our heart-to-hearts in the dugout?"

"Maybe we can call this our office." Amy's green eyes twinkled in amusement. Then she grew serious. "Tell me."

Lisa picked at the wood grain of the dugout bench before replying. "I got a letter from my father." Amy sucked in a breath. Lisa met her gaze. "Yeah, big shock, isn't it?"

"I imagine it is for you. Didn't you tell me he left before you were born, and you didn't know whether he was alive or dead?"

"I guess he's been keeping up on me over the years. Obviously, he's never contacted me until now." Lisa bit her lower lip. "He's not well."

"Oh, Lisa, I'm so sorry."

"Congestive heart failure. It's treatable, but apparently he needs to clear his conscience before he dies." Lisa didn't hide the bitterness in her voice.

Amy didn't say anything right away.

"What do you think, Aim?"

Amy waited a long while before answering. "What do I think? I think you need to do what feels right to you."

"If it were you…"

"If it were me, I'm sure I'd have the same reaction and feelings you're having. But it's hard for me to be totally objective. Both of my parents are dead now, and I'd give anything to see them and talk to them again." Amy blinked away her tears. "That's me, though. You're facing a different situation. My dad didn't walk out on my mom when she was pregnant."

Lisa sighed. "That's a big part of why I'm angry. Not only for me, but for my mom and how hard she struggled while I was growing up. It was tough. He was never there. Not a phone call. Not a letter. Nothing. My mom died with only me by her side. He didn't see how she suffered with cancer." She gave a humorless laugh. "Now he's the one with a serious illness."

Murphy pointed at Amy and waved her out on the field.

Lisa lifted her chin. "You have to go. I should get back to work, too."

They stood up, and Amy gave Lisa a quick hug. "Let me know if you need to talk some more. I'm always here for you. Try not to be too hard on yourself for feeling the way you do, Lisa. It makes sense." She hustled back onto the field.

"Fuck," Lisa said under her breath. She grabbed her reporter's notebook off the bench and left for the press box.

* * *

Amy took her lead off first in the top of the eighth with the Reds down 3-2. She peered at Pete Servace for the signs. He went through them again for Nick.

Hit-and-run.

Alex Timlin, the Giants left-hander, checked Amy one last time and made his move to the plate. Amy took off. She snuck a peek at the plate. It was a horrible pitch out of the strike zone. Nick lunged for the ball, doing his part of the hit-and-run. He didn't make contact, so Amy had to reach second ahead of the throw from the strong-armed catcher. She tried a sneaky slide to the outside of the base, but she was a foot from the bag when the second baseman caught the ball and tagged her out.

She got up and trotted toward the Reds dugout. Nick, obviously disappointed he didn't make contact, swung his bat hard a couple of times before stepping back in for the next pitch.

Murphy smacked her on the butt when she passed by him in the dugout. "Not your fault, Perry. Nick's either. Just a bad pitch to try it on."

Nick flied out. When he came into the dugout, he made a move like he was going to throw his batting helmet. Instead, he pushed it into the open slot and stomped down to where Amy sat.

She slapped him on the thigh.

"Lighten up, Sandy. It wasn't your fault," she said, echoing Murphy's words.

He flopped down onto the dugout bench and scowled at the scoreboard.

"Check the score lately, Perry?" he snapped.

"I know what the score is." She frowned at him.

"Check the standings?"

"Yes, I'm aware of where we are in the standings. Jesus. What's wrong?"

"Nothing." After the last out, he grabbed his glove and ran out on the field.

Damn, she thought. First Lisa, now Nick.

The Giants tacked on an insurance run in the bottom of the inning, and the Reds were quietly retired 1-2-3 in the top of the ninth.

When they got into the clubhouse, Amy watched Nick carefully and listened to his answers to the reporters. He wasn't rude, but he also wasn't as accommodating as usual. Lisa gave Amy a questioning glance on her way to the press box. Amy waited until the rest of the reporters cleared out and Nick started taking off his jersey.

"Want to tell me what's wrong?" Amy asked.

"What makes you think something's wrong?" Nick stripped off his undershirt.

"Gee, I dunno. Could it be you almost bit my head off in the dugout? Come on, Nick. It's me here."

Suddenly, it seemed all the anger left him. He sank down on the chair in front of his locker.

"Nick?"

"It's Ryan." He kept his voice low so only she could hear him.

Amy decided to wait him out when he didn't say anything for several more seconds.

"I think he's having an affair," he finally said.

"What?" She didn't realize she raised her voice until Tim Rawls glanced over at her with a curious expression. "How can you be sure?" she asked in a lower tone.

"I've entered a room a couple of times when he was on the phone. He'd hear me come in and hurry to end the call."

"You got to have more to go on than that."

"He's not been acting like himself. He's been secretive and withdrawn. When we've been on the road, I get his voicemail."

"Still, Nick, that doesn't mean—"

"And the other night, I smelled cologne on his clothes that wasn't his or mine."

Damn.

He gave her a rueful smile. "Yeah. Nothing to say to that, huh?"

"Have you tried approaching him about it?"

"I'm almost afraid to. I mean, what if it's true?"

Amy gripped his hand. "But what if it isn't?" He didn't answer. She pushed a little more. "Think about talking to him, okay?"

Nick stood up, finished undressing, and wrapped a towel around his waist. He grabbed another towel out of his locker. "I'll wait until after this road trip."

Amy wanted to say more to encourage him, but instead she watched him walk away with his head down and his shoulders slumped. Both of her best friends were hurting, and she had no clue how to fix it for either of them.

* * *

"God, Stacy. I want to help them, but I don't know what I can do."

"Hon, you're doing all you can. You're there for Nick and Ryan. You talk to them when they need to talk, and you offer as much support as possible. Don't beat yourself up."

Amy heard her stifle a yawn. She glanced at the bedside clock. It was after 1 a.m. in Cincinnati.

"Shit. I'm sorry. I always forget the time there when we're on the West Coast."

"Don't apologize. You can call anytime."

"You promise you're feeling okay? You wouldn't lie to me, right?" She could almost see Stacy smiling on the other end of the line.

"Amy, I'm always honest with you, and yes, I'm fine. A little tired—"

"Here I am waking you up…"

"Stop right there. You needed to talk. Besides, I love hearing your voice, and I miss you, even though you've only been gone a day." Stacy again stifled a yawn.

"That's it. I'll let you go, sleepyhead."

"Try not to worry. Ryan and Nick will work it out. I don't think Ryan would do something like that."

"Yeah, me either. I'll call you tomorrow at a decent hour. Before we head over to the park. Love you and miss you."

"Love you, too. Get some sleep."

Amy ended the call, tapping her fingers on her chest. Maybe she should call Ryan…

*   *   *

"I don't think it's a good idea."

Amy looked across the table at Lisa at the restaurant. They'd decided to meet for breakfast before heading to the ballpark. She raised her eyebrows, curious to hear Lisa's reasoning.

Lisa stabbed at her eggs and swallowed a bite before continuing. "You're only giving me a hypothetical. I understand this is private between you and your friend. So, hypothetically, I'd say no. Let your friend work it out." She sipped her orange juice and leaned closer. "It's not Nick and Ariana Montegue, is it?"

Amy had taken a drink of her milk and almost spewed it onto her plate. She started coughing. With her eyes watering, she grabbed her water and downed half of it.

"I take it we're not talking about Nick and Ariana."

Amy coughed a couple more times. "No, I'm not talking about Nick and Ariana."

Lisa sat back in the booth. "Good. They seem like a cute couple, and I'd hate to see Nick get hurt."

Amy came very close to telling Lisa about Nick but stopped before she opened her mouth. Nick told her in confidence, and that's how it would stay. Whom he wanted to know was up to him. She changed the subject to what they had discussed yesterday.

"Have you thought anymore about seeing your dad?" She regretted it as soon as the words left her lips. Lisa visibly flinched. She reached across the table for Lisa's hand. "Hey, I'm sorry."

"No, it's okay, Aim. You're my best friend. We can talk about it." Lisa pushed her plate to the side, the food mostly uneaten. "I have so many mixed feelings running through me, like I told you before. Ironically, curiosity is one of them."

"I'm not sure that's so ironic. You're a reporter. That's part of your nature, isn't it?"

"Maybe you're right."

"So does that mean you're leaning toward contacting him?"

Lisa blew out a breath. "Let's say I'm leaning more today than I was yesterday. We'll see how I feel when we get back home from this road trip. I need to talk to Frankie some more."

"She's your rock, isn't she?"

"Just like Stacy is for you, my friend."

* * *

Amy took her lead off second and checked behind her to make sure the shortstop wasn't sneaking over for a pick-off attempt.

Come on, Nick. We need this run.

They were tied with the Giants 4-4 with two out in the top of the eighth on Sunday afternoon. They'd go to San Diego right after the game. Their buses were ready to take them to the airport with bags packed and stored.

Nick had seemed distracted during the series but had come up big for them in last night's game with a three-run homer that put the game out of reach in the ninth.

He fouled off the next three pitches. On each pitch, Amy took off for third. She trotted back to the bag and waited for his next swing. Nick leveled his bat. The pitch was to the outer half of the plate. Nick went with it and lined the ball into the right center gap. Amy didn't need Servace to tell her to keep going. She knew she'd score easily on the double. She slapped hands with Roberts as she headed to the dugout.

The run held up in the bottom of the ninth when Lopez shut down the Giants without a hit.

Amy entered the clubhouse after Nick and watched as he walked toward the showers with his head down. The group of reporters standing around his locker appeared a little peeved at the brushoff.

Okay, that's it, Amy decided. I'm calling Ryan. Screw the consequences.

* * *

Amy didn't get the opportunity to make the phone call until they arrived in San Diego later that evening. She tossed her luggage on the floor of her hotel room and checked the clock. It was 10:30 in Cincinnati, but she thought it was important enough to chance a call this late.

"Hello?" Ryan's voice was gruff.

"Ryan, it's Amy Perry."

"Amy? Is everything okay? There's nothing wrong with Nick, is there?" He sounded a little panicked, which to her was a good sign. If he was cheating on Nick, she didn't think he'd sound so concerned.

"Everything's fine." She hesitated a beat before continuing. "Listen, I wasn't going to call, but I couldn't put it off any longer. I'm not sure how to go about asking you or—"

"Amy, for God's sake, spit it out. You're worse than Nick when it comes to getting to the point."

"Fine. Are you having an affair?"

A couple of seconds of silence passed before Ryan burst out laughing.

Amy rolled her eyes. "I take that as a no?"

In between his laughs, Ryan managed to ask, "Where would you get an idea like that?"

"Nick has been moping around, and I finally asked what the problem was. He said you've been acting strange. Hanging up the phone when he comes into the room. Not being home when he calls. And he said he smelled a different cologne on your clothes."

"Oh my God."

"Please tell me that doesn't mean—"

"No, Amy. I am not having an affair." Ryan sighed. "I'm finally seeing this from Nick's point of view. I could see where he might get that idea. It doesn't help he's out of town so much. I'm sure that's stirred up his imagination."

"Yeah, he's been pretty shook up."

Ryan swore softly. "I never intended for that to happen, obviously. I planned a surprise for him when he gets home from this road trip. I guess the cologne was because I stood too close to the salesman when he showed me some rings. I was going to ask Nick to marry me after the season ends."

"Oh, Ryan. That's so romantic." Amy couldn't keep from smiling.

"Yeah, I thought so until you told me he's worried I'm having an affair."

"Can I tell him it's not what he thinks, but I can't say what it is?"

Ryan sighed again. "Damn it. I feel like I'm spoiling the surprise."

"Trust me. You're not. If it means I can stop watching him mope around the clubhouse and be distracted on the field, then I say it's totally worth it."

"Go ahead, and when you're done, tell the big lug to call me."

* * *

"Go on contact," Servace whispered in her ear.

It was the top of the ninth with one out. Amy was the go-ahead run on third. Nick had already struck out. When he got into the dugout, he shoved his helmet hard into the slot. There hadn't been an opportunity to talk to him before the game.

Amy took her lead off third. Roberts slapped the next pitch to the right side of the infield, and she broke for home at the crack of the bat. The Padres second baseman slid to his knees to get to the ball. He came up firing. Henderson motioned at Amy to slide, but she didn't need to see the signal. She knew the ball would come home. She went into her slide to the outer half of the plate and hooked her hand back. The catcher smacked his mitt on her hand, but she'd already touched the plate. The umpire ruled her safe. She got up and limped slightly to the dugout.

"You okay?" Murphy asked when she stepped down the dugout stairs.

"Yeah, just a bruise." She sat down by Nick on the bench.

"Are you really okay, or were you bullshitting Skip?" Nick said.

"Well, it doesn't exactly feel like I can go out dancing with you tonight, but I think I'll live."

He cracked a smile.

"Good to see you smile, Sandy. After the game, I think I'll give you more reason to smile."

He opened his mouth to speak, but the inning had ended.

She grinned. "Gotta be patient, big guy."

They were the last players in the clubhouse.

"Are you shitting me? You asked him?"

"Don't act so surprised, Nick. You've been moping around worrying about something that's not a problem. I wanted to check in with Ryan to give you peace of mind. I can't tell you what it is, but he's definitely not having an affair."

Amy grabbed her bag from the bottom of her locker. "I do believe you'll have some kissing up to do when you get home for wondering if he was cheating on you."

Nick's face fell. "Damn. I could never imagine him doing it, but still. It gets so weird being away from him sometimes. My imagination goes crazy." Amy remembered Ryan had used the same words. He gave her a sidelong glance as they headed out of the clubhouse. "I'm an idiot."

Amy bumped shoulders with him. They were far enough away from the team bus that they could continue their conversation. "No, you're in love, and sometimes during seven months of baseball, you're far from home." She thought back to last year in Atlanta. "To make you feel better, you weren't sitting in a bar, drunk, with a woman draped all over you. I was definitely an idiot last season."

"Okay. For one thing, I'd never have a woman draped all over me at a bar."

"Oh, shut the hell up. You know what I mean."

Nick laughed. "Yeah, I do." He stopped before they got closer to the bus. The parking lot lights cut a swath across his face and allowed enough light for Amy to see the earnestness in his expression. "You need to let that go, Amy. Stacy has forgiven you, and you'll never do something like that again. You got the help you needed to deal with your mom's death."

Amy blinked away her tears. "You're right. Thanks for reminding me."

"You're welcome." They walked to the bus door. "I still might need you to talk to Ryan."

Amy patted him on the back as he stepped up onto the bus. "Anything for you, my friend."

* * *

"Hey, Leese. Not a bad West Coast swing for the team, huh?"

Lisa set her bag down by the door, and she and Frankie kissed. "No, not bad at all. It started out rough losing the series to the Giants, but they finished up strong in San Diego. I think Murph and the team will take a 4-2 record every time."

"You hungry?" Frankie made a move toward the kitchen.

"A little."

"Good. I saved you some of my famous lasagna." She lifted a container out of the refrigerator and stuck it in the microwave. "Give this a few minutes. I'll warm up some garlic bread, too."

"It's okay. The lasagna's fine."

"Sure?"

"Yeah." With a sigh, Lisa sat down at the dining room table.

"You look beat." Frankie popped open a cold Coke, put it on the table, and sat across from her.

"I am." Lisa took a sip.

"Anything else?"

Lisa glanced up. Frankie was staring at her intently. Then Frankie's expression softened. "It's not hard to figure out what might be bothering you, Leese. You have a lot on your mind after that letter arrived."

The microwave dinged. Frankie got up and stirred the lasagna before sticking it back into the microwave and hitting the timer again. She leaned against the counter. "Do you want to talk about it?"

Lisa spun the knife on the table in front of her. She finally met Frankie's eyes. "It's crazy, but I'm seriously thinking of contacting him."

The microwave dinged again. Frankie grabbed a dish towel, picked up the dish, and carried it to the table. As she ladled out some lasagna onto Lisa's plate, she said, "It's not crazy at all. No matter what, he's still your father."

Lisa forked a bite of lasagna and swallowed. She took another sip of Coke. "He is that, if only by blood."

"Any idea on when you'll call him?"

"Probably during this home stand." Lisa kept her head down as she ate.

Frankie gently gripped her hand that rested on the table. "I'm here for you in whatever way you need me. Please don't shut me out."

Lisa swallowed the lump in her throat. "I know that, Frankie," she said in a rough voice. "I've never doubted it."

They were silent for a while as Lisa finished the lasagna and put her dishes in the dishwasher.

"Oh, hey. I almost forgot. Marge Tompkins called while you were gone. She lost your cell number. I talked to her yesterday and told her you'd be back this evening late."

"Any idea on what she wants?"

"She said, 'Tell that partner of yours I have something big I want to tell her.'"

"Somehow, I don't think that woman could ever do anything small, do you?"

"Uh, no."

Lisa glanced at the clock. "Probably a little late to be calling her now."

"She reminded me she was in Kansas City and an hour behind us. She said to tell you to call, no matter how late."

"Must be big if she's saying it's okay to call at this hour. Last time I did that, she about bit my head off. Well, not even 'about.' She *did* bite my head off until she found out I was calling about the steroid rumors on Amy."

Frankie handed the phone to Lisa with a piece of paper. "She said her cell number has changed since the last time you woke her up."

Lisa chuckled as she dialed the number. Maybe this phone call was what she needed to get her mind off calling her father.

"Lisa?" Marge's gruff voice came through loud and clear.

"Yes, Coach. It's Lisa Collins returning your call. Frankie said you wanted to talk to me."

"You're the first person I thought of, since you're the one who covered Amy's story. I have a player you might be interested in seeing. In fact, I'm certain you'll want to see her play."

Lisa was more than a little intrigued.

"She's the complete opposite of Perry in many ways—smaller

in stature and build, fast, and I mean really fast, cocky with a mouth on her. Where she's similar is in her hitting and fielding. Has one of the best eyes for the baseball I've seen. She plays second but is comfortable at short and has a shortstop arm on her."

"Are you telling me—"

"That's exactly what I'm telling you. I think she could make it, at the very lowest Triple-A. She has the potential to get to the show."

"Marge, I don't mean to doubt what you're saying, but we both know how hard it is to make it. It wasn't easy for Amy. In fact, it was hard as hell."

"You think I don't know that?" Marge snapped. "Sorry, Lisa. I'm not saying she won't have a rough way to go. She needs to get a little of the cockiness knocked out of her." There was a pause on the other end. "Listen, do me a favor. We're having a tourney against a men's team there in the Cincinnati area during the Reds home stand. The Reds have an off-day Thursday, right?"

"Right."

"The tourney's in Hamilton. I can give you all the info you need. Come see her play. That's all I ask."

"What time?"

"Starts at 7:00."

"Okay. I'll be there."

"Bring that best friend of yours, too, since it's an off-day. I have something I want to discuss with her. Oh, and invite Frankie and Stacy if you want."

"Will do, Marge. See you Thursday night." She hung up. "Guess we're going to a game Thursday night if you're up to it. Amy and Stacy, too."

"Oh?"

"Hotshot ballplayer Tompkins wants me to see."

"Why does that sound familiar?"

Chapter 9

"Did she give you the player's name?" Amy asked from the backseat.

"No. Marge said she plays second. Shouldn't be hard to miss." Lisa glanced up at the rearview mirror and caught Amy's pensive expression. "What are you thinking?"

"It seems almost surreal."

"Yeah, it does."

Frankie turned in her passenger seat to address Amy. "Did you ever think another woman could get the chance?"

Before she answered, Stacy piped in, "Oh, I don't believe Amy's ego would even allow that thought to enter her mind." Stacy winked at Lisa in the mirror.

Amy whipped her head around to glare at Stacy. "I don't think like that."

"I was kidding, honey. You've talked about this exact thing happening again." Stacy patted her leg. "It'll be fun to see another woman have a shot at it."

"You kids, behave, or we'll take you back home," Frankie said.

Lisa had a sense of déjà vu as she stopped the car in the gravel parking lot by the baseball field. Two years ago, she had pulled into a similar parking lot to see Amy practice with the Bandits at the University of Indianapolis.

They got out of the car and walked toward the bleachers. They had barely reached earshot when Marge bellowed, "Goddammit, Benson! I told you to knock off that behind-the-back shit, didn't I?"

Lisa tried to see which player had incurred the wrath of Marge Tompkins. The second baseman, the woman they'd come to see play, was laughing.

"It's not fucking funny, either!"

Apparently, Benson had been displaying some of the cockiness Tompkins had told Lisa about. Frankie and Stacy settled into the bleachers, while Lisa and Amy hung around the fence to watch the

Bandits take fielding practice.

Benson continued to grin as she took grounders.

"She is a cocky little shit, isn't she?" Lisa said.

Amy didn't say anything right away.

"Aim?" Lisa glanced at her. Amy's attention hadn't drifted from watching Benson's actions.

"She backs it up, though."

"Dee, Suz, and Kat," Marge said, "you get your swings in before the game." Dee and Suzie trotted toward the plate with Benson.

Dee waved at Amy and Lisa. As Suzie began her batting practice, Dee made her way to the fence.

"Damn, Perry. Good to see you, man! And you, too, Lisa." Dee's strong New York accent always made Lisa smile.

Amy took her hand in a buddy shake. Lisa did the same.

"I'm sure the two of you didn't drive over to see me play. Let me guess. You're here to see Kat Benson. The old lady give you a call?"

Lisa nodded as Suzie got out of the batter's box and Benson settled in. She wasn't very tall, definitely not as tall as Amy's six-foot frame. Maybe five-seven or five-eight, Lisa thought. Benson immediately began spraying the ball to all parts of the field.

Dee watched her hit. "First Perry, now Benson. How come you never cover my play, Lisa?"

"Well…"

Dee waved her off. "Never mind. I know the answer."

"Tina! Get in there and pitch to Benson now!" Marge bellowed.

A tall, muscled, left-handed pitcher replaced the woman on the mound. Benson moved over to the other side of the plate to bat right-handed.

"Switch-hitter," Lisa said, almost to herself.

"Yeah, no difference in her hitting either. Except for maybe a bit more pop. Watch." Dee nodded toward the plate.

Again, Benson smacked the ball all over the field. One inside fastball she lined to the fence on one hop.

"Show off!" Dee shouted.

Benson laughed and kept hitting.

"Remind you of anyone?" Dee grinned at Lisa.

"Yeah, quite a bit."

Amy remained quiet as she kept her focus on Benson in the batter's box. Lisa, though, noticed a woman weaving unsteadily toward the first row of the bleachers.

"That's it, baby!" the woman yelled out. "You show 'em how your mama taught you to play the game."

"Oh, God." Dee shook her head. "Just what Kat doesn't need."

"Who is that?" Amy asked.

"That's her mom. She's shit-faced ninety percent of the time I see her. Please don't judge Kat's play tonight. She always comes apart when her mom shows up."

As if on cue, Kat started swinging and missing at the majority of the fastballs Tina threw over the plate.

"Fuck." Dee jogged toward home plate when Marge waved off Tina's next pitch. Marge put her arm around Kat, who kept her head lowered as they walked over to the dugout.

"Shit," Amy said. "I hate to see that."

Lisa really couldn't relate to what Kat was going through, and neither could Amy. Amy had supportive parents. Although Lisa's dad took off before she was born, her mom had been an anchor in her life until she died from ovarian cancer.

Kat paced back and forth in the dugout as she removed her batting gloves. She tossed them against the bench, plopped down, and held her head in her hands. When she raised her head, she looked over at her mother.

"That's my girl," the woman was saying loud enough for Lisa and Amy to hear. "I taught her everything she knows." The older couple sitting next to her stood and moved up a few rows.

Dee had made her way into the dugout and sat down beside Kat. Kat kept shaking her head at whatever Dee was saying to her. She shrugged off Dee's hand on her shoulder, grabbed her glove, and ran back out to second base. When a ball was hit to her, she fielded it cleanly and fired it over to first with much more force than was necessary during batting practice.

Marge Tompkins approached them, muttering to herself. She finally reached the fence where Amy and Lisa stood.

"Goddammit. I didn't think her mom would show up. Kat lives

in this area, but I can't see her telling her mom about the game. She must've found out another way." Marge scrubbed her hand over her face. "She always plays tight when her mom's in the stands."

"Hey, it's okay, Coach," Amy said. "Lisa and I understand. From the bit that we walked up on, we can tell how good she is."

"Yeah, but she's raw. She has this fucking attitude that I'm pretty sure comes from her shitty home life. She moved out when she was eighteen, but that doesn't mean it didn't affect her. Dee lets her crash at her place in Kansas City. From what Dee has told me, Kat stays mainly to herself and is like a gym rat at the batting cage down the street."

Lisa could tell Marge had a soft spot for her player.

Tompkins waved in the general direction of where Kat's mother was sitting. "And now this shit."

Kat fielded another ball and fired it back to Mandy, the first baseman.

"Jesus, Kat. Take it easy." Mandy scowled at her.

Mandy was one of the few straight women on the team, someone Kat really liked. She knew she shouldn't be taking her embarrassment and frustration out on her. Kat glanced back to her mother in the stands. *Why does she always do this to me? She wonders why I don't call her for games.*

"Well, this is why, damn it," Kat said under her breath. After she tossed another ball over to Mandy, her gaze wandered to where Marge was talking to two women. Kat didn't recognize the blonde. But the tall, muscular one with brown curly hair was unmistakable. Kat's stomach did a little roll.

"Oh no," she whispered. "Not tonight. Not when my mom's here." She wanted to crawl under second base and hide.

Coach Tompkins was motioning her over. "Benson! Come here!"

Although Kat was hustling over because she knew how Tompkins hated to wait for anything, it felt like her feet were stuck in quicksand.

"Kat Benson, I'd like to introduce you to Amy Perry and Lisa Collins."

Kat remembered Collins was the reporter who'd followed Amy

Perry's career. She shook hands with them, at the same time glancing over at her mother. She shifted her attention back to Amy who was asking her a question.

"Who taught you to switch-hit?"

"My dad. He played in the minor leagues with the Chicago White Sox. He told me if Pete Rose could do it, I could, too. He always had faith in me to one day make it to the bigs. I still don't know about that." It was one of the few fond memories she had of her father.

"You definitely have the skills," Amy said. "But it takes a lot more than that. It takes grit and heart and putting up with a ton of shit from the other guys."

Before Kat could answer, a familiar voice called out. "There you are, Kat, hon." Kat's mom was weaving their way. She stopped just short of them. Lisa reached out to steady her when it was clear she couldn't stand up straight.

"Mom, can we do this later?" Kat felt her cheeks flush and the prickling of tears start to form. *I will not cry. I will not cry…*

"Why didn't you tell me you were playing tonight?" She turned toward Lisa and Amy. "And why aren't you introducing me to your friends? I taught you better manners than that." She grabbed hold of the fence, obviously to steady herself even more.

"This is my mom, Angela." Kat kept her head down while she made the introduction, not wanting to see the expressions of sympathy that had crossed Amy's and Lisa's faces. Marge simply looked pissed off.

As Angela reached out with the hand that had been holding the fence, she stumbled to the ground. Marge helped her to her feet. "Why don't we get someone to take you home, Ms. Benson?"

Angela brushed the grass from her jeans and shook off Marge's hand. "No, I want to… to… Hell, what was I here for?" Her brow furrowed as she clearly tried to focus on what she was saying. She motioned at Kat. "Oh, that's it. To see her play." She seemed like she could pass out at any moment. "But maybe you're right."

"You didn't drive, did you, Mom?"

"No, I asked Larry to drop me off. Damn fool said I wasn't fit to drive, which is bullshit."

Marge glanced at her watch. "We have about an hour before

game time. Your mom doesn't live far from here, does she, Kat?"

"No, about half a mile."

"Why don't you take her home? I'll have Dee go with you."

"Coach, I can do it myself."

"I'm sure you can, but it's okay if Dee comes, too, right?" Marge was now sporting the same sympathetic expression that Lisa and Amy had on their faces moments earlier.

"Yeah, I guess."

"Good, good." Marge turned toward the field. "Dee! Come over here a minute!"

Kat tried to ignore the faces from the crowd looking their way. Tried not to notice the shaking of their heads or the words "that's so sad" she imagined were being spoken. She hated this. Hated every last humiliating second of it.

"Yeah, Coach?" Dee said as she stopped next to Kat.

"Why don't you go with Kat while she drives her mom home?" Marge reached into her pocket. "Take my car, Kat. I'll get your mom to the parking lot."

Dee cut a quick glance at Kat. "Okay."

"It was nice to meet you, Amy and Lisa." Kat shook their hands again.

"Nice to meet you, too," Amy said. "We'll still be here when you get back. We're staying for the game."

"Thanks." Her mom was now holding onto the fence with both hands. "For everything."

"Sure."

Kat and Dee headed to the other side of the field to leave from the entrance to their dugout. Dee kept quiet, as if knowing Kat didn't need to hear any pep talks.

"Thanks, Dee."

Dee put her arm around her shoulder and squeezed.

On the drive to her childhood home, Kat thought of a happier time before her mom turned to alcohol to ease the heartache of losing her father to "the other woman." She could still hear her mom's laughter as they played chess. Kat was so competitive, even at age ten when her mother first taught her the game. If Angela won a match, Kat would insist that they play until she won one.

But the lighthearted Angela never returned once Kat's father left the picture. Her mother had liked an occasional drink before that. After her father told Angela he was leaving her for a family friend, someone Angela had thought she could trust, Angela began leaning on the bottle to drown her sorrows. One drink was never enough. Soon, it became three, then five… Angela grew up the daughter of an alcoholic, and she hadn't been able to escape the same fate.

All of this swirled through Kat's mind as she drove toward her family home. She glanced in the rearview mirror at her mom slumped in the backseat, passed out. The tears she'd tried to keep at bay sprung up in her eyes. She swiped at her cheeks

Dee patted Kat's thigh. "It's going to be all right."

Kat nodded, knowing deep down that, no, it wasn't going to be all right. It never would until her mom went into rehab and battled her addiction. She pulled into the drive at the tri-level that was her home for the first eighteen years of her life. As soon as she could leave the place, she did, moving in with a cousin in Kansas City. She got a job. In her spare time, she took out her frustrations by playing on a fastpitch softball team for the first few years she lived there. That is until Marge Tompkins showed up at one of her games. She approached Kat afterward and offered her a tryout for the Bandits. That was last summer, and she never regretted it for a minute. After she made the team, Dee hooked up with her as a roommate.

Kat switched off the engine. She glanced into the backseat again and sighed. "Can you help me get her inside?"

In answer, Dee got out of the car and joined Kat by the back door. Angela was slumped in the seat. Kat eased the door open, reached in, and gently shook her mom. When she didn't rouse, she shook her a little harder.

"Mom, we need to get you in the house."

"Huh?" Angela sat up and looked around her in confusion. "How'd I get here?" She turned to Kat, obviously trying to focus. "Oh, hey, baby. When does your game start?"

"Later. How about we get you inside?" She helped Angela to her feet and shut the back door.

Angela stumbled between Kat and Dee as they struggled to hold her upright. Her mother was slight of build, but her drunkenness added weight to their efforts to direct her.

"Her bedroom is second door on the right down that hall," Kat said as they entered the home.

"You remembered." Angela gave Kat a lopsided smile.

"Yeah, Mom, I remembered." Kat tried to overlook the state the house was in, although she shouldn't have been surprised. She'd been the one to pick up the empty vodka and rum bottles. Apparently, her mother didn't have anyone in her life now to clean for her. The living room was a mess. The bedroom wasn't in any better shape. Clothing lay strewn on the floor, and dirty glasses sat on the nightstands.

After Dee helped get Angela into bed, she backed up and motioned toward the door. "I'll wait in the living room for you, Kat."

"Thanks, Dee." Kat helped Angela out of her jeans and stained T-shirt and tugged the covers up. Her mom now had tears in her eyes.

"Don't look at me like that, baby. I'm fine. I just miss you."

Kat blinked to keep the tears at bay. She was afraid she'd break down once she started. "I love you, Mom, but you need help."

"Aw, I'm fine, like I said. I can quit anytime. Had a couple of drinks before Larry dropped me off."

Kat had a sudden urge to find Angela's so-called boyfriend and kick his ass. She was about to say more, but her mom was already drifting off again.

"Love you, Kat," she mumbled. She flipped onto her side and faced the other way.

Kat stood there as she tried to remember all the reasons her therapist had given her for not enabling her mother. She knew the symptoms of codependency. She'd lived it for her teenage years as she tried to maintain a normal life at school while caring for an alcoholic mother. Her father? She had no desire to see the man, despite the fact he had reached out to her. She leaned over and kissed her mother's temple. "I love you, too, Mom."

She returned to the living room. "I'm ready to go back to the field." As they neared Marge's car, Kat held out the keys. "Can you drive?"

Kat was glad Dee didn't question her. There was really nothing to say.

"There they are," Marge said as Dee and Kat appeared near the dugout.

The other team had taken the field for their batting and fielding practice. Amy had been chatting with Marge ever since Dee and Kat left. Lisa seemed distracted since the encounter with Angela. Amy wondered if she was thinking about her father.

Marge was already walking toward the dugout.

"Everything okay, Lisa?"

Lisa jerked at the question. "What? Oh, yeah." She glanced toward the Bandits dugout.

Amy followed her line of sight. "Tough to see her mom like that."

"It was. Even though I have no idea how my dad led his life these past thirty-something years, I can't help but compare him to Kat's mother and what Kat's had to endure."

"You said you were going to reach out to him, though, right?"

"After seeing Kat's mom, I wonder if I'm doing the right thing."

"For what it's worth, I think you are. If you don't, you'll always have this 'what if?' hanging around you."

Lisa kicked at the grass. "I'm sure you're right."

"At least give it a shot. If nothing comes of it, then nothing comes of it. You can say you tried your best."

"Right."

The other team finished their pregame practice, and the pitcher was getting in his warm-up tosses.

"They're about ready to start," Amy said. "How about we go sit with Stacy and Frankie?"

They walked toward the bleachers. Lisa bumped shoulders with Amy. "Thanks, buddy."

"I don't know if I helped any."

"Oh, you did, Aim. You always do."

As they neared the stands, Stacy gave Amy a questioning look. Amy shook her head slightly.

Frankie stood up. "Anyone want something to drink from the concession stand?"

"You know we do! I'll go with you, Frankie," Stacy said.

Amy and Lisa settled onto the bleachers.

"Why does it always seem like I'm accompanying you to cover stories?" Amy asked.

"It did seem like that when we first met, didn't it?"

"If I recall, our first 'date' was a high school football game."

"You recall correctly. Hey, Benson is leading off. Let's see what she's got. She may shake it off with her mom not here."

Against the right-handed pitcher, Kat stepped into the batter's box to bat from the left side. She had more power from the right, but she could jump out of the box faster from the left. She peeked at the third baseman for the Hamilton Mustangs, the semipro team they were playing tonight. He was positioned well behind the bag. The first pitch hit the inside edge of the plate for a strike, but it wasn't the pitch she wanted. Something on the outside would do for what she had in mind. The next pitch was a fastball on the outer part of the plate. Squaring up to bunt, she deadened the ball so that it headed up the third baseline on a slow roll. She sprinted out of the box and easily beat the third baseman's throw.

Jo, the first base coach, smacked her on the butt. "Nice one, Benson."

Kat immediately stretched her lead off first and dove back with the pitcher's throw over. Now, it was a matter of timing and reading his move. She gauged his next three tosses over. The crowd booed. Even though the Mustangs were the home team, apparently the fans wanted to see some action.

Finally, the pitcher threw one toward home. Kat made a break for second. She glanced briefly at the plate to make sure she wouldn't be doubled up on a line drive. Dee had been taking the pitch all the way. The ball arrived a split second after Kat slid in headfirst and hooked her hand around the bag to keep from sliding past.

"Safe!"

She called time, stood up, and dusted herself off. This was what she needed. The game. It was always the game that kept her mind off her mother and her alcoholism. Over the years, the game had become a lifesaver for Kat. And she wasn't ashamed to admit it.

The Mustangs won 4-3, but Kat Benson was the star of the night for the Bandits. She finished 3-4 with one of her hits making it over the left field fence for a two-run homer.

As the Bandits players gathered their gear, Marge walked over to where Lisa and Amy stood next to the fence. Frankie and Stacy headed toward the car.

"What did you think, Lisa?"

"I think you're right, Coach. I think Benson has a lot of raw talent. Probably a good feature story there, but if you don't mind, I'd like to talk to my friend Sarah Swift of *Baseball Weekly* about doing the story. I'm the Reds beat writer. She'd be a much better person for the job."

Marge nodded. "All right. I trust your judgment. I remember the articles you two wrote when Amy and my team were accused of steroid use." Marge's face reddened at the memory.

Amy was glad when Lisa cut in before Marge started on one of her rants. "I think we probably need to be heading home." Lisa held out her hand. "Thanks for calling me, Coach. I'll have Sarah get in touch. I think she'll be able to travel to wherever you're playing, too."

"Look forward to hearing from you." Marge grasped Amy's arm. "Can I talk to you a minute?"

"Sure."

"We'll wait for you at the car, Aim."

"See you in a few." After Lisa left, Amy addressed Marge. "What's on your mind?"

Marge chewed on her lower lip. Amy had never seen her nervous about anything. Ever.

"I'm not sure how you'll feel about this, but you're the only one I trust to take over. So, what the hell. I'm going to give it a shot."

"What are you talking about?"

"I'm getting too old for this shit, Amy. The recruiting and putting up with attitudes as we break in new players each year. But I don't want the Bandits to go belly up with me leaving. I have no idea how long you plan to play the game. In the interim, one of the other coaches could take over, but ultimately, I want you to manage the team."

"Coach, I—"

Marge held up her hand. "No, let me finish. You have the right mindset for this. You're easygoing, levelheaded. You've played for the team, so you definitely know the ins and outs of managing it. And when I say interim manager, the team would be ready for you whenever you leave the game. Even four or five years from now, if that's what you decide to do."

Amy didn't know what to say, so she kept silent.

"Do me a favor and mull it over."

Amy watched as the players loaded their gear into the three team vans. "It's funny. I was talking to Stacy about maybe retiring after this year."

"Shit. I didn't think you'd leave the bigs so soon."

"Well, I told her if we won the Series this year, that would be the ultimate high for me as a player. But not as a person. As a person, the ultimate high would be if we were able to have a child. She of course told me to take time after the season, to not make any hasty decisions about quitting right now."

"You both are talking of having a kid?"

Amy smiled. "Yeah."

"Please don't tell me you'd be the one to carry the baby."

"What is it with everyone thinking I couldn't handle being pregnant!"

Marge burst out laughing. Amy glared at her until she, too, started laughing. "Okay, okay. I get it. You can quit now, Coach."

Marge opened her mouth to say something but started laughing again.

"I said you could stop."

Marge grabbed hold of her shoulder. "Sorry, Perry. I can't see it. Stacy, yes. You?" She bit her lip in an obvious attempt to hold the laughter at bay.

"You don't need to rub it in. Anyway, before you get so caught up in making fun of me, Stacy's already visited a fertility doctor. We'll know soon if she got it on her first try. I told her I wouldn't have a problem retiring with a Series win. I don't want to miss out on watching our kid grow up."

"For what it's worth, I think you'd both make great moms."

"Thanks." Amy thought of something. "I don't think I could do it. The managing I mean. I wouldn't want to pick up our lives and move to Kansas City. Stacy's family is in Indianapolis. We have good friends there, too. And Frankie and Lisa would just be a little over a hundred miles away when the Reds are in town."

"That's just it, Amy. If you were to manage the team, you could move it to Indianapolis. A new women's baseball league is starting up. Only a few of the Bandits players have close ties to KC. The others would jump at the chance to have Amy Perry manage them, especially with your experience at the major league level. Kat could sure use your guidance. A lot."

Amy thought about the fiery player and the demons she faced with her mother's addiction.

Marge made her last push. "At least give it some thought."

"All right. I will. I'll talk it over with Stacy."

"Of course. I would expect that."

"Marge! We're ready!" One of the coaches waved Marge over.

"Well, that's my cue." Marge held out her hand for another shake. "Thanks for coming out and thanks for listening. Good luck with the season."

"I'll keep in touch, Coach."

"Thank Lisa again for coming out, too."

"Will do."

Amy slid into the backseat next to Stacy. "What was that about," Stacy asked.

"We'll talk about it later." Amy quickly changed the subject. "What'd you really think, Lisa? About Benson?"

"Oh, I was being honest with Tompkins. She's got a lot of raw talent. She may need to temper her attitude some. I'll definitely fill Sarah in on her story."

Chapter 10

"Want a beer?" Frankie asked as she and Lisa entered their apartment.

"Yeah, I think I'm going to need one before I make this call."

Frankie handed her a Michelob and opened the other bottle for herself. "Your father?"

"Thanks." Lisa took the bottle. "Yes. I need to do this."

"Is that what you and Amy were talking about?"

"How do you know we weren't talking about Kat Benson the whole time?"

"Maybe because I know all your expressions by now, and you were definitely talking about something more serious than another woman clawing her way up the ladder into majors."

Lisa leaned in to give Frankie a kiss. "Guess you know me, and I'm glad you do." She took a sip of her beer and picked up the envelope from the end table. She pulled out the letter with her father's contact information at the bottom. As she took a big gulp of beer, Frankie moved to stand beside her.

"Are you ready for this?" Frankie asked quietly.

Lisa let out a sigh. "As ready as I ever will be." Carrying her beer, she started toward the balcony. She stopped, tucked the letter under her arm, and held out her free hand. "Come with me."

"I don't want to intrude."

"Frankie, you're my partner and my number one priority. You can never intrude. Come and sit out here with me. Please."

"You don't have to say please." Frankie took Lisa's hand. They went out onto the balcony and settled into chairs next to each other.

Lisa set her beer down on the side table and stared at her father's scrawl a moment longer. Finally, she muttered, "Fuck it," and dialed the number on her cell. She almost hoped it would click over to voicemail as it went through four rings, but on what would've been the fifth ring, a raspy voice answered.

"Hello."

Lisa gripped the phone tighter. Frankie clasped her other hand that was holding onto the arm of the chair for dear life. Frankie gave her a smile of encouragement.

"Yeah. Hi," she finally said. "This is Lisa." She couldn't bring herself to say, "Dad," and doubted that day would ever come… or at least not anytime soon.

"Lisa? Oh, thank God. I'm so glad you called." Her father's voice broke. Lisa could hear him quietly crying. After a long moment, he cleared his throat. "I'm so glad you called," he repeated. "I didn't think you would."

"I didn't think I would, either." Lisa heard the bitterness in her tone but didn't try to quell what was over thirty-five years of anger toward her father for abandoning them. Images flew through her mind. Her mother crying when she didn't think Lisa could hear her. The awkward Christmases and birthdays spent with only the two of them. Lisa remembered staring at the empty chair by her mother and trying her best to picture what her dad would look like on that particular day. She had only one photograph—an old and faded one that her mother tucked away in the dresser by her bed. Without her mother's knowledge, Lisa would sneak into her bedroom and sit on the edge of her bed to stare at the image of the two of them together so many years ago. So young, so happy.

"Are you there?"

Her father had said something she didn't catch. "What?"

"I told you I'm so proud of you and who you've grown into as a woman. I keep up on your writing and have since you started writing professionally."

A spark of anger pulsed through her body and flew out of her mouth. "Please don't make this into some sappy *Lifetime* movie where you tell me you showed up at my graduations or whatever without me knowing, but didn't want to approach me."

He didn't respond at first.

Lisa scrubbed her hand over her face. As quickly as the anger had rushed in, it left. "I'm sorry. This is all a shock to me. What do I call you? And don't say 'Dad.' That, I can't handle."

Surprisingly, he chuckled. "No, I wouldn't guess I've earned that right. How about you call me Ken?"

She knew her dad's name, of course, but it was still weird to believe she was actually talking to him. "Okay, Ken." She heard him wheezing on the other end of the line and remembered again how sick he was. "So, I guess it doesn't look good for you?"

"No. Congestive heart failure. I take medication, but I still get winded with it."

Lisa couldn't hold back the question any longer. "Why? Why did you leave Mom when she was pregnant?" She felt the tears slipping down her cheeks. Frankie gave her hand a little squeeze. Frankie's eyes were glistening in the light filtering out from the living room. Enough time went by that Lisa didn't think he'd answer. "Fine. If you don't want to talk, fine. This should be enough to ease your conscience." She was about to hang up when his voice stopped her.

"Wait. Don't go, Lisa. I… I want to see you if you'll let me."

Lisa sucked in a shaky breath. It was her turn to wait a long time before answering. "This was hard enough. I'm not sure I can sit down with you."

"Don't completely dismiss the idea." He spoke hurriedly. "Please."

He said the last word with such a sound of desperation that Lisa's resolve faltered.

"I'll think about it, okay?"

"Yeah, sure. I understand. I'm glad you reached out."

"I'll call you again."

"Good. I won't bother you. You make the move."

"Okay. Bye."

"Goodbye, Lisa."

Lisa clicked off her phone. She watched the lights of a riverboat passing by. So often, that sight gave her comfort. Tonight, she felt empty even though she'd just hung up after speaking with her father.

"You all right?"

"I don't know, Frankie. Hell, I'm not sure what I'm feeling."

"That's only natural."

Lisa shook her head. "I guess."

Frankie stood up and held out her hand. Without speaking, Lisa took hold of it and allowed Frankie to lead her back inside. Frankie shut off the lights on their way to the hallway to their bedroom. Slowly, she undressed Lisa and took off her own clothes. She eased Lisa down on the bed with her and held out her arm. Lisa pushed into her side and placed her head on Frankie's chest.

Lisa finally broke the silence. "He sounds so weak."

Frankie was rubbing Lisa's back. She paused for a second and then continued the motion.

"He wants to meet."

"I gathered from hearing your side of the conversation."

"I don't know if I can do it, Frankie." Lisa leaned up on her elbow and stared down at her. "Does that make me a bad person?"

Frankie caressed Lisa's cheek. "No, sweetheart, that makes you human."

"I really don't want to talk about this anymore tonight. What I'd really like is for you to make love to me."

Frankie kissed Lisa softly. "You don't have to ask me twice," she said as she rolled Lisa onto her back.

* * *

Amy and Stacy entered their condo. Stacy went to the kitchen. "Do you want a bottle of water?"

"No, I'm good." Amy flopped down on the couch.

Stacy came in, sat next to her, and gave Amy a look.

"What?" Amy asked.

"Are you going to let me know what you and Lisa were so engrossed in discussing?"

"Oh, her dad sent her a letter and wanted to meet with her. She told me about the letter in the middle of Nick's crisis about Ryan's supposed cheating, and I forgot to tell you. I guess her dad's not well at all."

"Didn't you say he left her mom before Lisa was born?"

"Yeah. She asked me what I thought. I told her she should make the effort or she'd always be wondering 'what if?'"

Stacy took a sip of her water. "Did she agree?"

"I think she might call him tonight."

"I'm glad you both remained such good friends."

"That never bothers you? That I'm still best friends with my ex?"

Stacy shook her head. "I remember how good she was last year when you were going through your mother's death. A friend like that, you don't want to lose."

Amy teared up at the memory. "Lisa will always be special to me."

Stacy poked her in the arm. "What did the boss lady have to say to you when we went to the car?"

"This you'll find interesting. She's talking about retiring and asked when I decided to leave the game, if I'd want to take over as manager."

"Marge is ready to hang it up?"

"That's what she said. I told her about us trying to have a baby."

Stacy arched her brow.

"All right. *You* trying to get pregnant. Trust me, she had a good laugh thinking about me being the one having the baby."

Stacy giggled. "You have to admit, Amy, that it is a bit of a stretch."

"Before you go into hysterics again about it, let me finish."

Stacy bit her lip and nodded.

"I told her I'd think about it. She told me I could relocate the team to Indianapolis if I agreed. Which would work, considering your sisters and mom live there."

Stacy set her water bottle on the coffee table. "You're really serious about this retiring thing, aren't you?"

"I told you. If we happen to win it all, it's definitely something to consider. Marge said if I kept playing a couple more years, there'd be a coach to fill in for me. But when I was ready to leave the game, the team was mine."

"I could see you coaching."

Amy stared off at the far wall. "Me, too. I think I could help out players like Kat Benson."

"Yes, you could. I saw what shape her mom was in. I felt sorry for Kat."

"Marge was telling me she needs a little guidance."

"Which you could provide."

"I think so."

"Well, tonight's not the night to make any big decisions. Remember what we discussed. Wait until you see how the season plays out before you decide to retire, because this isn't as cut and dried as you think it is. Promise?"

Amy leaned over and kissed her. "Promise."

Amy flipped through the sports channels on their TV in the bedroom. It was quiet in the bathroom. Stacy had gone in to take her shower, but Amy hadn't heard any water running.

"Honey? Everything okay in there?" she called out.

Stacy didn't answer. Instead, the door opened. She stood in the doorway, staring down. When she raised her head, she had tears in her eyes.

Amy instantly jumped to her feet and rushed to her. "Sweetie, what is it?"

Stacy held out the instrument Amy hadn't seen in her hand. There was a large, easy-to-read, minus mark in the middle of the small screen. "I'm not pregnant."

"Oh, honey." Amy took her into her arms. Stacy let Amy hold her for a while before she pulled away and threw the pregnancy test in the bathroom wastebasket. Amy led her to bed and again held her. "It'll be okay. It's only our first try. We're not going to give up."

"But my mom and Darlene got pregnant on their first tries."

"That doesn't mean anything." Amy pictured Darlene's wild, two-year-old twins. She grimaced. Please don't let our kid be like that.

"What's the face for?"

"Nothing."

"You're disappointed in me, aren't you?" Stacy started crying again.

"No, no. That's not it at all." Amy leaned over and kissed her. "I'm sorry I wasn't being honest. I was thinking about Mitchell and Michael."

"The little hellions?" Stacy wiped the tears from her cheeks.

"Yeah."

She slapped Amy lightly on the stomach. "You can't compare them with how our kid will be."

"Good."

"Although the fact that they're two years old has a lot to do with their behavior."

"When our child is two, can we ship her to your mom and ask

your mom to return her when she's, oh, three-and-a-half?"

Stacy laughed. "It doesn't work that way. I see you're still expecting us to have a girl."

"Absolutely. I have to teach her how to play baseball, after all."

"Amy, you do know you can teach our son to play baseball, don't you?"

"Not the same."

Stacy laughed again. Amy kissed her, pleased that she had helped lift Stacy's sadness. The kiss became a little more heated.

"Still want to take that shower?" Amy asked.

Stacy stood up and started toward the bathroom. "Only if you join me."

Amy sprang to her feet. "Oh, hell yeah."

* * *

Amy followed through on her swing and watched the flight of the ball. It hit a few rows up into the left field stands. She used batting practice to work on her situational hitting, but sometimes, it felt damn good to connect and launch a ball into the lower deck.

"How about another one of those fat ones right about here, Wally?" She held her bat over the middle of the plate.

"Of course, Perry. Whatever you want," he said in a sarcastic tone. He tossed a ball over the heart of the plate that might have hit 85 miles per hour on the radar gun.

Amy almost jumped out of her cleats as her bat connected with the ball. This one hit the facing of the upper deck. A low whistle got her attention.

"Damn, Aim. Why don't you try that in the game tonight?"

Amy glanced out of the corner of her eye. Lisa was leaning against the netting. The next ball was one of Wally's crazy knuckle balls. She waited on the pitch and lined it into center field. She waved him off. "That's it for me, Wally."

She stripped off her gloves and left the cage. "Do you have time to talk?" she asked Lisa.

"Always have time for you."

Amy pointed toward the dugout. "Why don't we head to our office?"

"Sounds good."

They settled onto the wooden bench. Lisa didn't speak, seemingly waiting for Amy to make the first move.

"Tompkins asked me if I had any interest in taking over coaching the Bandits."

Again, Lisa let out a low whistle. "So, I guess you're thinking more seriously of retiring?"

"I told her it wasn't certain yet, that Stacy and I needed to talk it over more. She said she could even have an interim manager take over until I was ready to manage. Then I told her it might be sooner rather than later that I quit the game."

"You'd move to Kansas City?"

"No. Marge said I could relocate the team to Indianapolis."

Lisa gazed out at the field as one of the Reds players peppered line drives around the outfield.

"Lisa?"

A slow smile creased Lisa's lips. "Marge couldn't have picked a better successor."

Amy returned the smile. "Yeah?"

"You'd be perfect, Aim."

* * *

"So, did you work everything out at home?" Amy asked Nick Sanders.

He spit out sunflower seeds before answering her vague question. Both of them knew what she was referring to.

"Yes, we did. There was a lot of making up to do. Not on my part, mind you."

"Oh, no. Never." She clapped when Ferguson slapped a run-scoring single to left field. She slapped hands with Cruz as he passed by in the dugout after scoring. The Reds were up 5-0 in the bottom of the seventh against the Chicago Cubs. It was the first game of a nine-game home stand, after which the Reds would leave on a ten-game road trip against their Central Division foes, starting in St. Louis, then up to Milwaukee, and ending the trip in Chicago against these same Cubs.

"Tell me more about this player you saw last night." Nick spit out another sunflower seed.

"She's got raw talent. I think she could make it in the minors. I don't know what level, but she needs some more coaching first."

"What's that ol' manager of yours think?"

"Marge is definitely high on her." Amy hesitated before continuing. "She approached me about something."

Amy's tone must've caught Nick's attention. He raised his eyebrows in question.

Hell, she already told her best friend. Might as well tell Nick, too. "I'll talk to you later about it."

They grabbed their gloves and hustled onto the field after the last out.

* * *

"Remember I told you I was thinking about retiring after this year?"

Amy had taken her shower after the other guys had finished and gone. Nick hadn't left. He said he was curious to know what she had to say.

She spotted one of the clubhouse staff picking up towels. "Let's wait to talk while we go to our cars." She stuffed her gear into her bag and lifted it to her shoulder. They didn't speak again until they reached her car. Amy tossed her bag in the back and slid into the driver's seat. Nick slid into the passenger side.

"What else can you tell me that would shock me as much as you walking away from the game? You said Tompkins approached you about something."

"It seems everything is happening at once. When we went out to see this player, Marge came up to me after the game. She asked me if I'd be interested in managing the team. She wants to retire."

"Goddamn. You're right. Everything *is* happening at once. What'd you say?"

Amy relayed the rest of her conversation with Marge Tompkins.

Again, Nick grew quiet. Enough time went by that Amy had to ask. "What do you think?"

"What do I think? I think we need to bust our asses and win the fucker this year."

Chapter 11

Kat wiped the tears streaming down her face and sniffed as quietly as possible in the darkness of the hotel room. She didn't want to wake Dee, asleep in the other bed.

"Do you want to talk about it?"

Kat rolled toward Dee's voice. "I didn't mean to wake you."

Dee switched on the bedside lamp. "You didn't, Kat. I've been worried about you for a while. You've closed up on me. You never do that. I'm your best friend, remember?"

Kat pushed herself up and leaned against the headboard. "Yeah, I remember. I… I don't know what to say."

Dee swung her legs over the bed and sat up on the edge while she faced Kat. "How long has she been like that?"

She didn't need to say whom she was talking about.

"She started drinking when my dad left her for her best friend."

Dee grimaced. "You never told me. God. That sucks."

"Yeah, it did. Still does. I don't want anything to do with either of them, my dad or Irene."

"Her name's Irene? How old is she? Eighty?"

Kat couldn't help but laugh. Dee knew what to say to lighten the mood.

"No. Same age as my mom."

"So, the drinking started then?"

"She had drinks on occasion before that—parties, outings, sometimes when we went out to eat. But it was never bad. Once my dad left, it's like someone flipped a switch. She started buying the biggest bottle of vodka. I'd come home from school and find her passed out on the couch." The sick feeling hit her stomach like it was yesterday. The first time it happened, Kat hoped, prayed even, that it was a one-time thing. Unfortunately, the pattern repeated itself for days and weeks following her dad's leaving.

"And it didn't stop?"

Kat shook her head. "I didn't think it was possible, but it got worse."

"What about her job?"

"She got fired from the law firm where she worked."

"She was an attorney?"

Again, the sudden urge to throw up assaulted Kat. Thinking about her mother's promising career and how quickly it fell apart did that to her. "Family law."

Dee got up. "Scoot over."

Kat gave her a questioning look.

"Get over yourself, Benson. I'm not making moves on you."

Kat shifted over so Dee could sit next to her.

Dee draped her arm over Kat's shoulder and pulled her close. "You looked like you needed a hug."

Kat leaned into the embrace. "Thanks," she mumbled.

"No problem." Dee was quiet for a moment. "The firm where she worked, didn't they try to get her help?"

"It was my mom's first trip to rehab." Kat remembered how hard her mom worked in that facility. Part of the therapy was to have family members join in sessions with the therapist. She recalled the spiteful words she threw at her mother. About how embarrassed she was to have anyone over. That wasn't the worst of what she said. It was honest, which is what the therapist had asked her to be. But Kat shouted that she wished she had a different mom, and the anguish on her mother's face still haunted Kat. Something had withered and died inside her that day. Afterwards, when her mom returned to drinking and Kat would put her to bed each night, Angela would reach up, caress Kat's cheek, and say, "I know you wish you had a different mom. I'm sorry. I'm so, so sorry for what I put you through." Angela would pass out before Kat had a chance to respond.

Dee squeezed her shoulder. "What were you thinking about?"

"How much words can hurt someone."

"Hey, Kat. Whatever you said to your mom, it's okay. It must have been so hard for you. No sisters or brothers. Your dad left. Your mom turns to drinking. How the hell did you make it through school?"

"One day at a time."

"How does your mom get by without a job?"

"Disability."

Dee gave her an incredulous look. "You're shitting me."

"Alcoholism is a disease." Kat didn't mean to sound defensive, but she did. Yeah, her mom shouldn't spend the money on more booze. But she needed money to feed herself. Kat tried to help as much as she could. She didn't have the funds, though, to make sure her mom had food in the house. Kat still had to worry about her own living.

"I'm sorry, dude. I know alcoholism is a disease. I have an uncle who's a recovering alcoholic. Before he went on the wagon, he put his family through hell. It's that sometimes, I wonder about the government giving money to someone who's probably going to spend it on the very thing they shouldn't."

Any rancor Kat felt quickly dissipated. She nudged her shoulder against Dee's. "I get what you're saying. Believe me. It's that sometimes…"

"It's that sometimes you think you're the only one who understands. That you're alone in this."

Kat couldn't speak for fear she'd break down. She bit her lip and nodded.

Dee hugged her again and patted her hair. "That's where you're wrong. I'm here for you, Kat. Coach is, too." Dee swiped at a stray tear on Kat's cheek. "She comes across as a hard-ass, but I remember how she was with Amy when her mom died. Amy told me, too, about when Marge drove into Cincinnati and helped her straighten out her hitting. She's got a heart of gold but doesn't want anyone to know about it."

"She's been good to me, although I wonder why. I drive her crazy with the shit I pull on the field."

"Remember flipping the ball between your legs to me at second to start that double play two weeks ago?"

Kat jumped up from the bed and imitated Marge stomping over to her at the dugout entrance when Kat ran off the field. She dropped her voice an octave. "You try that shit again, Benson, and your fucking ass is on the bench for the rest of the game. You hear me?"

Dee held her sides as she rolled around on the bed. "Oh my God. You could always nail her voice."

A pounding on the wall stopped them cold. A very familiar voice cut into the room. Only this time, it was the real deal. "These walls are thin, you two! Cut out the shit and get to sleep!"

They covered their mouths as they attempted to hold in their laughter. Dee got up from Kat's bed and moved toward her own. Before she had a chance to get into it, Kat grabbed her and hugged her tight.

"Thanks," she whispered.

"Anytime, Kat. Anytime."

Chapter 12

"What are you thinking about so seriously?" Sarah asked Lisa.

They were in Chicago. The Reds had played well on the trip, sweeping St. Louis and taking two out of three from the Brewers. They'd split the first two of a four-game series with the Cubs and were down 6-3 in the top of the eighth for the rare Saturday night game at Wrigley Field.

"I'm not sure I like all the new-fangled changes they made to Wrigley." Lisa had already started on her article. The team was playing flat tonight, which could be from fatigue.

"Oh, don't give me that shit. It's more serious than that."

Lisa really didn't want to talk about the decision she'd made. It frankly scared the crap out of her. "What did you decide about going to a Bandits game?" she asked.

"I get it. You're changing the subject."

Amy smacked a double down the left field line to lead off the inning.

Lisa idly wondered if they could come back this late in the game. Their bullpen had been overtaxed in Milwaukee.

"Collins?"

"You answer mine, and I'll answer yours."

"All right. Fine. I spoke with my editors at *Baseball Weekly*. They want me to fly into KC next month."

"Good. She deserves a look-see."

Sarah challenged her with a glare. "And? What's your story?"

"Right now, I have it that the Reds are beat down some from this ten-game road trip."

"Not that story, damn it."

"My dad wrote me and wants to meet me."

"Is that the letter you got awhile back?"

"Yup."

"Is this the same dad you've never seen? The same dad who took off when your mom was pregnant?"

Lisa blew out a breath. "Yeah, that one."

"What'd you decide?"

"I called him when we were home. Told him I'd think about it."

They stopped talking long enough to type on their laptops when Nick Sanders followed up Amy's double with one of his own. They might come back in this game, Lisa thought.

"That's got to be rough on you."

Lisa was surprised at Sarah's serious expression.

"What?" Sarah asked when she caught Lisa's glance. "I can't be sympathetic?"

"I didn't say anything."

"You didn't have to." Sarah sounded a little hurt.

"I'm sorry, Sarah. I've been in kind of a tailspin since I got his letter. Talking to him on the phone only added to it. He's not well."

"What does Frankie think?"

"Frankie said it's my decision to make, but I have a feeling she wants me to meet with him." Roberts, the next batter, popped up to the second baseman. "Amy thought I'd regret it and have a lot of 'what if's' if I didn't try."

"You talked to Amy?"

This time, there was no mistaking the hurt in Sarah's voice. Lisa reached over and grabbed her arm. "I apologize for not telling you sooner. It's been weighing on me. You're a good enough friend I could've confided in you, too."

"It's okay, Lisa. I know how close you and Amy were and still are as friends. If it had been me, I would've stayed closemouthed about it, too."

The next hitter knocked in Sanders from second, but a double play ended the inning for the Reds. It didn't surprise Lisa when the Reds bullpen gave up two more runs in the bottom half of the inning. The pitchers had to be running on fumes. They'd played three extra-inning games, two in St. Louis and the last one in Milwaukee, a seventeen-inning affair. The Reds didn't get any hits in the top of the ninth, and the game ended with the Cubs up 8-5.

Sarah and Lisa walked down to the elevator to the clubhouses.

As they waited for the elevator, Sarah said, "I'm heading out to the West Coast for the next few weeks to cover some teams. I'll finish up with the Mariners."

The doors slid open, and they stepped inside.

"I'll miss you, but I'm glad you'll get to visit with Mary."

"Yeah, that'll be pretty sweet." Sarah grinned. "So, you'll miss me, huh?"

Lisa play-shoved her as they got off the elevator. "Don't let it go to your head."

They entered the Reds clubhouse, and Sarah got some quick quotes before leaving for Chicago's clubhouse. Lisa left Max Murphy's office to catch one of the relief pitchers. She got the typical "we need to keep grinding" and "there are no excuses for not coming through for the team" quotes. She approached Amy but not for any further quotes. She simply wanted to talk with her friend.

Amy had finished stuffing gear in her bag when Lisa stood next to her.

"How's it going?" Lisa asked.

"Oh, hey, Lisa. Eh, could be better. I was hoping we'd get this one so we'd have a chance to take three of four."

"You still had a good trip, though. Especially against the Cards and Brewers."

Nick approached his locker, a towel still wrapped around his waist. "It's all yours, Perry."

"Thanks, Sandy." Amy turned to Lisa. "How is everything?" she asked softly. Nick had started dressing.

Lisa kept her focus on Amy. She was used to seeing the players in all manner of undress.

"I'm going to call him and set something up."

"Call…"

Lisa didn't say anything, not wanting to get too personal in front of Sanders. She hoped Amy would catch on.

"Ohhh. You think you'll be all right meeting with him?"

"I think so."

"I'll see you in the bus, Amy," Nick said. He nodded at Lisa and left the clubhouse.

"Sorry. I didn't mean to bring this up in front of him."

"Nick's fine, Lisa. He didn't know what we were talking about, and even if he did, you can trust him enough that he'd never mention it." She gripped Lisa's shoulder. "Call me if you need to talk, because I'm guessing you mean you'll call your dad after we get home from this trip."

"I figured it would be a good time. Monday's an off-day. I can call him tomorrow night when we get into Cincinnati."

"Where will he be coming from? I'm assuming he's coming to meet you and you're not traveling to meet him."

"You're right. He's in Steubenville."

"Isn't that up around Cleveland?"

"It is. Of course, he may not be well enough to travel."

"I have a feeling he'll make every effort to see you, even if it's to meet you halfway. Maybe you can get together in Columbus."

"That might not be a bad idea."

Amy hooked her thumb toward the showers. "I'd better get in a quick one or they'll leave without me."

"Oh, sure." Lisa started to leave.

"Lisa?"

"Yeah?"

"I'm glad you're making the effort. I don't think you'll regret it."

Lisa didn't say anything. As she walked back to the elevator that took her to the press box, she whispered, "I hope you're right, Aim."

Chapter 13

On their drive up to Columbus to meet her father, Lisa tried to think of anything other than the impending visit.

"Damn. I forgot to tell you the news about Amy, didn't I?" Lisa said.

"Considering I don't know what it is, you're probably right," Frankie said.

Lisa told her about the possible retirement and about Marge's offer to manage the Bandits.

"Retirement?"

"It's not definite yet. But she's considering it."

"Wow. That would disappoint a lot of people. But it's her decision to make."

Frankie was quiet for a few miles. "Manage the Bandits, huh? I could see it, though. Amy has the right temperament. She definitely has the knowledge to pass on."

"That's what I thought."

The rest of the miles passed quickly until they reached the outskirts of the city. Frankie took the ramp that led to the restaurant. After a couple more turns, they arrived at their destination.

"You're sure you don't want me to go in with you?" Frankie asked as they sat in the parking lot of Schmidt's Sausage Haus in Columbus.

Lisa rubbed her sweaty palms onto her jeans. "I think so." She'd been certain when she got off the phone with her father and during the discussion last night in bed with Frankie that she could handle this on her own. Now that they were here and it was time for her to meet a man she'd never met in her thirty-seven years of life, she suddenly had developed cold feet.

"Hey, look at me."

Lisa met Frankie's dark eyes that were full of love. They softened even more as Frankie brushed Lisa's hair off her forehead.

"You can do this, sweetheart, but there's no shame in asking me to go with you."

Lisa chewed on her lower lip as she contemplated it one last time. No. She needed to do this alone. Despite the anger she still harbored toward her father, she wanted to be fair to him and didn't want him to feel intimidated.

"Let's keep it the way we discussed it. You don't mind going to another restaurant and waiting for my call?"

Frankie cupped Lisa's cheek and leaned in for a soft kiss. "No."

"Thank you." Lisa unbuckled her seatbelt, opened the car door, and got out. "I'll call you soon," she said as she peered down at Frankie.

"Take your time. But remember, if you need me to come sooner, I'm a phone call away."

With that, Lisa shut the door and took her first shaky step toward the restaurant entrance. She'd told her father she'd meet him inside. She'd only been to the restaurant one other time when visiting a friend several years ago. She remembered it could be a little loud and wasn't really an intimate location for a heart-to-heart. But she wanted it that way. As she told her father on the phone, this wasn't a *Lifetime* movie. It wasn't going to be easy.

"May I take your name?" the young woman asked at the hostess station.

"No, I think—"

"I've already given them my name," a familiar voice said behind her.

Lisa hesitated for a beat, took a deep breath, let it out, and slowly turned around.

The first thing she noticed was she had her father's hazel eyes. In fact, she felt she was looking at a version of herself, albeit a male version, in another twenty years or so. His hair was completely gray. His eyes were watering. Lisa wasn't certain if it was because of his poor health, or if he was truly touched to see her. For one of the few times in her life, she was at a loss for words.

"You might not be comfortable with a hug, but how about this?" he stuck out his hand.

Almost on autopilot, Lisa offered hers and was struck at how familiar his touch seemed. It was like an out-of-body experience, as if she were a baby and he was gripping her fingers as only parents do when they're in awe at the birth of their child. The feeling increased when he closed his other hand over hers.

"You have no idea," he choked out. "No idea how… how…" He released her hand and swiped at his cheek. "Ah hell."

"No, I think I do have an idea." Lisa was surprised at the lump that formed in her throat. Fuck.

"Collins." The hostess's voice cut into their words.

"That's us." Her dad winked at Lisa.

They followed the young blonde around waiters and other patrons until she led them to a two-seat table in the very corner of the back of the restaurant. Damn, Lisa thought. It was about to get more intimate than she anticipated. She noticed how the sound diminished here. Other voices murmured around them in broken conversation, but it definitely wasn't loud.

"Jeremy will be with you shortly," the hostess said as she laid the menus on the table.

They sat down across from each other. Again, sweat broke out on Lisa's palms. She discreetly put her hands under the table and wiped them on her jeans once more.

The virtual stranger—hell, he was a stranger—across from her gave her a tentative smile. "You're a beautiful young woman, Lisa."

She laughed nervously. "I don't know about young."

"Well, you are to me."

"And I don't know about beautiful," she continued as if he hadn't spoken.

"That you can't argue with. As your father, I have the right to speak the truth."

It seemed he was trying too hard, and Lisa couldn't have that. Not if they had any chance at an honest discussion. "Ken…"

Her father stared down at the table.

"Sorry. I can't call you 'Dad.' We already had this conversation."

He raised his head. "I understand."

"This isn't going to work if we're not completely honest with each other. You don't need to butter me up with compliments."

"I wasn't—" he stopped. "Hell, maybe I was. But I meant every word."

Right at that moment, their server showed up and set two glasses of water on the table. "Hi, I'm Jeremy. Do you have any idea of what you'd like to drink?"

Lisa had to bite her tongue to keep from saying "a whiskey sour—make it a double."

"I'll stick with the water," her dad said.

"Me, too."

"Do you still need more time to look over the menu?"

"Yes, if you don't mind," Lisa said.

"I'll be back in a bit."

Lisa watched him walk away. When she turned back to the table, she found her dad studying her.

"What?"

"You look a lot like your mother. Well, maybe a slightly older version of her."

Lisa sat back in her chair. "That's kind of funny. When I met your eyes, I felt like I was looking at myself in about twenty years."

"No, you definitely have her bone structure."

She wondered briefly if this would be the extent of their conversation—talking about Lisa's appearance and her resemblance to him and her mother.

"Thank you again for agreeing to meet with me, even if this is the only meeting we ever have. I hope it isn't," Ken hastily added.

"I had to think about it." Anger built inside her, and she was uncertain if she could tamp it down if it bubbled out.

"You have every right to be angry at me. Disappointed. Every emotion you're feeling is completely justified. Believe me, I know that, Lisa."

Lisa glanced around her, leaned her elbows on the table, and lowered her voice. "Do you, Ken? Do you really? How the hell can you possibly know when you've not given a good goddamn about me and about Mom all these years?"

It was Ken's turn to sit back in his chair. He opened his mouth to speak then stopped.

"Go ahead and say what you've come to say. It's obvious I'm not holding back," she told him.

His hand shook as he ran it through his hair. "I'm not going to give you any excuses for why I ran out on you and your mother."

"Caroline. You mean me and Caroline. She had a name."

"I was in love with her, so yes, I know her name."

Jeremy strode up to their table. His gaze flicked back and forth at them. He shifted in place. "Um, would you like more time?"

"Not really," Lisa said. She opened her menu and picked out the first thing that she saw. "I just want an order of your pretzel nuggets." She didn't have an appetite.

"Do you mind if we split them?" her father asked.

"Fine with me."

Jeremy scribbled down the order and swooped up the menus. "It won't be long on these."

After he left, Ken said, "I was in love with her, Lisa. Had been since the moment I met her."

"But not enough to stay."

"It was compli—"

"I swear if you're about to say 'it was complicated,' stop right there. Or I'm getting up and leaving this place. Seriously, how complicated can it be? From what Mom told me, you were together almost two years before she got pregnant. What happened? Was I the cause of you leaving?" Lisa willed the tears to stay at bay. It was something she'd fretted over all her life, despite her mother's assurances that it had nothing to do with her.

Ken reached across the table, but Lisa yanked her hand away. His hurt expression didn't give her pause.

"It wasn't you, Lisa. It was never you."

"Mom said the same thing. Can't you see where I'd think that, though? You find out Mom's pregnant, and you leave? I mean, what the hell was I supposed to believe?"

"Your mother never told you anything else?"

Lisa shook her head slightly but then remembered the one night where her mother had started to share some of her past with Lisa. She'd clammed up as fast as she opened up. "I think maybe she was going to tell me something once, but she didn't say."

"I was from a very conservative family. Fundamentalist, actually. They didn't care for your mother. They didn't think she was good enough for me. They especially didn't think she could be my future wife. For one thing, she was Catholic, and I was raised Southern Baptist. At that time, marrying her was like condemning myself to hell. In their minds. Not mine." Her father gazed out of the window, obviously lost in his memories. "When she told me she was pregnant, I decided then and there we'd get married. Even if it would be by a justice of the peace. We'd be married, and we'd all live happily ever after." He faced Lisa. "But my parents found out. Before I even knew what was happening, my family was packing up to leave."

"You could have stayed, though. You could have gone against them."

"You're right. I could have. But I was nineteen years old, Lisa. Nineteen and afraid of losing my family."

"What about Mom and me? Didn't you think about us?"

"Oh, yes. Yes, I did. I was foolish to go along with the move out west. We settled down in Iowa."

He stopped speaking as Jeremy returned with their order and refilled their glasses.

After he left them, Lisa asked, "Did you ever try to contact Mom?"

"I did. But she was so hurt, she didn't want to talk to me. Not that I blame her."

"It broke her heart." Lisa didn't try to hold in her tears this time.

"Mine, too."

Lisa was about to say she found that hard to believe, but the forlorn expression on his face appeared to be an honest one. To avoid meeting his gaze any longer, she grabbed a pretzel nugget and dunked it in honey mustard.

After a period of silence between them, Lisa finally spoke. "Was there ever anyone else?" She stopped short of asking if she had any half-brothers or half-sisters.

"You mean did I ever marry?"

"Well, yeah."

"No."

Lisa tried to hide her surprise.

"Caroline was the only woman for me. Don't get me wrong. I dated over the years. A few women thought they had me caught, but I couldn't go through with it." He reached into his pocket and took out his wallet. He pulled a worn, colored photo from inside and slid it over to her.

She carefully lifted it from the table as if it were an artifact from an ancient time. It was a photograph of the two of them in happier days. Her father sat on the trunk of an old Camaro. Her mother stood in front of him, her grin wide, her eyes bright as he draped his arms around her from behind.

"You both seem so happy." It reminded her of the only other photograph she'd seen of them together.

"We were." He took the photo from her and carefully slid it back in his wallet. "About two months later, I was gone."

"What about all the years in between? You could have broken away and contacted us. Don't give me that bullshit about your parents' influence, either."

He barked out a laugh.

"What's so funny?"

"You. Feisty like your mom."

She folded her arms in front of her chest when she thought he wouldn't answer.

"I have no excuses, Lisa. None. Once your mom said she wanted nothing to do with me, I took her at her word. Then a year went by, another one, and another. Pretty soon, ten years had passed. Twenty years. It was too late."

"It's never too late." Lisa heard the bitterness in her voice and didn't try to hide it. "Mom died of ovarian cancer when I was twenty-five. If you couldn't contact her, you could've reached out to me."

"And how would've you reacted? Honestly."

Lisa poked at a nugget on her plate. She hated to admit he was right. She would've refused to see him.

"It's okay, though. Believe me. You might not think I do, but I understand."

For the first time since they sat down, she did believe him about his understanding.

She let out a deep sigh. "Let's set all that aside for now. Tell me about your health."

"I'm on medication to treat it. I have my good days and bad."

Lisa remembered again that Amy's mother died from the illness, but she wondered if it worked like cancer—that there were stages.

Her dad continued. "I have to be careful. Sometimes I can tell my lungs are filling up with fluid and know it's probably time for a hospital stay to drain them. Most of the time, the medication I'm on works."

His solemn words hung over them and limited their conversation to questions about Lisa's work, if she enjoyed the travel, anything other than discussing his health. Eventually, their conversation dwindled down to nothing. Her father grabbed the bill and left a tip on the table. Lisa called Frankie while her dad was standing in line at the front register.

They stepped out of the restaurant. Lisa spotted Frankie, and she waved. Her father craned his neck to see who she was waving at.

"Who's that?"

Without any hesitation, Lisa said, "Frankie, my partner." She awaited what she feared would be his homophobic reaction.

"Good for you. I'm glad you've found someone. Don't let her go, you hear?"

"N-no. I don't plan on it."

Ken stared down at his feet before he raised his head. "Do you think we can meet again? I can drive down to Cincinnati."

Lisa surprised herself by saying, "That's a long drive. You sure it's not too far?"

"No. It's fine."

"All right. It's something to think about."

His grin threatened to overtake his face. "Great. Great." He stuck out his hand, but Lisa hugged him. It was quick…but it was a hug.

"Thanks again for meeting with me, Lisa. Contact me when you're ready."

He headed toward a blue pickup truck, and she waited until he got inside. He tooted his horn and waved. She went to their car and slid into the passenger seat.

"How'd it go? You hugged him, so I'm assuming it wasn't too bad."

Lisa watched her father's truck pull out into traffic. "You're right. It wasn't too bad."

Chapter 14

After discussing with Sarah how hot the Reds had been in her absence, Lisa relayed the conversation she and her father had at Schmidt's.

"So, in other words, you two cleared some air?" Sarah asked. The National Anthem ended at Citizens Bank Park in Philadelphia, and the Phillies players jogged out to their positions. After a home stand that saw the Reds go 4-2, they were only one-and-a-half games out of first in the Central Division behind the Cards going into the third week of June.

"Yes, we definitely cleared some air. It was a little testy, but I think he understood how I felt."

"Are you going to see him again?"

"I think so. He said he could drive down to Cincinnati."

Sarah looked surprised.

"I wondered about the drive, too," Lisa said. "But he seemed to think he could make it."

"And his health?"

For the first time, Lisa felt a stab in her stomach at the thought of her father dying. "It doesn't sound good. I kept thinking about Amy's mom dying from the same thing."

"Damn, Collins. I'm sorry."

Lisa didn't say anything and, instead, focused on the play below. The Phillies ace, Tim Fairchild, the same pitcher who hit Amy with a pitch at the start of the season, had retired the first two Reds in order. Amy strode to the plate. She leaned her bat against her knees as she adjusted her batting gloves, one of her pre-at-bat rituals. Lisa wondered what was going through her mind, considering Fairchild's comments the last time they faced each other.

* * *

Amy's mind really wasn't on the game. Before the Reds flew out of Cincinnati last night, Stacy was in tears—another failed attempt at having a baby. This time, when Amy tried to console her, she wasn't as successful. Amy reminded her that they'd just started the process, to be a little more patient. With that comment, Stacy stomped out of the bedroom. Amy let her cool down. About an hour later, Stacy returned, slid into bed and into Amy's open arms.

Amy scuffed her right foot in the back of the batter's box and settled in. Because her mind was over five hundred miles away, she wasn't ready for Fairchild's first pitch, a fastball under her chin. She quickly backpedaled out of the way, lost her balance, and fell to the dirt. The crowd cheered.

Bill Phelps, the home plate umpire, immediately issued a warning to Fairchild and both benches. Normally, Phelps might have let it go. But with Fairchild's actions the last time the two teams met, plus his inflammatory remarks after the game, Phelps apparently wasn't taking any chances.

Amy got to her feet. She clamped her teeth together so hard, it surprised her that none of them cracked. She didn't need this shit. Not today. Well, not ever. But especially not today.

Fairchild snatched the ball into his glove when the Phillies catcher tossed it back to him.

With a deep breath, Amy eased back into the box. She leveled her bat, ready for whatever Fairchild would do. He glared at her over the webbing of his glove, kicked his leg high, and threw another fastball at the middle of her body. She turned in time to have it plunk her in the back.

All of her frustration bubbled to the surface like a volcano ready to spew its lava. Stacy. The failed attempts at having a baby. Stacy's sad expression when Amy said goodbye at the airport. And now, this fucking, macho jackass trying to make a statement by hitting her with another pitch.

She dropped her bat at the plate and charged the mound. At first, Fairchild's eyes widened with surprise. Then he tossed his glove aside and yelled, "Bring it, bitch!" The words had barely left his lips before Amy swung hard at his jaw. He ducked enough that it was a glancing blow. Before she could make another move, someone grabbed her from behind.

"You made your point, Perry." Third base coach Pete Servace

held her tight and yanked her toward the dugout.

"Let me go, Pete! Let me at him!"

Amy struggled to free herself as he led her away from the field. She caught the blur of Nick rushing by. He barreled into Fairchild and tackled him to the ground. All hell was breaking loose in the infield as Murphy, the Phillies manager, coaches, umpires, and players tried to break up mini-skirmishes.

"Fuck you, Fairchild!" Amy screamed as Servace yanked her to the dugout steps. "You mother fuckin' asshole!"

"Get her off the field," Phelps told him.

"What do you think I'm trying to do, Bill! If you haven't noticed, she's a little pissed off."

When it was clear Amy didn't have a chance to get back into the action, she relaxed. "It's okay, Pete. It's okay."

"Sure?"

"Yeah," she muttered.

"All right." He released her but kept his hand against her stomach as if anticipating another attempt to charge onto the field.

Her teammates grabbed their hats they'd lost in the free-for-all. She couldn't help but smile at Nick whose uniform shirt was now untucked from his belted pants. His face was beet red. But what made her grin even wider was the sight of Fairchild wiping blood from his nose. She only grazed him, but it appeared his luck ran out when Nick got to him.

"You're out of here, number twenty-two." Phelps pointed to the dugout.

"Yeah, I figured." She headed down the stairs and glanced back one last time as the umpires sorted out who to toss from the game.

"Holy shit, Collins. Holy shit."

Lisa didn't have anything to add to Sarah's observation. When Amy got hit by a ninety-five-mile-per-hour fastball, dropped her bat, charged the mound, and landed a glancing blow against Fairchild, the whole scene burned into her brain.

Several minutes went by before the umpires restored order. Along with Fairchild, Sanders, and Amy, two other players were out of the game, one from each team. The umpires also tossed the Phillies manager, Brayden, because of the earlier warning to both benches.

Lisa and Sarah typed furiously on their keyboards. Lisa imagined Sarah's story had changed as dramatically as her own. The outcome of the game was an afterthought once everything settled down, with the Reds coming out on top 3-2.

Lisa followed Sarah into the Phillies clubhouse. She wanted to hear what Tim Fairchild had to say before she interviewed Amy and the other Reds players, especially since he was the one who instigated everything.

She gathered with the other reporters, both print and TV, as they peppered Fairchild with questions.

"No comment," Fairchild repeated to each reporter.

Yeah, not so cocky now after Amy got to you and Nick clocked you into next week, Lisa thought. Eventually, he stalked away with a bag of ice held to his face.

Lisa and Sarah made their way to the Reds clubhouse and had to push through the pack to get to Amy.

"I don't know what the league office will do," Amy was saying as Lisa and Sarah got closer. "But I won't appeal. I can only hope they're fair in the suspension time."

There was an edge to her voice. Lisa thought she was talking about Fairchild's punishment. She silently hoped the league would hit him the hardest.

The reporters turned as Nick's voice rose next to them. "I'm telling you he better never try that shit again. He needs to know we've got Amy's back. We're a team, and we look out for our own."

Lisa didn't miss Amy's small smile.

"That's it, everybody," Nick said. "Gotta get this iced." He held up his right hand. "Seems it ran into something hard." The reporters laughed. "Let's go, Perry. You need to get your back checked out, too."

The reporters parted to let them through. Lisa scribbled down quotes from the other players and from Murphy. All said the same thing, that this better be the end of it. Left hanging in the air above them, like a thought balloon in a comic strip, was the unspoken threat of retaliation if Fairchild tried it again.

"Jesus Christ, Perry," Nick said. "Seeing your back makes me want to go to the Phillies clubhouse and beat the shit out of Fairchild again."

Amy twisted to try to get a glimpse in the mirror behind the trainer's table. She winced in pain. "Fuck."

"Pain means 'don't do that,'" Tom, the trainer, said. "You haven't learned this valuable lesson yet?" He placed a bag of ice against her back and wrapped it in a bandage. "Keep this on for a bit before you take your shower."

She grunted.

"Glad you agree." Tom motioned at Nick. "Let me see that hand."

Nick stood in front of him as Tom took the fingers through several range-of-motion exercises.

"I don't think you broke anything, but we'll X-ray it to be sure."

Max Murphy marched into the room. "How are my two pugilists, Tom?"

"Sore."

Max raised his eyebrows at Amy. "How you feeling?"

"Tom got it right. Sore."

"And you?" Max asked Nick.

Nick flexed his fingers. "Don't think anything's broken."

Max motioned at the door. "Get your ass to the X-ray machine. Doc's waiting on you." After Nick left, Max said, "Well, Perry. This is one time I'm not going to yell at you for losing your cool. It'll cost us a few games without you and Sanders, but you had every right to charge the mound. I think you shocked the shit out of that prick Fairchild, though."

Amy started to laugh, but she stopped immediately when pain shot through her back.

Max took a step forward. The expression on his face reminded her of her father's overprotectiveness when she'd been injured during a Little League game.

"It hurts like hell, Skip. But like you said, I think I'll have a few days off for it to heal some."

"I just hope Sandy is okay."

"I don't think it's broken," Tom chimed in.

"Good. Good." Max hesitated and then said, "Perry, I think you found out your teammates have your back if this crap ever happens again. As long as you don't fly off the handle at a brushback." He held up his hand when Amy started to interrupt. "Which you've never done. Don't think I haven't watched for it. Tonight, like I said, you had every right to do what you did."

"Thanks, Skip."

"All right. Time to get my own shower in."

Amy eased off the training table.

"Ice that off and on after your shower when you get to the hotel room," Tom told her.

"Will do."

On her way to her locker, she passed teammates in various stages of undress. Each of them gave her words of encouragement. Although she was hurting, she couldn't help but stand up a little straighter. Tonight, she felt truly accepted. The thought made the pain in her back ease a little bit.

* * *

"Want to make some bets on the suspension times?" Sarah peered at Lisa over her bottle of beer.

"Should be seven games for Fairchild, especially since it's the second time he's gone after Amy, plus some of the shit he said before should come into play. Probably five games for Sanders since he really got to Fairchild pretty good." Lisa couldn't hold back her grin.

"Yeah, I figured you'd like that."

"It was nice to see."

"Three for Amy?"

Lisa sipped from her Michelob. "Probably. They may take into account that she'd didn't go after him the first time. That's why I think it'll be three instead of five games."

"Hell, I won't even bet you since we agree."

They grew quiet. Lisa thought of something. "If I ask you a question, take into consideration you don't have to answer."

"Why, thank you for your permission, Collins."

"You're welcome. Are you thinking of moving back to Seattle?"

Sarah sputtered on her next sip of beer.

"I take that as a yes."

"You don't have be so smug about it," Sarah said as she wiped off her hand and the table. "Like I said, I did make some inquiries at the *Times*."

Lisa made a circular motion with her hand. "And? I swear, getting information from you is ridiculously hard."

"You're a reporter. You're supposed to drag shit out of me."

"God, you're a pain in the ass."

"Damn proud of it, too. Before you jump across the table and strangle me, they still don't have anything, but they'll keep me in mind."

"Good, Sarah. I'm happy for you."

"In case you missed it, I don't have a job yet."

"I'm happy for you because of Mary, silly."

Sarah blushed. Lisa almost teased her about it but let it drop.

"You mentioned you'd be checking out Kat Benson. When are you heading out to Kansas City?" she asked.

"Next weekend."

"Trust me, you'll be impressed."

"Figured, or you wouldn't have told me to give her a look-see. Amy seemed impressed, too, when I asked her about Benson."

Lisa thought about Kat's mother and the tough life Kat must have had growing up. Hell, even now. She almost said something to Sarah but decided to leave it alone. Sarah had her story in Kat Benson's play on the field.

* * *

"Why is it I'm always having this conversation with you on the phone?"

Amy shifted on the bed. This ice pack crap really was getting old. "Hon, I'm fine. Honest."

Stacy gave a very unladylike snort on the other end of the line. "You would tell me that if you were limping around on crutches. God, this is so frustrating!"

"More important, how are you?"

"How I am at the moment isn't the issue."

"It is to me."

"I'm fine, Amy. Wishing you were here with me so I could take care of you. But otherwise, fine."

"I hated leaving you. Especially now. Since we started this baby thing, every time I leave seems more magnified."

"You really are a guy. 'Baby thing'?"

"You know what I mean, Stace."

"Yeah, I do. Am I right that you may be getting some time off because of tonight?"

"Yes. How long, we won't know until the league reviews the tapes."

"That bastard pitcher better get a lot more suspension than you."

"I have a feeling he will. Nick may be next in line for most time off, unfortunately. With me, I'm not so sure." Amy shifted and moved the ice off her back. "As soon as they announce it, I'll serve the time. I charged the mound and took a swing. Would like to have connected a little more."

"Me, too. But that look on his face? When you dropped your bat and started for him? Oh my God. That was priceless."

"It was something I won't forget."

"Wish we had a picture. Maybe we can get a still off the tape or something."

"You're too much, Stace."

"I'm not too much for you, though, am I?"

Amy thought she heard some worry behind her words. "Don't ever think that. We're going to have this baby, and she'll be beautiful like her mother."

"Thank you, sweetheart. I'll let you go. It's past midnight, and you're tired. I'm glad you called. I was about to ring your cell."

"I thought you might be a little worried, so I beat you to it."

"I love you, babe."

"Love you, too, Stacy."

Amy ended the call and placed the cell phone on the nightstand. She got up, walked to the window, and gazed out over the lights of Philadelphia. Having time off from the game for a few days wouldn't bother her. With thinking like that, she wondered if she was more than ready to step away from it all.

Chapter 15

"Hey, who's that woman talking with Coach?" Kat tilted her chin toward Marge Tompkins and a woman with short, dark, graying hair.

Dee glanced over and tossed the baseball back to Kat. They were warming up before one of the Bandits games in the all-women's baseball league. "Dunno. Maybe a reporter. She has one of those notebooks."

Interesting, Kat thought. They finished warming up their arms and were in the process of stretching out their quads when Marge called out and waved.

"Benson! Come over here!"

As Kat rose, she heard Dee mutter, "Where have I seen this before?"

Kat trotted over.

"Kat, this is Sarah Swift with *Baseball Weekly*. They want to do a feature on you, maybe even follow us to a few out-of-town games."

Sarah stuck out her hand. "Been hearing good things about you, Kat."

"Thanks." Kat gripped Sarah's hand.

Marge said, "Difference between this one here and Perry is Benson isn't shy. Sometimes I gotta knock her down a couple of pegs." Marge looked like she was trying to maintain her dour expression, but her mouth slid into a smile. "Still a helluva ballplayer. I'll let you two get at it. Remember we still have a game to play, Benson." She clapped Kat on the shoulder on her way back onto the field.

"I know we can't talk long," Sarah said. "I wanted to get introduced and give you a heads-up as to why I'm here. I'll still cover the Bandits for a short time, but my main focus is on you and your play. From what Lisa Collins and Amy Perry told me, you may have a shot at the lower minors."

Normally, Kat would blurt out something like, "Hell yes, I have a shot!" But hearing that Lisa Collins, whose work she followed and admired, and *the* Amy Perry thought she had a shot? She didn't know what to say.

"Guess Tompkins's got you wrong. Seems like you're a little shy."

Kat felt the blush hit her cheeks. "It's not that. It's a surprise to hear Amy Perry thinks so highly of me."

"Collins and Perry are discerning. Trust me. Is it okay with you that I do a feature and follow you some on the road? I don't have to get your permission, but it helps if you're cooperative."

"I don't have a problem with it... I mean, thank you, Ms. Swift."

Sarah snorted. "Kid, do *not* call me Ms. Swift. I feel old enough as it is. Sarah's fine."

Kat offered her hand again. "I look forward to talking to you more, Sarah."

"Me, too, Kat."

Kat hustled into the dugout.

"Let me guess. She's going to feature you in some articles," Dee said, her voice dripping in sarcasm.

"Um…"

"Damn. You and Perry need to pay me some money. I seem to be a good luck charm with this reporter shit."

"Once I hit it big, I'll spot you some dough, Terrell."

"Gee, thanks. Instead, why don't you take me along for the ride?"

For a second, Kat thought Dee was serious. Then she caught the sly grin.

"You can always be my agent."

"That's not such a bad idea."

"Benson and Terrell, get your asses on the field," Marge barked at them.

"Right," Kat mumbled. Silly to be caught up in the hype. Nothing was certain yet.

The game progressed into the late innings with the score tied in the bottom of the ninth. The team playing against them, the Monarchs, was one of the best in the league, trailing the Bandits in their division by a game.

Kat led off the inning with a walk. Jo, the first base coach, put her arm around Kat's shoulders and said in a low voice, "You know what we need you to do." Of course, Kat knew. Speed was part of her game.

She took her lead, edging a little farther away from the bag with each throw the pitcher made home. The count got to 2-1. Kat always had the greenlight to steal, so she didn't even glance at Marge, who was the third base coach. The Monarchs pitcher fired a fastball to the plate. Kat immediately took off for second, churning faster with each lift of her leg. She easily beat the throw, popped up from her slide, and called time. As she dusted herself off, she checked out Marge's series of signs. Nothing for Dee to do but hit away on what was now a 2-2 count. Dee's job, though, was to hit to the right side to allow Kat to get to third with one out. She could then score on a sacrifice fly.

But Dee came through with more than grounding out to the second or first baseman. She lined the next pitch, a curve ball on the outside part of the plate, into right field. With the path of the ball, Kat knew she had a chance to score. She focused on Marge, who was waving her around third but at the last second threw up the stop sign. Kat's momentum already had her headed toward home. She ran through the sign. She heard the roar of the crowd, fans from both teams. The Bandits fans screaming for a win. The Monarchs fans screaming for a throw out at the plate. The Monarchs catcher was standing upright, not crouched yet to take the throw. Then she changed her stance. Suzie, the on-deck batter, yelled at Kat to slide. Kat did exactly what you're not supposed to do at home plate... she slid headfirst. The ball and mitt arrived at the same time. She already had her hand on the plate when the catcher's mitt slammed into her face.

"Safe!"

Kat rolled onto her back and lay there, dazed, staring up at the darkened sky. Suzie arrived first and reached to pull Kat to her feet.

"That was friggin' awesome, Kat!" Suzie's expression changed, and she let her hand drop. "Oh, Jesus. You're bleeding." The color drained from her cheeks. Kat remembered Suzie was especially squeamish around blood.

The umpire leaned over her. "You okay?" Kat didn't respond and didn't move, and the umpire motioned to Marge. "I think she needs some help."

Marge's face came into view above her. "What am I going to do with you?" She reached down and gently lifted Kat into a seated position. "You do know when I throw my arms up, that means you stay on third, right?"

"Yeah." The bitterness of the blood coated her mouth. She spit some off to the side and tried to ignore the color. She let Marge help her to her feet. Her teammates surrounded her.

"Easy on the backslaps, everybody. We need to get some ice on Benson's mouth."

"Damn, Kat," Dee said. "You're not supposed to stop her mitt with your face."

"Funny."

Marge kept her hand tucked under Kat's elbow as she led her to the dugout bench. Edie, an assistant coach, had a bag of ice ready.

"Dip that towel in the ice water and hand it to me first, Edie." Marge motioned to a towel on the bench. "Let's get this blood cleaned off." Edie dipped the towel in the cooler, twisted out the water, and handed the towel to Marge. Marge, her brow creased with obvious concern, gently dabbed at Kat's mouth. Kat didn't see this side of her coach that often. Dee had told Kat about a time before Kat was on the team. Dee had slid into second base hard and ended up with a badly sprained left ankle. Marge took Dee to the hospital for X-rays, and according to Dee, sat in the recliner at Dee's apartment until the next morning, frequently checking on the swelling throughout the night.

Marge took the bag of ice from Edie and placed it against Kat's lower lip. "Hold this there, will you?"

Kat complied. She jerked as the cold shot through the cut on her lip.

"It's going to hurt." Marge glanced at Dee, who was leaning over Kat with her hands on her knees, her forehead creased with concern. "You make sure she takes care of this tonight. She'll still have a fat lip, but the more we ice it, the better it'll be."

Sarah Swift walked up behind Dee and Marge. "At least you were safe, huh?"

Marge glared at her.

"Damn right," Kat said.

"Guess that in-depth interview will have to wait a little while longer." Sarah reached into her back pocket, pulled out her wallet, and slid out a business card. "Call me, and we'll set up a time to talk tomorrow. I need to check in with my editors and write about tonight's game while it's fresh in my mind."

Kat took the card. "Thanks for coming out."

"I'm going to have fun following you." Sarah gave a little salute and left for the parking lot.

Dee shook her head.

Kat glared at her. "Don't say it."

Dee threw her hands up in the air. "What? That you're about to become the second-most-written-about star from the Bandits?"

"Give it a rest, Terrell," Marge told Dee.

"Just kidding, Coach."

"Why don't you both head on home."

"You up for leaving, Kat?"

"Yeah." Kat stood and swayed a little. "Whoa."

Marge immediately gripped her elbow. "That's it. X-rays for you to check for a concussion."

"But—"

"No arguments. Dee will drive you over to St. Luke's ER. Edie and I will follow."

"But—"

"Quit wasting my time, Benson, and go!"

Dee tugged Kat out of the dugout and toward the parking lot. When they got out of earshot, she said, "What? You think you could win an argument with Tompkins? Maybe you do have a concussion."

* * *

Later, at their shared apartment, Dee said, "Why don't you shower first? That way you can get settled in faster."

Kat wasn't going to argue. The trip to the hospital had been tiring. They'd waited in the ER for an hour. Once the nurse took her back, it had been a fast exam and X-ray. No concussion. Marge told her to rest and not come to the next day's game. Guess she could still do that interview with Sarah Swift.

After her shower, Dee leaned into her room and asked if she needed anything. Kat was about to speak when her cell phone rang on the nightstand. Kat didn't recognize the number.

"Hello?"

"Is this Kat Benson?"

Kat's heart started beating faster. "Y-yes."

"This is Larry Richardson. Listen, I wanted to tell you I drove your mom to the hospital tonight."

Kat jumped to her feet. "What's wrong?"

"She fell and hit her head on the side of the coffee table in the living room. Got a nasty cut. She'd been… uh… drinking again."

"What about you, Larry?" Kat snapped.

"What do you mean?"

"What do you do when my mom's downing all that vodka?"

"Well, I—"

"Never mind. Which hospital?"

"Fort Hamilton. It's the closest."

"Is she okay?"

"She's going to be fine. A few stitches. They wanted to keep her overnight because of her condition."

"Her room number?"

"Ah, hell, Kat, I don't remember."

"I'll call the main desk." Before Larry could offer up any more lame information, she hung up on him. She started pacing in the small bedroom.

"Your mom?"

Kat nodded.

Dee put a hand on her shoulder. "Hey." Kat tried to pull away. "Hey, come on." Dee led her to the bed. They sat there for a long moment in silence. Dee finally spoke. "You said your mom tried rehab?"

"Twice. The time I told you about when her law firm advised it and one other time. She couldn't stick with it." As she spoke the words, Amy Winehouse's song rang in her head, taunting her about not going to rehab. "I should get home."

"And do what, Kat? You told me yourself that you can't live

her life for her. She won't go until she's ready."

"What if she's never ready? What if I lose her?" Kat sniffed and pushed her finger across her nose.

Dee held her close. "Don't talk like that. I think we have a road trip coming up to Indianapolis. We're supposed to play three exhibition games against some local teams. Marge said something about giving us some time off. It'll be close to July Fourth. Maybe you can drive over to Hamilton. Heck, I'll go with you for company, if you want."

"You'd go?"

"Absolutely."

Kat managed a weak smile. "I'd like that."

"Good." Dee squeezed her shoulder. "Time to get some rest." She stood up and walked to the door.

"Thanks, Dee. I'm going to call the hospital first and check on my mom."

"After that, go to sleep. I don't want to have to answer to boss lady if you don't." Dee pointed at her and left.

Kat Googled the hospital on her phone and dialed the number. As the call connected, she said a silent prayer for her mom.

Chapter 16

Amy sighed with contentment as she held Stacy in bed.

Stacy stroked her fingertips between Amy's bare breasts. "Can I say that you having these three days off is pretty nice?" She grinned up at Amy.

Amy was still tingling from a mind-numbing orgasm. "Can I say I agree?"

"What a way to celebrate the Supreme Court's decision to legalize same-sex marriage, huh?"

"Definitely. I'm thinking we'll be celebrating that one for the rest of our lives."

"That's not a complaint, is it?"

"Hell no, sweetheart. Making love to you is like breathing. I can't live without it."

Stacy leaned up and kissed her gently. "God, you say the most romantic things."

"Don't let Nick hear you say that. He'll never let me live it down."

"Speaking of Nick, I'm sorry he got the five games, but I'm glad that asshole Phillies pitcher got seven."

Like her, Nick didn't appeal. But Fairchild had appealed to the league to get his suspension shortened. "Anymore thought about me retiring?" she asked Stacy.

Stacy pushed herself up, baring her breasts as the sheet fell away. "Right this moment isn't the time to be asking me that loaded question."

Amy stared at Stacy's hardened nipples. "Yeah, I get your point... so to speak."

"Ha-ha." Stacy scooted closer and threw her right leg across Amy's body. She leaned down and brushed their lips together. "I never want you to live with regrets."

Amy held Stacy's hair back so she could focus on her eyes. "Sweetheart, you are my life." She let her other hand drift lower to cup Stacy's stomach. "This baby will be my life."

Stacy bit her lip as Amy's hand drifted even lower.

"Raise up a little," Amy told her. She slid her fingers through Stacy's wetness and easily entered her.

Stacy began thrusting with her hips, her brow creased in concentration. "God, you're going to make me come so hard."

"That's the general idea," Amy said with a grin.

In a matter of seconds, Amy had her right on the edge. When she could feel Stacy's inner walls begin to flutter, she dropped her other hand to Stacy's left nipple. She pulled and tweaked it in the same rhythm as the thrusts of her right hand. "That's it, Stace. Now."

Stacy tensed and her body froze, impaled on Amy's fingers as she shouted her release. Amy pressed her thumb against Stacy's twitching clit. "Oh, Jesus! I'm going to come again." Amy gently eased out and continued rubbing Stacy's clit until she cried out once more. She collapsed into Amy's arms.

Amy held her and rubbed her back as Stacy slowly came down from her climax. Amy could feel Stacy's heart beating hard against her chest. Stacy slid off and lay beside her, her arm thrown over her eyes.

"Goddamn, Amy," Stacy said in a shaky voice.

Amy leaned on her elbow and gently lifted Stacy's arm from her face. She bent down and placed the softest of kisses on Stacy's forehead, cheeks, and lips. "I love you."

Stacy tugged Amy down even more to give her a bruising kiss. "I love you. So much." She started to tear up.

"Hey, hey. What's this all about?" Amy took Stacy into her arms as Stacy quietly cried. "Did I do something wrong?"

"No, sweetheart. Are you kidding? You did everything right." Stacy snuggled even closer. "I want to give us a baby. With all my heart and soul, it's what I want. You'd make such an awesome mom, Amy."

"So will you, Stace. It will happen. Don't worry."

"You're not disappointed in me?"

"I could never be disappointed in you, especially not about this. It'll happen. I can feel it."

"I need to have your faith."

Amy kissed the top of her head. "Let me have faith enough for both of us." She kept up her gentle stroking of Stacy's back. Stacy's breathing shifted to the point that Amy thought she'd drifted off.

"Does it bother you?" Stacy asked.

"The baby?"

"No. That you probably won't make the All-Star Team again this year. It's a change in subject, but I was thinking about it earlier today. I checked out the voting. It looks like Adrian Gonzalez is going to make it. I was hoping with Pujols moving to the American League, you'd get a shot at it."

Amy shook her head slightly but realized Stacy couldn't see the action. "With my stats this year, I don't think I was worthy." Going into July, she was batting .272 with 10 homeruns and 40 RBIs. Decent numbers. But not All-Star worthy. Not to her.

"But Nick's going."

"Yes, as he should be. I'm glad to see with the big lead he has at his position, he'll get voted in, too, and not picked. He has the numbers to back it up." Nick's average was .302 with 22 homeruns and 58 RBIs. She still found it hard to believe he'd be retiring at the end of the season.

"I'm glad you're not too disappointed. You're sure you don't mind me heading to Indianapolis for a few days?"

"You've not visited with your sisters or your parents this summer. It'll be good for you all to meet up."

"I wish you could be there, but you'll be back on the road again here soon."

"Wish I could be there, too." Being around Darlene and the kids was tiresome, but she always enjoyed seeing Stacy's other sister, Stephanie. She was like a younger version of Stacy, full of fire and passion. Stacy said she worried sometimes about Stephanie finding the "right woman" to tame her.

Stacy cupped Amy's breast and rubbed her thumb against her nipple.

Another gush of wetness pulsed between Amy's legs with the move. "What the hell were we talking about?" she mumbled as Stacy dropped her hand lower and swiped against her clit.

Stacy chuckled. "Baseball and my family. But I think we need to get back to the topic at hand." As she spoke the word "hand," she slid into Amy's center.

Amy slammed her eyes shut. "Oh, yes."

* * *

"You're getting together with your dad again during the All-Star break?" Frankie shouted from the bathroom.

Lisa sat up in bed as she typed out some article ideas on her laptop. She was waiting for Frankie to finish up after her shower. "That's probably the best time to see him. We'll be in Cleveland in September, but…"

Frankie entered the bedroom. "But?" Then her expression softened. She got into bed and slid under the covers. "You don't know how he'll be feeling then."

"Or if… if…" Lisa couldn't finish. She swallowed hard.

"Save what you're working on there." Frankie pointed at the laptop.

Lisa hit Control S, shut her laptop, and set it on the bedside table.

Frankie leaned over and switched off the light. She reached for Lisa and held her tight. Some time went by before Frankie spoke again. "Lisa, you can't know exactly how this will play out. From what I understand about congestive heart failure, it's different for everyone. There's medication for it. The doctors stay on top of it. I have a feeling some of this is you remembering Amy's mom and what she went through."

"Yeah, you're right."

"His color wasn't good when I saw him in the parking lot."

"No, it wasn't."

"I hate this. I hate that he didn't reach out to you until he was afraid he didn't have many days left on earth."

Lisa patted Frankie's stomach. "It's all right, Frankie. I've not had him all of my life. The few times I see him are more than I ever had before. I'm a big girl. I can do this." Frankie's jaw was tight. She patted her stomach again. "Don't be mad."

Frankie peered down. "For you, I won't be mad."

"Promise?"

Frankie slid down to lie on her side next to Lisa and cupped her cheek. "Promise."

Lisa grabbed Frankie's hand and kissed her palm. "I'll call him tomorrow to set up the next day we'll meet. Maybe Wednesday evening, Thursday at the latest the week of the All-Star break."

"You want me to join you this time?"

"I'd like that. I think he would, too."

Frankie kissed her. "Then that's where I'll be."

Chapter 17

"I read the piece in *Baseball Weekly*. Sarah Swift's good. At least she made you look good." Dee lay on her back on her hotel bed, tossing a baseball up toward the ceiling.

On the third toss, Kat reached up and grabbed it on its descent.

Dee jumped out of bed.

"Hey! Give it back."

They tussled on Kat's bed until she finally handed it over. "God, you're such a baby. 'Give it back!' Waa, waa, waa."

"Oh, shut up. You're pissed because you went 0-4 tonight."

"Eh. Maybe." Dee probably had a good point. There was a cute brunette sitting behind their dugout next to a woman who looked a lot like her, only older. "Did you see the two chicks sitting behind our dugout?"

"Ooh, Kat noticed a babe. Alert the papers! Sometimes I think you could join a nunnery, Benson."

"Because I'm not a slut like you?"

Dee backhanded her in the stomach. "Shut up. I simply like to sample the merchandise. Besides"—she reached into her pocket and pulled out a slip of player—"the one with the longer hair, the one who couldn't keep her eyes off you all night, she gave me her number."

Kat felt deflated. "So? Why would I care if she gave you her number?"

"Ah, now you're jealous."

"God, Terrell. I don't know why I room with you when we go out of town. The one time I could get away from you and your smart mouth."

Dee ignored her as she peeled open the paper. "Unfortunately, for some unknown, bizarre reason, she asked me to give *you* her number." She dangled the paper in the air.

Kat attempted to snatch it away.

"Ah, ah, ah." Dee leaned forward and turned her ear toward

Kat. "Not until I hear the magic words."

"Give it here!" Kat lunged for the paper again.

"Nope. Those aren't the words." Dee moved the paper from hand to hand each time Kat got close.

"All right, all right. I'm sorry?"

"What? Is that a question? Can you possibly make it a statement?"

"I'm sorry I said that stuff about you. Hell, you're my best friend."

"Better." Dee handed her the paper.

Kat read: "I'd love to meet you for coffee while you're in town.—Stephanie McCrady." Her number was scrawled under the message.

Dee peeked over her shoulder. "I'll be damned. I didn't want to tell you that the one chick is Amy's wife. I've met her. I've never met her sister, though. Don't you remember seeing Stacy in Hamilton?"

"No, not really." Kat's mind had been on other things, like avoiding the embarrassing confrontation with her mother.

"If she's anything like her sister, she's a find. Can't for the life of me understand what she sees in you."

"Hey!"

"I'm kidding. You're so easy to tease." Dee nodded at the paper. "You going to call her?"

Suddenly, Kat felt very insecure. Dee was partially right. She didn't date that often. She may come across as cocky and sure of herself on the field. But in life and in matters of love, she felt inadequate, often bumbling, around another woman. Especially one as pretty as Stephanie.

"Don't."

Kat snapped her head around. "Don't what?"

"Don't overanalyze this. You said we're best friends. Don't you think I know you by now? For some reason, you've always sold yourself short with the women. You shouldn't. You're cute, kindhearted, smart…"

Kat threw up her hands. "Stop, stop! You're embarrassing me."

"I do tease you… a lot. I'm not now. I'm serious. Give her a call." She grabbed Kat's cell phone and held it out to her. "If you don't, I will and pretend I'm you."

Kat narrowed her eyes at her. "You wouldn't."

"Try me."

She snatched the phone from Dee. "Fine." She punched the numbers written on the paper.

"Hello."

Kat's bravado fizzled to nothing at the sound of Stephanie's soft-spoken voice.

Dee smacked her on the arm. "Say something," she mouthed.

"Um, hi. This is Kat. Kat Benson."

"Oh. Hi, Kat. I'm glad you called."

Kat could hear the smile in Stephanie's voice. "Yeah, me, too. So, did you like the game tonight?"

"Lame, lame, lame," Dee muttered as she plopped back onto her bed and started tossing her baseball again.

"Shut up," Kat mouthed to her.

"Is there someone there with you?"

Kat thought Stephanie sounded a little disappointed. "Yeah, my teammate, Dee."

"Oh. Please thank her for giving you my number."

"She said to thank you," Kat told Dee.

"Tell her I'm not sure what she sees in you," Dee replied as she tossed the ball into the air.

"Dee said she was happy to pass on the note."

"That's not what I said, Stephanie!" Dee shouted.

"Hang on, Stephanie." Kat put her hand over the microphone. "Can you leave and give me some privacy?"

Dee hopped up. "No problem. Remember, though. No phone sex on the first call," she said as she reached the door.

Kat snatched her pillow and threw it at her. Dee managed to dodge the pillow before she shut the door.

"Sorry about that, Stephanie."

Stephanie giggled. "Did she say what I thought she said?"

"Oh, God. You heard her?" Kat buried her face in her hand.

"It's okay, Kat," Stephanie said around her laughter. "Dee's funny."

"She's definitely something."

They both grew quiet.

"So… you wanted to meet for coffee?" Kat asked.

"Or how about an early lunch? I have tomorrow off from work."

Curious, Kat asked, "Where do you work?"

"At a small art gallery downtown."

"We don't have to be at the ballpark until five tomorrow night. I could meet you in the late morning or even for lunch as long as you pick me up. I don't have any transportation."

"I'd be happy to. Where are you staying?"

Kat told her about the Marriott. "Hang on. Let me get you the exact address." She picked up the paperwork from the desk and relayed the information to Stephanie.

"You're practically down the street. I don't live far from downtown. How about eleven? That'll give you some time to sleep in if you want, plus plenty of time to talk before you need to get to the ballpark. I'm driving a red Elantra."

"Sounds good."

"Thanks for calling, Kat. I look forward to seeing you tomorrow."

"Me, too. I mean, I look forward to seeing you."

"Kat?"

"Yes?"

"You don't need to be nervous. I already think you're cute."

Before Kat could respond, Stephanie ended the call. Kat couldn't stop smiling. "She thinks I'm cute."

Dee tapped on the door and entered when Kat didn't answer right away. "What's that goofy grin for?" she asked as she shut the door.

"She thinks I'm cute."

"Oh, God help us all."

Chapter 18

Kat dressed in her best pair of jeans and the one shirt she always kept hung up when they traveled on road trips on the off chance they had to go to some place fancy to eat. It was a navy blue, short-sleeved, cotton blouse with white stitching across the chest. She'd gotten compliments on it before. Well, Dee had teased her mercilessly the first time she wore it but had since told her she wore it well.

She nervously tugged on her leather belt and stared down at her shoes. If only she had a nice pair of loafers to wear, but her new, white sneakers would have to do. She caught a flash of red out of the corner of her eye. The Elantra pulled to a stop in the hotel roundabout. Kat opened the passenger door and slid inside.

"Hi," she said softly as she buckled her seatbelt.

"Hi." Stephanie gave her a shy smile that showed off a deep dimple on her right cheek.

Kat's heart skipped a beat when she met Stephanie's gaze. Holy crap, she thought. I hope I'm not in over my head here. She realized Stephanie had asked her a question. "I'm sorry?"

Stephanie's smile grew even wider. "I asked if you trusted me as to where we'd go for an early lunch."

"I don't know Indianapolis. I'm up for whatever you have in mind."

Stephanie checked behind her before driving out of the roundabout and into downtown traffic. "I hope you don't mind. It's where my sister used to work. She still does when she's in town, if only for a day. Heck, I don't even know if she asks for pay anymore with Amy in the majors making the nice money she does. Stacy told me once she enjoys seeing everyone and keeping in touch that way. It's the Watering Hole. Frankie, Lisa Collins's partner, still owns it. But Billie manages it for her now. God, listen to me. I'm babbling, aren't I? I told you not to be nervous last night, but I can't seem to shut up."

"It's okay, Stephanie. I'm still a little nervous, but I think once we sit down and get to know each other a little, that'll all go away."

"You're right." She glanced at Kat as she made a turn. "Going to the Watering Hole is good with you? I don't drink, but they have awesome lunch specials. Janine is an excellent cook and makes the best tenderloin sandwiches in town, heck, maybe even in the state."

"That's quite an endorsement."

"Trust me. If you like tenderloins, you won't argue once you have one of hers."

Somehow, Kat already felt comfortable enough to trust Stephanie. Yes, she was a little nervous, but there was something about the dark-haired beauty that made Kat believe everything she was telling her. "I trust you."

Stephanie flashed her that dimpled smile again. "Yeah?"

"Yeah."

A few more turns and they were on a street called Massachusetts Avenue that was at a forty-five-degree angle to the other streets in the area.

"This is the arts district. It used to be more of the gay district, but you know how that goes. We move in and get everything going, and the straights decide that it's a good place for them to live, too. Pretty soon, our businesses are pushed out because of high rent. The art gallery I work at is just down the street." Stephanie parked the Elantra in front of a brick building with high front windows. "The Watering Hole" was etched on the glass, along with an image of a woman raising a pole with a rainbow-colored fish on a hook.

Stephanie approached the door first, but Kat hurried to open it for her.

"Why thank you," Stephanie said. "You're very gallant."

"You're welcome." Kat followed her in and while Stephanie walked in front of her, took in Stephanie's shapely ass that fit into her khaki shorts just right. Her sleeveless, collared, white blouse showed off her dark tan.

"Let me introduce you." Stephanie motioned to a butch behind the bar in the back of the room. "Billie!"

The butch, who had short-cropped hair and a tight tank top that revealed toned muscles, turned toward Stephanie's voice. "Little sis! Haven't seen you in here in a while. I know you aren't fond of the drinking, but shit, you could at least stop in to say hi."

"Sorry, Billie."

"Ah, hell. Give me a hug." Billie stepped from behind the bar and hugged Stephanie. She looked over Stephanie's shoulder and caught Kat's eye. "You're here on a date?"

Stephanie's cheeks reddened with an adorable blush.

"Yes. Kat Benson, this is Billie, manager of the Watering Hole for the past couple of years."

Kat held out her hand. "Nice to meet you."

"You, too."

"Kat is the second baseman on the Bandits. I thought she'd enjoy Janine's cooking."

"Can't go wrong there," Billie said. "Yet another player from the Bandits, Stephanie? You trying to keep it in the family?"

Stephanie slapped her on the arm. "Stop it! You're embarrassing me."

A door near the bar marked "Office" opened up and the older version of Stephanie emerged.

"Stacy. I'm glad we caught you while you're still here. This is Kat Benson."

"I know. I saw her play last night, silly, and the other night in Hamilton." She shook Kat's hand. "Very nice to meet you, Kat. If my sister proves to be too annoying, feel free to let me know, and I'll share some deep, dark secrets that'll keep her in line." She winked at Stephanie.

"Okay, clearly coming here might have been a mistake," Stephanie mumbled.

Stacy nudged Stephanie. "Quit being so sensitive. Billie, whatever they're having, I'm buying."

"Stacy—"

"No arguments." Stacy glanced at her watch. "Sorry I can't stay and chat, but I promised Amy I'd give her a call around this time."

"She's back playing, right?" Kat asked.

"Tonight's her first game back. They're playing the Rockies in Denver. They still have a couple more games without Nick Sanders. Thank God they've only lost a half game in the standings while those two have been out."

Billie got behind the bar again. "Still glad she went after that punk."

"She wishes she'd landed a better punch," Stacy said, "but I think Nick took care of that for her."

Billie grinned. "It was nice seeing that blood running down Fairchild's face."

Stephanie held up her hand. "Let's hold off further discussion about blood. It's not one of my favorite topics. Especially when we're getting ready to eat."

"All right, all right," Stacy said. "I'll see you later at the house?"

"Once I take Kat back."

"Kat, again, it's nice to meet you in person. You're a heck of a player. Amy doesn't dole out compliments that often, and she thinks highly of you."

Kat felt her face warm. "Thank you, Stacy."

"You're very welcome. Have a good lunch." Stacy waved on her way back into the office.

"What are you having?" Billie asked as she swiped down the bar with a wet towel.

"You ready for those tenderloins?" Stephanie asked Kat.

"How could I not be after your endorsement?"

"Two tenderloins and, what, a soda, Kat?"

"Do you serve Pepsi?"

"We do," Billie answered.

"I'll take a Pepsi then."

"One for me, too, Billie."

Billie moved toward a door that led to what must have been the kitchen. They heard her shout their order. She then headed out to the tables and chatted with some of the customers.

"Would you feel more comfortable at one of the tables rather than sitting here at the bar?" Stephanie asked.

"If you don't mind."

They moved from the bar and Stephanie called, "Billie, we're over here in the corner."

"Of course you are," Billie said with a big grin.

"I swear, between her and Stacy, I'm questioning why I picked this place," Stephanie muttered.

Kat pulled out her chair for her. "I think it's because they love you."

"Wow, thanks again. I've never had a date open a door for me, let alone pull out a chair for me.”

“Maybe you’ve been dating the wrong women.” Kat sat down across from her.

Stephanie’s dark eyes sparkled in the light shining in from the large window. “Maybe I have.”

Billie brought over their Pepsi. “Tenderloins should be right out.” She greeted two women who entered and settled onto stools at the bar. They seemed to be regulars because Billie poured Budweiser from the tap into glasses and slid them in front of the women without being asked. Kat realized Stephanie had said something to her.

“Hmm? God, I’m sorry.”

“You’re not bored with my company already, are you?” That dimple that looked so much like her sister’s reappeared in Stephanie’s right cheek.

“No. I’m probably still a little groggy.”

“Did I get you up too early?”

Kat shook her head. “No, you didn’t.”

“My question was the typical ‘tell me a little about yourself.’”

Kat’s heart thudded hard in her chest. This is where she usually stumbled in dates because she wasn’t sure how much she wanted to reveal about her background, but Stephanie seemed safe. Actually, she made Kat feel safe—something she hadn’t felt in some time.

Stephanie furrowed her brow. “I’m sorry, I didn’t mean—”

Kat reached across the table and squeezed her hand. “You’re fine. I’m an only child. I’ve been on my own since I was eighteen.” She rubbed her fingertips across the worn wood of the table, contemplating what she’d say next. When she raised her head, she met only open interest in Stephanie’s gaze. Kat went with her gut instinct and latched onto the safe feeling that Stephanie offered. “I left as soon as I could and moved to Kansas City to live with a cousin. A few years after moving, I landed on the Bandits team. Well, I guess I should say Marge saw me playing and offered me a tryout.”

“Why did you leave home so young? Not that there’s anything wrong with that,” Stephanie hastily added.

Kat cleared her throat. “My mom… my mom’s an alcoholic and…” Kat was shocked when she choked up.

“Hey. You don’t need to say any more.”

Kat plowed on. “My dad left my mom for her best friend. After that happened, she started drinking. Not that much at first, but more as time went by. My therapist keeps telling me that it's okay, that I shouldn't enable her, but sometimes I feel guilty about leaving her."

"Your therapist is right, Kat. You can't cure her. Has she ever sought out help?"

"She's gone through rehab twice. I got a call recently that she was in the hospital with stitches in her head from a fall." Kat stopped talking when Billie delivered their tenderloin sandwiches.

"Oh, God, Kat. Again, I'm so sorry," Stephanie said after Billie left.

Kat grabbed the ketchup and doused her tenderloin and fries. "Not your fault."

Stephanie stopped her before she picked up her tenderloin. "It's not my fault, but I can tell you're in pain. I'm sorry for that. For you."

Kat blinked rapidly to stave off the tears. "You're very kind." They stared at each other before they both dove into their sandwiches. "This is fantastic," Kat said around a bite.

"Didn't I tell you?"

For the rest of the meal, Kat listened to Stephanie talk about her two sisters and her home life as they grew up. Her very normal, very healthy home life. She tried not to be jealous, but it hit her when talking with a friend who sometimes took their relationship with their family for granted.

"Don't get me wrong. We still fought," Stephanie said as she finished off her fries. She motioned at Kat's uneaten fries. "You going to eat those?"

Kat pushed her basket over. "Nope. Have at them." She was happy Stephanie felt comfortable enough to ask. As Stephanie scarfed down the remaining fries in the basket, Kat asked, "Would you like to go out again?"

Stephanie gave her a bright smile. "I'd love to see you again."

"We're here for a few more days. Maybe after the game tomorrow? It's a late afternoon contest. I could be showered and ready about seven-thirty, if that's not too late."

There was that cute dimple again. "That's absolutely not too late."

Chapter 19

"You sure you don't mind driving with me to Hamilton?" Kat shot a quick look at Dee and returned her attention to I-74.

"I told you I'd like to come along to support you. I'm glad Tompkins was nice enough to let us use one of the coaches' cars."

Marge had not only been nice, as Dee said, but she'd also told Kat if there was anything she needed or anything she ever wanted to talk about, that she'd be there for her.

They drove a few miles in silence.

Dee said, "You didn't say too much about how your date went with Stephanie. In fact, you were pretty quiet at the game. Even when I was razzing you about your home run. Then again, you couldn't quit staring at her in the stands."

"Could you keep from staring?"

"Let me think about that a sec. Um. No. And she didn't ask me out."

"I hope…"

"You hope…"

"I hope I don't screw this up. I can see me maybe falling for her, and, well, I've never really had a girlfriend. I guess you could say what I've had is some quickies. Fumbled shit. Mainly to satisfy a need. Nothing that ever felt permanent or remotely serious."

She could feel Dee's stare. "What?" she asked.

"You're getting a lot out of one date."

"Haven't you ever had that, Dee? Someone you thought you really clicked with?"

A flicker of pain passed across Dee's face in a millisecond, but it was long enough for Kat to suspect something had happened in Dee's past to put it there.

"There was… someone," Dee said softly.

"Hey, I didn't mean to bring back bad memories."

Dee shook her head. "You didn't know. Besides, it was three years ago. You'd think I would be over it by now."

"You've been out on dates, though. I've seen you in Kansas City."

"Nothing lasting and nothing worthwhile. Like you described it, a way to ease the longing by satisfying a need. It wasn't the same."

"You'll meet someone again, Dee. Someone who'll treat you right. Someone who deserves you and your love."

For once, Dee didn't have a quick rejoinder. She kept her attention out the window at the passing farmland. "You really think so?" she asked in a quiet voice.

"I know so."

A couple more miles on their hundred-mile journey churned up under the tires before Dee spoke again. "How will you approach this with your mom?"

"Not really sure. First, I guess I'll see what kind of shape she's in and go from there."

"Whatever you need me to do, I'll do it, Kat."

Kat parked the car in the drive of her mother's house. She was relieved to see no other cars but her mom's. She didn't want to have this conversation in front of Larry.

When they approached the front door, Kat almost used her old key. Then she thought better of it and knocked. There was no response, so she knocked again. When her mother didn't appear at the door, Kat felt the same lurch of fear from childhood hit her stomach, like a rock hits a glass window. She pulled out her key and unlocked the door.

"Mom?" she shouted.

No answer. The silence was almost eerie.

"Mom?" She moved faster down the hallway, but her mom wasn't in any of the bedrooms. She heard moaning coming from the bathroom and hustled to the closed door. She knocked hard. "Mom? Let me in."

There was a garbled response. Kat tried to push the door open, but it was blocked. She pushed a little harder and was able to open it enough to see her mother sprawled on the floor, her face lying in vomit.

"Jesus," Kat hissed. She shoved hard against the door, helped

Angela into a seated position, and leaned her against the wall in front of the toilet. She heard Dee behind her in the doorway. Without turning around, she said, "Can you get me some washcloths and a towel? They're in the pantry to the right."

Dee reappeared shortly and, without any instruction from Kat, ran water over the washcloths. She handed them to Kat, plus the towel. "Is there anything else I can do?"

"Once I get her cleaned up, I'll need you to help me get her to the bedroom." The usual humiliation Kat felt in situations exactly like this didn't wash over her. Instead, she felt a deep sadness… and a determination that she'd get her mom to admit that rehab was the only solution.

First, she cleaned the vomit off Angela's face and shirt. She used the other washcloths to clean up the mess on the floor. She grabbed the towel beside her and dried Angela's shirt off as best she could. Once they got her up from the floor, they could then change her clothes.

"You ready for me?" Dee asked.

"Yeah."

With the two of them lifting Angela's dead weight, they were able to help her to her feet. They shuffled out of the bathroom with Angela between them, much the same way as the last time when they drove her home from the ballgame. They managed to get her in bed. Dee helped Kat slip off the soiled clothes.

"Does she have a nightshirt or something?" Dee asked.

"Behind you in the second drawer of her dresser."

Dee retrieved the shirt and handed it to Kat. With Dee's help, they lifted Angela up enough to pull the shirt over her head.

As Angela fell back onto the pillow, she opened her eyes.

"Kat? What are you doing here?"

"I came to see how you're doing since your trip to the ER." Kat brushed her fingers over the sutures on Angela's forehead.

Angela lightly gripped Kat's wrist. "It's nothing, baby. A scratch. I was a little clumsy." All of her words were slurred and almost unintelligible. Unfortunately, Kat had plenty of practice over the years to understand her mother when she was drunk.

"Mom, we both know better. You were drunk, and you passed out and smacked your head on the coffee table."

"Larry found me, though. No biggie."

"It *is* a big deal." Kat was silently counting the sutures. Fourteen it looked like. "You could've lost a lot more blood."

"Baby, you worry too much."

Angela's eyes fluttered shut. Kat wanted to keep talking, especially about her reentering rehab. She could see it was a hopeless cause. Angela wasn't waking again, probably for several hours.

Kat rose from the bed. "I need to call Marge to let her know we won't be back until later today. It'll take Mom that long to sleep this off. Damn, Dee. I didn't think we'd both miss this afternoon's game."

"Don't worry about it, Kat. The important thing is taking care of your mom. Besides, Joely and Marcia have been chomping at the bit to play. They can take our places today. Remember, it's an exhibition and not a tournament."

"Still…"

"There is no 'still.'"

"Can you call her?" Kat asked.

Dee took out her phone and left the room. Kat heard her quiet murmurings down the hall. She met Kat's gaze when she came back in. "It's taken care of. Marge's main concern was you. Let that guilt thing go." She glanced at Angela. "Why don't we go get a bite to eat and come back later and wait for her to wake up? How does that sound to you?"

"There's a great hamburger joint down the street."

"Let's go then. Maybe your mom will wake up a few hours after we get back."

Kat wasn't so sure. When Angela got this bad, it sometimes took her twelve hours to come out of a binge like this. Kat hated to think how much drinking she'd done in the past couple of days.

They left the house and drove about a mile away for lunch. Once they were seated and ordered their food, Dee started discussing the Bandits and some of the things they both needed to work on. Kat got the impression she was trying to distract Kat. Kat couldn't love her friend more for Dee's sensitivity in what felt like an awkward situation.

About two hours later, they drove back to the house. When

they entered, Kat checked on her mother. She was tossing and turning in the bed, so much so that Kat thought she'd wake up soon. She rejoined Dee in the living room.

"I think my mom is going to be up sooner than I first thought." She sat on the couch next to Dee. "She's pretty restless in there."

"Do you think you'll be able to talk to her?"

"Talk to me about what?" a familiar voice said behind them.

Kat's mother stood in the hallway, oblivious to the fact she was only in a nightshirt and panties. She didn't seem to register that Dee was there, too.

Angela pushed her hand through her disheveled hair as she swayed slightly in the hallway. Her tone of voice and the deep frown that creased her forehead showed that she was irritated. Kat had seen this look before, and it usually meant there would be no reasoning with her.

Kat stood up from the couch and approached her. "Mom, we really do need to talk."

"If this is what I think it's about, no we don't, Kat." She brushed past Kat on the way to the kitchen. "Now I know why you're here." Kat noticed she must not have slept it all off because her speech was still slurred.

Kat followed her. "Don't you even wonder how you got into the bedroom? Does that kind of stuff even register to you?" She tried not to sound angry, but this side of her mother's addiction always unearthed childhood memories of her mother's tantrums when Kat tried to withhold alcohol from her. This had all the makings of one of those knockdown-drag-out fights.

"I'm guessing you put me there." Angela opened cabinets above and below the counter. "Damn it. I know I still have some stuff left."

"After cleaning you up from where you threw up and passed out in the bathroom, yeah, I did put you to bed."

Angela didn't seem to be listening. Her actions became even more frantic in her search for liquor. Suddenly, she wheeled around. "You sure as hell better not have hidden my shit." Her expression had morphed into an angry, red mask of frustration.

Kat heard Dee enter the kitchen, probably because Angela's voice kept rising with each pass through the cabinets. Angela veered toward the pantry, but Kat tried to block her.

"Get out of my way, Kat."

"Mom, you have to stop this. Can't you see it's killing you?"

Angela shoved her aside and lunged at the pantry door. She managed to open the door and grab a half-full vodka bottle. Kat tried to wrench it away from her. They struggled with the bottle. Angela, her face ugly with fury, yanked it free from Kat's grip. The bottle flew up and connected hard on Kat's right cheek. She cried out in pain as she grabbed her face. When she pulled her trembling hand away, blood coated her fingers.

Angela's rabid expression immediately changed to one of worry. "Oh, God, baby. I'm so sorry." She made a move toward Kat.

Kat peered through the fingers of the hand she held on her cheek. She held her other hand up. "Don't come near me."

Angela's eyes filled with tears. "I didn't mean it. You have to know I didn't mean it."

Kat reached for a hand towel at the sink and held it to her cheek. "You never do, Mom."

Dee lifted Kat's hand away, her brow creased in worry. "I think we need to have that checked out."

Kat moved her jaw back and forth. She glanced at the towel. Most of the bleeding had stopped. "I just want to get out of here." She turned back to her mom who was quietly crying. "I'm done, Mom. Until you get some help and really dry out and stay sober, I'm done. I can't do this anymore." She motioned to the front of the house. "Come on, Dee. Let's go."

"Wait!" Angela grabbed her arm. "Wait! You can't leave like this. I still need you."

Kat's gaze shifted to the bottle that Angela still held. "You've got what you think you need. And it's not me."

Kat left the house with Dee, certain it would be the last time she'd ever visit there. She pulled the keys out of her pocket and handed them to Dee.

"I'll let you drive." Kat could already feel the swelling in her cheek.

"We need to stop at a store on the way and get some ice for that."

Kat was about to argue but was too damn tired. "Fine," she said in a defeated voice.

As the car moved away, Kat laid her head on the headrest. She heard her mother's muted cries for them to come back. She closed her eyes and wished with all her might that when she opened them, the world would have changed and all would be okay.

But life wasn't that simple.

* * *

Later, when they got to their hotel room, Kat returned Stephanie's calls she'd ignored on the drive back to Indianapolis.

"Hey," Stephanie said in a hurt tone. "I thought we were supposed to get together tonight after your game."

"Something came up. I'm sorry I didn't call you earlier."

There was a beat of silence. "It wasn't something I did, was it?"

Kat touched her swollen cheek and winced in pain. "No, no. Something else." In her mind, she pictured Stephanie's kind, dark eyes. She wanted to give into that kindness and let it heal her tattered soul… but she couldn't allow herself that hope.

"Did it have something to do with your mom?" At Kat's sharp inhalation of breath, Stephanie quickly said, "You don't have to tell me. I wanted to make sure you're okay."

Kat hesitated for a split second. "Yeah. It was pretty rough. We didn't make it back in time for this afternoon's game."

"Do you want to talk about it?"

"Not right now, Stephanie. Maybe later. It's too hard right now."

"I understand. You leave for Kansas City in the morning, right?"

"We do."

"Um… listen… um… we've only had one date, but I felt something between us. I don't know if you felt it, too."

Kat smiled. "I did."

"Do you think you'd mind if I came down to Kansas City sometime to see you? I mean, I get it if you think it's too fast, or if—"

"I'd love it if you'd come down."

"Oh, God. I'm so glad to hear that. Well, you have my number. I'm going to leave it to you to call me and let me know when's a good time."

"All right."

"But don't wait too long."

"Oh, I won't."

"Good. Because I really like you, Kat."

"I really like you, too, Stephanie."

Neither spoke for a long moment.

"I'll let you get some rest," Stephanie finally said. Her voice softened even more. "I'm sorry about your mom."

"Thanks. Me, too. I'll tell you about it sometime. Just not right now."

"Kat, you don't ever have to tell me if you're not comfortable with it."

"I feel safe with you, though. I've never felt that with anyone before."

"Not anyone?"

"No."

"I look forward to being the last one." Stephanie's voice drifted over the line like a soft caress.

"I hope so," Kat said quietly.

After they ended the call, Kat lay staring up at the ceiling, a mixture of pain and joy battling inside. She wanted to see Stephanie again… soon.

Chapter 20

Amy took her lead off first but kept her eye on the catcher, who was known to throw behind the runner. She dove back into the bag when Sullivan, the Giants pitcher, tried a pick-off throw. The Reds were in the top of the eighth of a tied game. Nick Sanders was down 1-2 on the count. This last game of their West Coast road trip was the final game before the All-Star break. They had kept pace with the first-place Cardinals in the Central Division, only a game and a half back. If they could pull this one off, they'd return home with a 6-3 record against the West Division.

She was glad they had Nick back. Thank God his absence hadn't hurt the team, and hers hadn't either. Everyone picked up their play while they were out of the lineup.

She focused on Sullivan's move again and stepped back to the bag easily this time when he sidearmed his next throw to first.

She checked Servace's signs at third. A straight steal. A little unusual, but maybe Murphy was trying to catch them off guard. Amy had decent speed with eight stolen bases so far. She moved a little farther off the bag. As Sullivan threw to the plate, she took off for second, her focus on the bag and on the second baseman who moved to straddle it in anticipation of the throw. The catcher's throw was high, and she managed to slide in under the tag.

Sullivan picked up the rosin bag and tossed it to the back of the mound. He glanced at Amy before toeing the rubber. He went into his stretch, checked Amy one last time, and fired to home plate. Nick easily backed away from the high and tight fastball. He checked Servace for the signs. Amy did, too, even though she figured it would be for Nick to swing away at whatever he liked.

Sullivan again checked her at second. He hurled another fastball, but he left this one in the middle of the plate. The crack of the bat against the ball sounded like a cannon shot. Amy immediately knew it was gone but couldn't help but admire the trajectory of the ball as it arced through the night sky and landed halfway into the stands in left. She rounded third at a good clip, remembering how fast Nick trotted around the bases after a homer. She crossed the plate in time to see him rounding third.

"Way to go, Sandy." She smacked hands with him at the plate.

"Not bad for an old dude, huh?"

"Nope." Amy followed him into the dugout where they slapped hands with their teammates.

The game ended with the Reds on top 4-2. The Pirates, the team right behind them in the standings, had lost earlier in the afternoon, so the Reds managed to pick up a game in the Wild Card and one game on the Cardinals, who also lost. Amy and the rest of the team were well aware of how last season ended. Winning the division was still their number one goal. Who knew how a one-game playoff to get into the divisional round would go? Like last year, it could be one and done.

In the clubhouse, Amy talked to the *Chronicle*'s reporter before Lisa ambled over.

"Great win for the club, Aim. Anxious for the All-Star break?"

"I am. It'll be nice to spend time with Stacy." What Amy didn't say was they'd be making a trip into Dr. Rodriguez's office for another attempt at having a baby. "What about you?"

"I'll enjoy my time with Frankie, but we're also going to meet up with my dad. Both of us this time."

"Sounds like you're not as nervous about it as you were before."

"I think it's a process. Something we can't rush. I don't think it would work out if we forced it."

Nick walked by, draped in a towel tied around his middle.

"Hi, Lisa."

"Nick."

"Time for your shower, Perry. All the guys are done."

"Guess I'll see you later, Lisa." Amy gathered her stuff.

"See you, Aim."

* * *

Amy held Stacy's hand as they waited for Dr. Rodriguez to enter. Stacy had already stripped down and donned a hospital gown.

Amy was dragging from getting into Cincinnati late the night before, but she wouldn't have missed this for the world.

Stacy squeezed her hand. "You ready to try again?"

"Yes. I have a good feeling about this one."

"You won't be disappointed if we have to keep trying, though, right?"

"Honey, what matters to me is you. We can try as many times as it takes, but you need to know I love you regardless of what happens." Amy leaned over and brushed her lips against Stacy's. There was a tapping at the door. Amy drew back. "Come in."

"Good morning," Dr. Rodriguez said as she and Kim entered the room. She approached the sink and washed off her hands with sanitizing soap and water. "You ready to try again? Third time can sometimes be the charm."

Amy held Stacy's gaze.

"We're ready," they said at the same time.

The other two women laughed. "Well, I'd say that's a definite positive." Dr. Rodriguez went to the instrument tray with Kim by her side.

Amy stroked Stacy's hair as Dr. Rodriguez completed the procedure.

"Okay. We let that settle like we did before. I'll leave you two alone for a bit, and we'll get you scheduled to return in the morning."

After she and Kim left the room, Amy again bent over the exam table and continued running her fingers through Stacy's hair. "You're beautiful, sweetheart."

"I love the way you look at me."

"I'm glad. Because I'm never going to stop."

* * *

"Heya, Lisa! How goes it?" Billie shouted to her as she entered the Watering Hole.

"Doing fine. Nice to have a break away from the grind of covering the team, though." Lisa motioned toward Frankie's office. "I'm assuming she's in there?"

"And where else would she be? Gotta check on the orders and

how we're doing."

As Lisa moved past Billie, she asked, "So, how are you and Alexis?"

Billie's face lit up. "Still going strong."

Lisa gave her a light punch on the shoulder. "I'm happy for you."

"Thanks, man."

Lisa opened the door to the office and stuck her head in. "Too busy?"

"Get yourself in here and give me a kiss. I've not seen you for almost two weeks. What makes you think I could be too busy for you?"

Lisa bent to give Frankie what started as a chaste kiss and ended with both of them pulling apart and trying to catch their breath.

"Wow," they said at the same time and then laughed.

"You about done?" Lisa asked.

Frankie tapped a flourish of keys on her PC's keyboard and shut off the hard drive. "I am now. You ready to go to Cincy?"

"Let's swing by the house first. Then we can head on down."

"Oh yeah? What's at the house?"

"Oh, I don't know. Our bed maybe?"

"You little dog, you."

"Hey, you can't blame me for wanting you," Lisa said.

"Did I say I was complaining?"

Frankie stacked some papers on her desk and grabbed her briefcase. She followed Lisa out of the office and shut the door.

"Billie, the bar's all yours. We're driving back to Cincy later."

"Anything I need to know about or do, boss?"

"We need to order another case of Jack Daniels, and it looked like we might be running a bit low on Budweiser. The bottles of course. I don't remember off the top of my head what else there is. I listed it on a sheet. It's on the desk."

"Crap. I tried to keep on top of everything."

Frankie clasped Billie's shoulder. "You're doing a great job here. I probably don't tell you that enough. I trust you with my baby. Don't ever forget that."

Billie ducked her head, and a full blush hit her cheeks.

"Thanks, Frankie. What you think means a lot to me."

"You're welcome. Call me if you need me."

"You got it. Be careful on your drive home."

Awhile later, they lay in each other arms, their skin covered in a fine sheen of sweat from their lovemaking.

"Damn, Leese. Where'd that come from?" Frankie stroked Lisa's shoulder.

"From right here." Lisa tapped Frankie's heart. "I really missed you."

"I can tell. The feeling is mutual in case you didn't notice."

Lisa leaned up on her elbow. "Oh, I noticed all right. About three orgasms ago."

"What time is it? We should probably head out soon."

Long shadows were pushing their way into the room as if to urge them out of the bed and on their way.

Lisa glanced at the digital clock behind Frankie. "It's six. How about we take a shower together."

"There's another thirty minutes or so before we get ready to leave."

"Is that a problem, Ms. Dunkin?"

"Why, no, Ms. Collins, it's not."

* * *

Once they settled into their apartment late Tuesday afternoon, Lisa called her dad to set up a time to meet for lunch or dinner on either Wednesday or Thursday. Friday, she'd be leaving with the Reds on a ten-game road trip to Milwaukee, Chicago, and St. Louis—all Central Division teams. They'd return home to play the other team in their division, the Pirates.

Her father answered the call on the second ring. "Hello, Lisa." He sounded a little stronger today.

"Hi. Listen, I have a break now with the All-Star Game. I thought you could meet Frankie and me for lunch or dinner some place. Maybe tomorrow or tomorrow night?"

"I'd love to. Like I told you before, I have no problems driving down there."

"You're sure? We could still meet in Columbus somewhere."

"I'd like to drive to Cincinnati. Where would you want to go?"

"Do you enjoy pub food?"

"Absolutely."

"How about the Red Roost Tavern on Fifth Street?"

"I have a GPS in my truck. Give me the exact address. You want to meet for a late lunch, early dinner around 3:00?"

"That works for us." Lisa opened her laptop, Googled the address to the tavern, and rattled it off.

"See you tomorrow at 3:00."

Lisa clicked off her phone. "Guess we're set. You ready to meet my dad?"

"I want to be there for you, but yes, I'm ready to meet him. He sounds like he's trying to make the effort to get to know you better. As long as he treats you right, that's all that matters to me."

Lisa and Frankie entered the restaurant. Lisa was about to approach the hostess when she spotted her dad waving at her from a table in the middle of the room.

"There he is," Lisa said.

As they drew nearer, Ken's face creased into a smile. "So glad we could meet again." He hugged Lisa but kept his gaze on Frankie over Lisa's shoulder. He held out his hand. "You must be Lisa's partner, Frankie. I'm honored to meet you."

"I'm honored to meet you, too, sir."

"Please. Call me Ken. Sir makes me feel like I'm in the military."

They seated themselves around the table, ordered water, and sat in awkward silence until Frankie spoke.

"I'm glad you contacted Lisa, Ken." She glanced at Lisa and took her hand that rested on the table. "It means a lot to me because of how much it means to her."

Lisa met her gaze and then met her father's.

"I was so happy to hear from you again, Lisa. The first time we met, it might have been an obligation thing for you."

Lisa started to object.

"No, it's how I saw it, or how my insecure mind saw it. But hearing from you last night meant that you cared. For that, I'm very thankful."

The waiter showed up with their water and asked for their drink orders. He left, allowing them time to choose their meals. They all decided on steaks and baked potatoes.

When the waiter returned and took their orders, Ken joked, "Guess we're kind of redundant, aren't we?"

The server smiled. "We're known for our steaks here, so it's not that unusual."

He left them, and they fell into a comfortable conversation. Ken asked about Frankie, and Frankie described the Watering Hole, how long she'd owned it, how she and Lisa met. Lisa talked more of her work as a reporter and how the travel sometimes wore her out—mostly how much she missed Frankie during the weeks away.

Their meals arrived, and they settled in to eat. Lisa listened while Frankie asked Ken about his work at the Steubenville chemical plant. He retired early when his health started deteriorating.

Eventually dinner and conversation wound down. Her father insisted on paying for their meals. Lisa tried to object but gave up when she thought that maybe it made him feel even better about their time together. She thanked him instead.

Out in the parking lot, they stopped by Lisa's car.

"I guess it's time to say goodbye." Ken's reluctance was obvious in his voice.

Suddenly, Lisa choked up. She cleared her throat. "Let's say it's goodbye for now. We'll definitely get together again."

"Good." Ken embraced her. When he went to shake Frankie's hand, she hugged him and patted his back.

"Glad I got to know you better, Ken," Frankie said as she withdrew from the hug.

"Me, too. Lisa is a lucky woman to have you."

Frankie caught Lisa's eye. "I'm the lucky one. I tell her that as often as I can. So far, she's not grown tired of hearing it."

Lisa put her arm around Frankie. "We have mock arguments about who's luckier."

Ken got into his Ford F-150 and waved as he pulled out.

"I couldn't be happier for you, Leese," Frankie said as she returned his wave. "Listening to the two of you talk during dinner, I could tell how much you needed this."

"I definitely don't regret contacting him. Thanks for your encouragement and support." Unmindful of who might be nearby, she leaned in and gave Frankie a gentle kiss.

"Mmm. Nice," Frankie whispered.

"There's more where that came from."

"Is that so?"

"An endless supply, as a matter of fact."

Chapter 21

Nick left the batter's box after he finished his last swings of batting practice. He hung around the cage as Amy stepped in. Only the two of them were near the cage, but he still kept his voice down.

"Given any more thought about what we discussed the other day?"

At first, Amy didn't know what he was talking about, but it hit her as she smacked a line drive into left. "Not really. It kind of depends on the other thing we talked about."

Their speaking in code was sort of funny to her, but no way was she going to openly talk about this maybe being her last season with the Reds while she was on a baseball field getting in her batting practice.

They were at the start of a three-game series in St. Louis's Busch Stadium, on the last leg of their ten-game road trip. They'd taken three of four from the Milwaukee Brewers and swept the Chicago Cubs. Nearing the end of July, they trailed the first-place Cards by only one game.

"How's that other thing going?" Nick asked.

Amy watched the flight of the last ball she hit. It bounced against the left field wall.

"Not bad, Perry."

"Thanks." She took a few more pitches then waved off Wally. "That's it for me!"

"Glad I could help out, princess," he shouted back.

The teasing was something Amy finally accepted as Wally's way of telling her she was okay by him. At first, she took it the wrong way. The longer she was around him, the more she realized he truly respected her as a member of the team.

Amy stripped off her batting gloves and walked with Nick back to the dugout and down into the visitor's clubhouse. Luckily, they were alone and able to talk freely.

Amy said, "We went to the doctor again before the start of this road trip. We should know soon if it took."

"That's some highly technical terminology there, Perry."

She punched him lightly on the shoulder. "You know what I'm saying."

"Ryan keeps asking, so you need to let me know as soon as you find out. Otherwise, I'll have one pissed-off boyfriend to deal with."

Amy grabbed a bottle of water from one of the refrigerators and handed another one to Nick.

"What about you, Nick? Have any regrets about this being your last year?"

"I thought I would. Maybe a little. But the deeper we've gotten into the season, the better I feel about the decision. It'll be nice to kick back with Ryan. We're getting married in the fall. You and Stacy are invited, of course. We plan to have the wedding at our house in the backyard. I'd like you to be my best man."

Amy took a swig from her water. At Nick's pronouncement, she started choking.

"Jesus, Perry. It's not that big a surprise, is it? After all, Ryan bought me that ring."

She finally caught her breath. With eyes watering, she said, "No, it's not a surprise. It's so funny how you spring shit on me. Like when you told me you were retiring. You could be reciting the next-day weather forecast. Is that a guy thing? Because even though I'm a butch, I don't spring shit like that on people like it's nothing."

"Gotta keep you on your toes."

"You're definitely doing that." She clasped his shoulder. "In answer to your question, I'd be honored to be your best man."

"Good."

Sitting at their lockers, they stripped off their practice jerseys. As they buttoned up their playing jerseys, they talked about the series against the Cards and what they'd need to do to take two out of three. Two out of three would mean they'd head back to Cincinnati tied for first place in the Central Division.

While they went over that day's opposing pitcher, Amy couldn't help but wonder how much she would miss this if she left the game. As quickly as that thought entered her mind, she pictured herself holding their baby. The feeling that washed over her, one of complete and utter fulfillment, was enough to push all other thoughts away.

Tyler Denks, the center fielder, led off for the Reds in the top of the fifth. They were trailing 3-0 and were having a hard time getting hits against the Cardinals ace, Joe Walker. Amy stood at the foot of the dugout steps, ready to go to the on-deck circle after Tim Rawls, the second baseman, came up to bat. Pete Servace went through a series of signs, one of which called for Denks to bunt.

Walker's first pitch was outside. Denks didn't show bunt, but Amy thought it was because the ball was so far outside, he didn't want to alert the third baseman too soon.

The next pitch, a curve ball, was one Denks could handle. He laid down a perfect bunt, deadened enough that it dribbled up the third baseline. The Cards third baseman could only watch it roll in hopes it would trickle foul. It stayed fair, and Denks reached first.

Denks took off on the first pitch to Rawls, and Rawls slapped a hit behind the second baseman who was moving to cover the bag.

Amy strolled to the plate, first and third and no outs. They had to get at least one run here. Even though it would plate a run, she wanted to avoid a double play. There was nothing like a double play to deaden any kind of rally.

Servace went through a series of signs. He might as well have been waving a real sign that read, "Just get a freaking hit," because he wasn't asking her to put down a suicide squeeze.

The first two pitches missed, outside and low. Walker wasn't giving her anything decent to hit and was obviously hoping for an infield ground ball. The next pitch was a curve ball that had too much of the plate. Amy hit a sharp line drive between the third baseman and shortstop. The shortstop dove for the ball and came up firing to second. Amy chugged down the line with "don't hit into a double play" screaming in her head. At the last second, she lunged forward and her left foot hit the bag an instant before the ball reached the first baseman's glove. Thankfully, she was safe. But she felt something pop in her left hamstring. She hobbled about five more feet and had to stop as her hamstring tightened up even more. She bent over and grabbed the back of her leg.

Jeffries, the first base coach, trotted up beside her and put his hand on her back.

"You okay there, Perry? Did you pull something?"

"It sure feels like it." She tried to jog back to the bag and came up short when pain ripped through her muscle. "Goddammit."

Max Murphy, Tom, and Barry, the assistant trainer, made their way out to the field. "Hamstring?" Murphy asked, the concern obvious in his voice.

"Yeah. Goddammit, Murph. This can't happen now. Not when we're in the middle of this thing."

Murphy waved for Brett Colston, their backup first baseman, to take Amy's place on the bag. Murphy kept his hand lightly on Amy's back as she limped to the dugout while Tom kept his hand under her left elbow. Nick met her halfway.

"You pull it?"

"Yeah. Fuck." She knew she was heading for the disabled list, and she hated it. "Win this one, Sandy."

"Damn right," Nick said.

Amy didn't even stop in the dugout. She limped down the steps with the assistance of Tom and Barry. They led her to the training room. Tom helped her get her uniform pants off until she was down to her sliding shorts that ended halfway down her thigh.

"Think you can make it up onto the table?"

"I think so." She pushed off on her right leg while she lifted her hip onto the end of the cushioned table. Tom and Barry helped guide her up.

"Let's have you do some stretches," he told her.

She gingerly moved onto her back.

Tom ran his fingers over the muscle in the back of her left thigh. "It's already swollen. I'm going to move it around a little."

"A little" morphed quickly into a lot of pain as he manipulated the muscle.

"Okay, let's get you sitting up."

Amy grimaced as she straightened on the table.

"We should probably get an MRI," Tom said. "It feels like a pull. To what degree, I don't know. I want to make sure you haven't torn anything." He must've noticed the look on her face. "It doesn't seem like it, so let's not get ahead of ourselves. In the meantime, I'll put some ice on it. Why don't you shower first? Did you bring some sweatpants to the ballpark?"

"Yeah."

"All right. After your shower, dress in those and we'll wrap an ice bag around it. They have an X-ray machine here, but I'd feel better if we take you to a hospital and run an MRI."

Amy simply nodded. There wasn't much else to say.

Later, after the game—a 4-3 come-from-behind victory for the Reds—Amy lay in her hotel room with her leg propped up on extra pillows. She was icing the leg as Tom had asked. Twenty minutes on, twenty minutes off. The good thing was the MRI showed no tear. They were dealing with a hamstring pull, but it would still be enough to put her on the fifteen-day disabled list. Murphy had informed her about her trip to the DL after the MRI results came back. He didn't want to be short on the team and would rather have her rest up in time for another brutal portion of the schedule in August. They'd go into interleague play and take on the Toronto Blue Jays and Tampa Bay Rays, two of the hottest teams in the majors.

As she was about to reach for her cell phone and call Stacy, it rang with Stacy's ringtone: the Bee Gees's "More Than a Woman." Stacy kept asking her to change the song, but Amy adamantly refused.

"Hey, Stace."

"I caught a highlight from the game tonight. I wasn't able to watch it earlier. I was driving back from Indy." Stacy was returning from visiting her family.

"How's everybody?"

"They're all good. More important, how are you? I saw where you went down in the fifth inning."

"A pulled hamstring. Murphy already told me I'm going on the DL."

"Oh, sweetheart. I'm so sorry, I know how hard you work to stay in shape to prevent injury."

"It'll be hard watching the guys play. I'll still sit in the dugout, though, and support them."

"Of course. I was glad to see you won tonight. You're in a tie for first. That's great!"

Amy loved Stacy's enthusiasm. "I hope we can take at least

one more game while we're here. It'd make for a nice flight back to Cincy, knowing we're in first place. Or a tie. Enough about baseball. How are you feeling?"

There was a slight hesitation.

Amy sat up straighter in bed as a jolt of anxiety rocketed through her body. "Stacy?"

"Honey, I'm fine. A little tired but fine."

"No more driving to Indianapolis, all right? Not until I get back home, and it's an off-day, and I—"

"Amy, please don't worry. I'm really fine. I haven't gotten a lot of sleep the past couple of nights, that's all."

"You're sure?"

"Yes. I think a lot of it is I'm missing you."

"Miss you, too, sweetheart," Amy said. "We'll be back on Sunday early evening unless we go into extra innings."

"Can't wait to see you. Why don't you try to get some rest? Have you been able to take anything for pain?"

"Some Ibuprofen. It's helped."

"Well, close your eyes and think of me. That should do it."

Stacy's words warmed her heart. "It always does, sweetheart."

* * *

Stacy was waiting curbside as Amy limped out of the terminal at the Cincinnati/Northern Kentucky International Airport. The only thing that made the pain tolerable was the satisfaction that the Reds had swept the Cardinals and were in sole possession of first place in the Central Division.

After unloading her bags, Amy slid into the passenger seat, leaned over the console, and gave Stacy a kiss.

"I missed you," Amy said.

"Missed you, too." Stacy pulled out of the terminal and onto the road that led out of the airport. "How does your leg feel?"

"Unfortunately, it feels like I pulled my hamstring."

"Don't worry. During your two weeks off, we'll find ways to keep you occupied at home."

Amy placed her hand on Stacy's thigh. "Oh, we will?"

Stacy shot her a sexy grin. "You can bet on it, and you won't even have to move."

About twenty-five minutes later, they pulled into their gated condo parking lot. Amy dropped her gear beside the door. As soon as Stacy locked the door behind her, Amy swung her around and took her into her arms. She bent her head to give her a thorough kiss. What she really wanted to do was lift Stacy into her arms and carry her into the bedroom, but she knew her injury would prevent that.

"Mmm. God, you can kiss," Stacy said with a moan.

"I'm pretty good at a few other things, too."

"Believe me, I know."

"Why don't you get that bottle of wine you brought home from Easley's Winery? I think it might help take the edge off this pain."

A hard-to-describe look flashed across Stacy's face.

"Okay. You go on into the bedroom. I'll meet you there."

Amy picked up her bags and carried them into the bedroom. By the time Stacy appeared, Amy had stripped down and dressed in her boxers and a tank top.

Stacy made a circular motion with her finger. "Let me see the other side of your left leg." Amy complied. "Oh, baby. It's bruised." Stacy set the bottle of wine and a glass on the bedside table. She knelt and placed a soft kiss to the back of Amy's leg.

Amy flinched, but it wasn't from pain. Arousal hit her between the legs.

"I didn't hurt you, did I?"

"Uh, no."

Stacy giggled. "I would say I'm sorry, but we both know I'm not." She rose to her feet. "Why don't you get comfortable in bed?" As Amy slid under the covers, Stacy poured the wine and handed her the glass.

"You're not having any wine?"

"Not quite yet." Stacy moved away. "I'll just be a minute in the bathroom."

Amy took a sip of wine. She glanced up when she heard Stacy enter the bedroom… and almost dropped her glass. Stacy was wearing a lacy black negligee. From where Amy was sitting, it appeared she'd left her panties in the bathroom.

Stacy's cheeks reddened. "Is this okay?"

Amy swallowed hard and tried to find her voice. To stall for time, she took infinite care in placing her glass on the nightstand. When she turned back to Stacy, Stacy was sauntering toward the bed.

"My God, Stace. You're beautiful." At times like these, when Amy was rendered almost speechless, she wished for the ability to pull romantic lines from the top of her head. But really, there were no words to describe how breathtaking Stacy was.

Stacy slid under the covers and pressed against Amy. She trailed her index finger across Amy's lips and bent down and kissed her, teasing Amy with her tongue. "I need to tell you something, but I wanted the time to be right."

Amy's heart felt like it would explode with desire. She hoped whatever it was Stacy needed to say wouldn't take long.

"Remember earlier when you asked me to drink with you?"

Amy nodded.

"Well, it's going to be awhile before I can drink alcohol." Stacy's eyes pooled with unshed tears. "About nine months to be exact."

Amy blinked. "About nine..." She suddenly shot up in bed, ignoring the pain that shot through her thigh. "Oh my God. Are you telling me what I think you're telling me?"

Tears were now streaming down Stacy's cheeks. "I found out this morning. We're going to have a baby."

"Oh, honey." Amy burst into tears, not even trying to hold it back.

"Hey." Stacy wiped her own cheeks and then Amy's. "I hope these are happy tears."

"Oh my God. I can't... Oh my God." Amy's speech had deteriorated to two- or three-word responses. "Do you even have to ask? This is wonderful news." With a long, passionate kiss, she showed Stacy just how happy she was.

Stacy moved to straddle Amy. Amy could feel how wet Stacy was through her boxers. She was answering with her own heat but thought of something. She practically lifted Stacy off her body when panic shot through her.

"Wait. Won't we hurt the baby? I mean, I don't want to... I mean I do..."

"Amy Perry, if you think I'm going without sex for nine months, you're freaking crazy. We are not going to hurt the baby. Now give me your hand." Stacy lifted up and pulled Amy's hand into her wetness. "Feel that? That's what you do to me." Stacy started to move against Amy's fingers. "I'm not hurting you, am I?" Stacy said.

"Are you kidding me? Let's take this off." Amy tugged the negligee over Stacy's head. She squeezed Stacy's nipples as she moved faster against her fingers.

"God, don't stop touching me," Stacy said with a gasp.

"Never. Never, baby." Amy watched in awe as Stacy strained for release. "You are so fucking hot."

"Right… right there." Stacy suddenly slowed and pushed hard against Amy's fingers. She cried out and held herself up before slumping into Amy's arms.

"I love you," Amy whispered as she kissed Stacy's hair.

Stacy raised her head and cupped Amy's face. "I love you, too, sweetheart. I know you just got in your boxers and tank top, but let's take these off." She helped Amy carefully undress. Placing soft kisses on Amy's cheeks and lips, she slowly eased her way down Amy's body. When she gently moved Amy's legs apart, Stacy's gaze burned with heat. "Let me show you how much."

Later, as they rested in each other's arms, Amy suddenly sat up. She winced in pain. "Damn. Forgot again about the hammy."

"Honey? What is it?"

"Can I call Nick and Lisa and tell them about the baby?"

Stacy chuckled. "I wondered how long it would take you to ask. Of course you can call."

Amy gingerly got out of bed, not even bothering to dress. She grabbed the portable phone on the bedside table. "I can't wait to tell them we're going to be moms." She glanced at Stacy when she didn't respond. Stacy was giving her a fond look. "What?"

"I love how enthusiastic you are, even without your clothes."

Amy suddenly realized she was standing there stark naked, ready to call two of her best friends. "I can't help it," she said sheepishly.

"I wouldn't want you any other way, sweetheart."

Chapter 22

Kat took her lead off first. She scraped a line with her right foot to mark how far out she could go and safely make it back to the bag with a dive. The opposing pitcher glanced over her shoulder. She took a long pause in her delivery, turned, and threw over to first. Kat dove back into the bag before the first baseman slapped the tag on her back. She stood up and brushed off her uniform. Edging off the bag, she gauged the delivery to the plate. When the pitcher committed to throwing to the plate, Kat took off for second. She didn't glance toward home but focused on her goal. She slid headfirst and made it before the second baseman applied the tag. Again, she stood up and brushed off her uniform. The other team's manager called for time and visited the mound.

While the infielders and catcher converged on the mound for a conference, Kat took off her helmet and wiped the sweat from her forehead. She tried not to think about the latest phone message from her mother, begging her to return the call. She was tempted to block the number but couldn't quite take the step where she would cut her mom off entirely.

The conference broke up on the mound. Marge gave the signs to Dee who was at the plate. Kat wished life were that simple that you could follow a series of signs as to what to do, to know what was for the best.

Dee singled to right. Marge waved Kat around, and she easily scored. The Bandits were now up 5-0 in the bottom of the seventh. After Suzie made the last out of the inning, Kat grabbed Dee's glove and handed it to her on the way out to her position at second. She fielded one of the practice grounders from the first baseman. After she finished her throw, she glanced into the stands. Sarah Swift was in town. After the publication of her in-depth piece on Kat, Sarah needed to cover a few more games and keep up with her play.

During the bottom of the inning, Kat's mind drifted to another phone call that she hadn't returned yet. Stephanie. They'd stayed in touch since Kat had visited Indianapolis, spending many hours on the phone. She wanted to wait until she had more time to enjoy a conversation without her mind ping-ponging to thoughts of her mom. She decided she would return Stephanie's call tonight, and they could discuss when Stephanie might be able to come for a visit.

While her mind was on Stephanie, the left-handed batter at the plate lined a ball right at Kat's face. On instinct, she raised her glove at the last second and snared it in the air for an out. When she started the ball around the infield, Dee gave her a quizzical glance. Kat shrugged her shoulders.

The game ended with the Bandits pitcher pitching a shutout, 7-0. After doing the good sportsmanship thing with the other team by slapping hands with them, Dee, Kat, and her teammates gathered their gear and headed for their cars. Kat was sliding her bats and glove into the backseat of her Forester when Dee approached her.

"Want to go with us to O'Hara's to talk about the game and bullshit?"

"I don't think so."

"Is it because it's a bar?" Dee asked, her tone sympathetic.

"No. I can sit around with you guys in a bar and bullshit for hours. That's not a problem. I'm just tired and want to head out."

"You sure you're okay?"

"I'm fine, Dee. Go and have fun. Tell everybody I'm sorry I couldn't make it."

In a quick move, Dee pulled Kat to her in a tight hug.

"What's this for?" Kat said.

"I think you needed it." Dee slapped her once on the back. "I'll see you later at the apartment."

As Kat drove, she thought about her call to Stephanie. When she got to the apartment, she carried her gear to the spare bedroom's closet. She took her cell phone into the living room and plopped onto the comfy couch that Dee and she bought together. She glanced around the room, wondering how it would all work out if one of them decided to move. They had made a pact, though, to divide the furniture, and if needed, one would pay the other her half of the lease-breaking fee.

The phone rang three times before Stephanie picked up. "Hey, you."

Kat's world righted itself, and with those two softly spoken words, the heavy burden she'd been carrying around eased.

"Hey."

"How'd the game go tonight?"

"We won 7-0."

"And you? I bet you went 4-4 with two singles, two doubles, and four RBIs."

Kat flushed with embarrassment and cleared her throat. "Close. I went 3-4 with a single, a double, and a triple, and I knocked in three."

"You amaze me, Kat. I can't wait to see you play again." Stephanie paused. "Speaking of which…"

"What about this weekend?"

"That's perfect. I can take Friday and the weekend off from work."

"You sure they won't miss you at the gallery?"

"It's been a little slow lately, so it shouldn't be a problem."

"You'll fly down, right?" Kat said.

"That'd be best. It would allow us more time together. I'll make the flight arrangements and give you a call back when I'm done."

"Okay." Kat was reluctant to get off the phone even though she was tired from the game and in dire need of a shower.

"We'll be together soon," Stephanie said softly.

It surprised Kat how easily Stephanie could read her. "How'd you know what I was thinking?"

"I know how I'm feeling about this visit, and I assumed you were anticipating it as much as I am."

"Definitely."

"How about you get some rest. I'll call you tomorrow once I get the tickets."

"Talk to you then, Stephanie."

After she ended the call, Kat sat for the longest time, staring at nothing. She couldn't quit smiling. She set the phone aside and went to her bedroom to grab her nightclothes. She stripped down in the bathroom and stepped into the shower. After she finished, she headed for the kitchen to fix a peanut butter and jelly sandwich. Her phone buzzed in the living room. Hustling to get to it before it went to voicemail, she didn't pay attention to the caller ID. It was probably Stephanie, maybe even telling her she'd already purchased the tickets.

"Missed me that much already?" Kat said as she answered.

"Kat. Thank God you finally took my call."

Kat's stomach plunged like she was riding in an out-of-control elevator and couldn't reach the emergency Stop button. She did have control of ending this call, though, and ran her thumb down to the red circle to hang up.

"Wait!" Her mother sounded desperate, more desperate than she'd ever sounded before.

Kat found her voice. "Why should I, Mom? I've heard it all before."

"It's different this time, baby. Way different. I've never hurt you before—"

"You hurt me every time you picked up a glass."

"I know I did, Kit Kat," Angela said in a soft voice.

Kat fought back the tears. "You… you haven't called me that in so long."

"You'll always be my Kit Kat, but the last time you were here, I really, really hurt you. Physically. I can't get it out of my head. The blood. The look on your face. I've let you down so much over the years, sweetheart. I want to change that."

Kat sank back in the couch as she listened to her mother speak. She'd said she'd change before. Many times. But she'd never sounded like this—almost like she meant every word. Right. Old hurt reared its ugly head, and Kat lashed out.

"I'm supposed to believe you now? After all the crap you pulled? Knocking me upside the head with a bottle has given you an epiphany?"

"I wouldn't call it an epiphany. I'd say it's a cold dose of reality. I'm ready to go to rehab. This time, I'm serious about it, Kat. Dead serious. I haven't had a drink since you left here."

Shocked at this revelation, Kat did the adding in her head. That was…

"Nineteen days. I've been sober nineteen days. But God, do I crave a drink. I need help, baby. I need counseling, and I can get that in rehab." Angela sniffed. Kat realized she was crying. "I have no right to ask you to do this. None at all. Will you come home and go with me when I admit myself to Riverside?"

Riverside Center was a short- and long-term rehabilitation facility in Cincinnati. That her mother wanted to be admitted there spoke volumes. Could Kat trust her this time? Trust her enough to put her heart out there again?

Kat took a deep breath… and a leap of faith. "When?"

"This weekend. Saturday."

Kat hesitated, her thoughts on Stephanie and her visit.

"If you can't or if you don't want to—"

"It's not that, Mom." Kat made a quick decision. "I'll drive in." She would've taken a flight, but she wasn't sure how long she'd be there and didn't want to pin herself down to a departure time.

Angela was quietly sobbing.

"Mom, don't cry. You're doing the right thing, and I'll be there, okay?"

After some audible breaths, her mom seemed to have composed herself. "You'll never know how much this means to me, especially after… after…"

"Let's forget that. The important thing is you're going for treatment." If that one incident was the impetus for her mom to reenter rehab, it was worth the pain, she thought. "I'll call you Friday when I'm on the road."

"All right, sweetheart. I love you."

"Love you, too, Mom."

Kat ended the call and immediately contacted Stephanie.

"This is nice. Twice in one day," Stephanie said as she answered.

"I hate to do this to you, Stephanie, but I need to cancel this weekend. Something's come up at home."

"Your mom? Is she all right?"

"Yeah. She's fine. Thanks for asking." Kat hesitated, wondering how much she should share. Then the feeling of safety and trust Stephanie instilled returned in Kat's next heartbeat. "It is about my mom. She's admitting herself into a rehab facility this weekend. She asked that I be there. I told her I'd come."

"Of course, Kat." Stephanie didn't speak for a moment. When she started talking again, her words came out haltingly. "Um…

listen… um… I don't know how you'd feel about this, but… um… if you want, I could join you."

At first, Kat was shocked. The shock quickly became wonder… wonder at this tender-hearted soul who'd entered Kat's life exactly when she needed her the most. The question was, though, how far would she let Stephanie in?

Stephanie spoke into the silence.

"I understand if you want to go by yourself. If you could let me know how your mom is doing—"

"Yes."

"Yes? You'd want me to join you?"

"Yes, I'd like you to join me. I'm driving. I can swing by Indianapolis to pick you up. It's actually on the way. Then we could hop on I-74 leaving Indy. Are you sure you want to do this, Stephanie?"

"I wouldn't have offered if I didn't mean it. I want to be there for you. You've had a rough go of it for a long time. This could be life-changing. I feel like something special has already started with us, that we clicked the first time we met. I'd like to get to know you even better."

Kat was pleased that what she was feeling wasn't one-sided. Stephanie felt the same way.

"I'm leaving here really early Friday morning and should be in Indianapolis around one. I'll call you when I get close. I have GPS in my car, so if you give me your address, I can plug that in, too."

Stephanie relayed the information to Kat, and they chatted for a few minutes more.

"Thanks for doing this, Stephanie. I'll talk to you Friday."

"Thank you for trusting me enough to let me in."

Stephanie's soft voice stayed with Kat long after she ended the call.

Chapter 23

"You don't want me to go with you?" Dee sounded hurt as Kat packed her suitcase.

"It's not that, Dee. You've already been there for me. I don't know how long this will take."

"Stephanie's going, though. That's pretty interesting."

"It's not what you think."

"And what might I be thinking, Ms. Benson?"

"That we'll have hot sex in the hotel room."

"Do you want to have hot sex in the hotel room?"

Kat's heart skipped a beat, and sweat broke out on her forehead. Jesus. What was the matter with her? This was about her mom, not about getting Stephanie into bed.

"Earth to Kat."

"Huh?"

"Where were you just now?"

"Nowhere."

"Yeah, right," Dee said with a smirk.

Kat zipped up her suitcase and set it on the floor. "Nothing will happen, Dee."

"It wouldn't be a bad thing if it did. Right?"

"Well, it's not going to."

Dee threw her hands up in the air. "I won't say another word about it." She followed Kat into the living room as she wheeled her suitcase to the front door. "Call me when you reach Indianapolis so I know you're doing all right."

"Will do."

Dee hugged her and whispered, "I'm so glad your mom is doing the healthy thing, not only for her but for you, too."

"Thanks. She's the one she needs to focus on, though."

"From what you've told me, I think this time she will."

Kat walked to her Forester and put her suitcase in the back. "I'll call you in about seven hours."

"Be safe." Dee slapped the roof of the car as Kat started the engine.

* * *

"Hey, Stephanie. I'm turning onto Fletcher right now." Stephanie had told her she lived in Fountain Square, which was near the downtown area. She was standing and waving on the porch of her small bungalow.

"I see you."

Kat parked in front of the house. She got out and helped Stephanie with her suitcase. She accompanied Stephanie to the passenger side and opened the door for her.

Stephanie fastened her seatbelt. "I said this before, but you are so gallant."

"I think I'm being polite." After she got into the driver's seat, she was about to start the engine when Stephanie stopped her with a touch to her arm. Her breath hitched at the intensity of Stephanie's stare.

"I think you're incredibly sweet," Stephanie said softly. She shifted closer to where she was a couple inches from Kat's face. Stephanie's gaze drifted down to Kat's mouth. "May I kiss you?"

Kat didn't think she could answer even if she tried... so she nodded. They drew closer. Stephanie's lips were as soft as Kat thought they would be. At first, it was a whisper of a kiss, a gentle spark to a flame. Kat moaned, placed her hand behind Stephanie's neck, and pulled her even closer. She entered Stephanie's mouth with her tongue, tenderly exploring, letting Stephanie decide how far to take the passion. Stephanie answered by meeting each thrust before slowly withdrawing. She pressed her forehead against Kat's.

"I liked that," Stephanie murmured. "Very much."

"Me, too." Kat kissed her once again but kept it light. If not, she was very afraid she'd climb over the console and straddle Stephanie's lap. "I guess we should get going."

"Yes."

On the drive to Hamilton they got to know each other better. Kat opened up more about growing up as an only child of an alcoholic mother. She told about how she poured all of her passion into sports in high school, making all-state on her basketball and fastpitch softball teams. She had already told Stephanie about leaving the house at eighteen and going to Kansas City.

"After I made the Bandits, I moved out of my cousin's house. It had gotten a little awkward with my cousin bringing home boyfriends. So I jumped on Dee's offer to share an apartment with her."

"Do you like the travel?" Stephanie asked.

"I do. It's fun going to all these cities I normally wouldn't visit. We tend to stay within the Midwest, but we've also made some trips to California and to the East Coast."

"Amy told Stacy you have a shot to make it in the minors, at the very least."

Kat felt her face redden. "I don't know…"

"Kat, I might not know as much about baseball as Stacy does, but I do know good playing when I see it."

"I think I need to hone my skills a little more with Marge before moving on to a men's minor league team."

"I can see it happening."

Stephanie's confidence in her ability made Kat feel like a superstar.

"I told you some about my sisters before," Stephanie said, "but I didn't tell you the latest news."

Kat sensed it was something special. Stephanie was vibrating with excitement.

"Stacy's pregnant."

"Oh, wow! That's great. Do they have a due date yet?"

"April 3."

"I'm so happy for her and for Amy." Kat wondered about Amy still playing after the baby was born, but she kept her thoughts to herself. Stephanie seemed to have the same concerns.

"I bet it'll be hard for Amy to be away after the baby's born. She's so protective of Stacy anyway. Having a baby would only add to her need to be there for them both. She's already convinced it'll be a girl, despite Stacy telling her it could very well be a boy. Amy immediately pointed out that there are three girls in Stacy's family." Stephanie shook her head.

"Will they want to find out the sex?"

"No, they want to be surprised. Me? I think I'd want to know."

Kat's mind flashed to the two of them in an OBGYN office, finding out the sex of their own baby. Whoa. Where did that come from?

"You okay?" Stephanie asked.

"Uh, yeah."

They grew quiet for the remaining miles to Hamilton. Kat had taken the initiative to book a hotel room in Cincinnati for one night. She had discussed it with Stephanie, at first suggesting they get two rooms. Stephanie had said, no, get the one room with two queen-size beds to save on cost. Kat's heart rate had picked up as she thought about the two of them sharing a room. Then she had berated herself for acting very much like a teenager in heat.

"Do you mind if I go ahead and drive into Cincinnati to drop you off at the hotel before going to my mom's?"

Stephanie placed her hand on top of Kat's that rested on the console between them. "This is a very private time for your mom. I don't want to intrude."

Kat flipped her hand so she could intertwine their fingers. She lightly shook Stephanie's hand. "I do want you to meet her, though. Under better circumstances. She'd really like you." She paused. "I'm glad you came with me."

"I wouldn't want to be anywhere else."

Kat parked in her mother's drive in the afternoon after dropping Stephanie off at the Hampton Inn located near the rehab center. So far, she'd missed the heavy rush-hour traffic that would hit in an hour or so. This visit with her mom wouldn't take that long.

The front door swung open as Kat walked up the pathway. She stumbled at the sight of her mom. Her blue eyes were as clear as the sky above, clearer than anytime Kat could remember. Her mom had pulled her hair into a ponytail. She was wearing jeans and a long-sleeved white T-shirt. She looked like Kat's older sister, not like a forty-nine-year-old woman battling an addiction.

Kat stood in front of her. "Mom, I…" Unable to speak, Kat simply grabbed her mother and held her tight, relieved beyond reason that she didn't catch a whiff of alcohol.

"Kat, oh my beautiful Katherine." Angela kissed Kat's temple and moved aside for Kat to enter. She followed behind. "Are you hungry? Can I get you anything? I have some leftovers in the fridge. Or I can fix you a deli sandwich."

Kat realized how nervous her mother was and quickly tried to ease her distress. She reached out and clasped both of Angela's hands in hers. "You don't need to do any of that. I stopped by to tell you I made it into town. I'm staying at a hotel in Cincinnati. The Hampton Inn right by Riverside Center."

"You won't be staying here tonight?"

Kat heard the disappointment in her mother's voice. "A friend joined me for the drive, and we're staying together."

"Is it the same friend who came before?"

"No. This woman… well, I hope we'll be more than friends."

"Oh, Kat. I'm so happy for you."

Angela's enthusiasm warmed Kat's heart. "We met not too long ago. She saw me play in a game in Indianapolis. We went out for a lunch date. She was going to visit me in Kansas City this weekend."

Angela sat down on the couch and motioned at Kat to join her. "And I go and ruin it for you."

"You didn't. She was kind enough to ask if she could join me in driving here, so I picked her up in Indianapolis on my way. She understood that this is a personal thing for you. She wanted you and me to have this time alone. I'll be the only one going with you tomorrow morning when you check in."

"She sounds special."

Kat couldn't help but smile. "She is."

Angela touched Kat's cheek. "This looks good on you."

"What does?"

"Your happiness. I'd like to meet her sometime. That is if you'd want me to."

"Of course."

"Then that settles it. Once I finish treatment, we'll figure out a time when the three of us can get together."

"I'd like that. She would, too." Kat noticed the bag sitting by the front door. "You ready to go tomorrow?"

Angela blew out a breath. "I don't know if 'ready' is the right word. Frankly, I'm scared shitless." She laughed nervously. "Not the best of words to use, but it's how I feel. At least I'm honest, huh?"

Kat held her mother's hand. "There's nothing wrong with being honest. If you're feeling low tonight, call me. I'll be here in a flash. Otherwise, I'll pick you up tomorrow morning to drive you over, and I'll be there when you go in. I love you, Mom."

Angela's eyes filled with tears. "Love you, too, Kit Kat."

* * *

Kat was quiet when she and Stephanie went out for dinner. She'd not wanted to stay long at her mom's, and she hadn't. She was afraid the longer she stayed, the more she'd add to Angela's anxiety. With her head down, she pushed around the food on her plate until a light touch to her hand made her stop. She raised her head and caught Stephanie's compassionate expression.

"You've been pretty quiet since you came back from your mom's," Stephanie said. "Do you want to talk about it?"

Kat set her fork down and sat back in her chair. "I don't know what to say."

"How about how you're feeling?"

"Scared. Sad, but at the same time glad my mom's taken this step. Wondering if this time she'll stick with it." She tossed her hand up in a gesture of helplessness. "Pretty mixed up."

"Which is all normal, if you ask me." Stephanie glanced down at her own plate. "I couldn't eat another bite. Why don't we head back to the hotel and maybe chill in front of the TV until we get tired? Maybe catch a movie?" She quirked her mouth. "Or a Reds game."

"It doesn't have to be sports. It can be a movie."

Stephanie placed her napkin on the table. "All right then. Let's pay our bills and get out of here."

Kat waved down their server.

* * *

"You've never seen this movie?" Stephanie asked.

Stretched out on their beds, they lay on their stomachs with their pillows scrunched under their chins. "I'd get as far as the tornado scene and then turn it off. It scared the crap out of me as a kid." Kat watched in fascination as the flying monkeys made their first appearance in *The Wizard of Oz*. "Although those guys are pretty freaking scary, too. Kids watch this?"

"Every year. I can't count the number of times I've seen it."

"I guess so, since you've sung along to every song," Kat teased.

"Hey!" Stephanie pouted. "You have to admit they're catchy tunes."

"I've enjoyed listening to you sing." In fact, Kat thought she was adorable and had more fun watching the childlike expressions on Stephanie's face with each passing scene. She also enjoyed that Stephanie knew every line. It surprised her that she didn't find it annoying that she was hearing the lines spoken in stereo—from the actors on the screen and from Stephanie.

They had bought some candy and microwavable popcorn on their way back to the hotel and finished the popcorn about halfway through the movie. Kat polished off a box of Milk Duds while Stephanie munched on her Gummy Bears.

The closing credits flashed on the screen.

"You mean it was all a dream?" Kat asked, incredulously.

"Yeah." Stephanie took her empty Gummy Bears bag to the trash.

Kat felt cheated and wondered how all the kids felt when they saw the movie. "Man, what a rip-off."

Stephanie laughed. "You're so cute. You're like a little kid."

"I guess I am."

Stephanie grew serious. "Probably some of it is you didn't get to experience this when you really were a kid. It's all new to you."

Kat thought about it for a moment. Stephanie was right. Kat grew up much faster than she should have once her mom started heavily drinking. Taking care of Angela while trying to manage her studies and life in general caused her to grow into adulthood at an early age. Here she was at twenty-four, viewing *The Wizard of Oz* for the first time.

She thought about her mom and how Kat had treated her over the years, especially when Kat would get angry. Frustrated and angry. She flipped onto her back and wiped at her wet cheeks.

Stephanie sat down beside Kat on the edge of the mattress. "You're crying."

"I was so mean to her sometimes. I told her once that I wish I had a different mom. I even brought up the name of my best friend's mother, saying I'd take her over my own mom any day. At least she'd be there for me. I still remember the look on my mom's face when I told her that. She was devastated."

"Kat, you can't beat yourself up over it. What you were feeling was only natural. You were hurting, and you wanted to make it stop."

"I even imagined myself on that show *Who's the Boss?* They'd show reruns in the afternoon, and I'd see myself as Judith Light's other kid. She was the exact opposite of my mother. Cool, sophisticated, put together." Kat sighed. "Not a drunk." Again, the harsh words she'd thrown at her mom bombarded Kat's memory. "God, I was such an idiot."

Stephanie put her hand on Kat's shoulder. "Stop. I won't let you put yourself down anymore."

Kat's vision blurred. "I wish I could do it over. Maybe I could've helped her more, maybe I could've…" She stopped, buried her face in her hands, and started sobbing. The bed shifted and Stephanie pulled her into her arms and petted her hair.

"Shh. It'll be okay." Stephanie rocked her gently. "You're a good daughter, Kat. Don't ever forget that."

Eventually Kat's sobbing trickled down to sniffling. She shifted in Stephanie's arms. "I'm a mess. I bet you wish you hadn't come."

Stephanie cupped Kat's face and used her thumbs to wipe away the tears from her cheeks. "You couldn't be further from the truth. I wouldn't have offered if I didn't want to be here. I thought this would be hard on you. I wanted to support you in any way I could."

Kat wrapped her fingers around Stephanie's wrists and slowly and tenderly kissed each palm. "Thank you for… well, for everything."

Stephanie stared at Kat's lips, then she met her eyes and

dropped her gaze again to her mouth. She moved closer and brushed her lips against Kat's. Soon, Kat was caught up in a spinning, dizzying feeling of desire.

Stephanie ended the kiss. She held Kat's gaze, regret and desire warring in her eyes. "How about we both get some rest tonight? Tomorrow will be hard on you."

At first, Kat was disappointed. But Stephanie was right. It wasn't the time to take what was going on between them a step further. That Stephanie stopped what was about to start made Kat care for her even more.

Stephanie stood up and moved toward her bed.

Kat gently grabbed her wrist. Stephanie turned with a questioning look.

"Thank you," Kat said.

Stephanie smiled. "You're welcome."

As Kat settled under her covers, she drifted off to sleep with the memory of Stephanie's soft lips pressed against hers.

* * *

"You don't mind waiting? I don't know how long it will take."

"Kat, we've been over this. No, I don't mind. I'll be here when you get back."

"All right. I'll call you once my mom is checked in and I'm out of there."

"That's fine." Stephanie put her arms around Kat's waist. "Try not to worry."

"I'll try."

"You'd better go. It's getting close to the time your mom told them she'd be there."

Kat kissed her. "Talk to you soon."

On the drive to the house, Kat's mind filled with the memory of what almost happened last night with Stephanie. She thought that prospect would fill her with fear. Instead, her heart was full of anticipation over what came next. Romance was no longer something scary for her to avoid at all costs.

Kat turned onto her mother's street. Approaching the house, she spotted Angela sitting on the front step, her suitcase by her side.

She was dressed in pale yellow linen slacks and a white, short-sleeved, buttoned blouse. Kat couldn't remember the last time she'd seen her dressed up.

She pulled into the drive, killed the engine, and got out. Angela picked up the suitcase and started for the car. "Let me get that, Mom." Kat quickly grabbed it from her hand, and while she placed it in the back, her mom got in the car. Kat slid into the driver's seat. She glanced over and noticed for the first time how pale Angela was. She looked so scared. Kat gripped Angela's hands, clasped so tightly together that the knuckles had whitened. "This is all good. There's no reason to be scared. They'll help you, and you'll come out stronger than you ever have before." Kat swallowed hard and continued. "I think I've let you down the past few years. I—"

"No," Angela said forcefully. "Don't you ever say that, Kat. After what I've put you through? You're the only blessing in my life. Without you, I don't think I could've kept going. So, don't you ever say you've let me down. I'm the one who let *you* down. I can't make up for all those years. But starting today, I can live the rest of my life sober and try to be the mother to you that you should've had from the very beginning."

"Let's make this the start of a new life," Kat said. "Let's move on from this day and have no regrets."

"Part of AA is owning up to everything you've put your loved ones through, though."

Kat patted her leg. "We'll cross that bridge when we come to it."

Angela leaned over the console and kissed her cheek. "Thank you."

* * *

Angela completed the last form and signed her name. She carried the clipboard up to the front desk.

"Someone will call you back soon," the woman told her.

Angela sat back down next to Kat. Kat grabbed her hand and held it tight. Neither of them spoke but said their words through a quiet understanding. Five minutes later, a woman with round-rimmed glasses and kind eyes called Angela's name. She held out her hand. "I'm Renee Larkins, one of the counselors here at Riverside. Come on back."

They followed the counselor to a room where it was only the three of them.

Renee took her time to read over Angela's paperwork. "You're here for your alcohol treatment?"

"Yes, ma'am."

"Oh, please, no need to 'yes, ma'am' me. It's Renee. We're all on a first-name basis here, even the doctors."

Angela gave her a tentative smile. "I'll keep that in mind."

Renee covered the regulations and rules for the facility. Although Angela had gone through this twice before, it helped to hear them again. Renee wound down in about an hour. "We know how incredibly difficult this is for you, but we also know that today you're making the first step in taking your life back." She stood up. "It's time to say goodbye to Kat for now. Kat, you're welcome to visit in a few days."

Angela also stood. "Honey, why don't you wait and come back in two weeks."

Her request took Kat by surprise. "I can visit sooner than that."

"I need this time to start healing on my own. We'll talk when you come back."

Kat rose from her chair. "I'll do whatever you need me to."

"You have your whole life ahead of you, sweetheart. I need to take responsibility for my own life now." With that, Angela embraced Kat for a long moment. "I love you," she whispered in Kat's ear.

Kat tried to speak around the lump in her throat. "Love you, too, Mom."

Renee led Angela through the other door. It clicked shut and Kat felt empty and alone. She rubbed her chest as if she could wipe away her loneliness.

The feeling lingered on the drive back to Indianapolis. Pensive and preoccupied, she kept mostly quiet. She could tell Stephanie was trying her best to draw her out, but she wasn't successful.

They reached downtown Indianapolis, and she slowed to a stop in front of Stephanie's home.

"Come inside." Kat was about to decline the invitation, but

Stephanie stopped her. "Please. Don't shut me out."

Kat melted at the plaintive sound of her voice. She answered by taking out Stephanie's suitcase and carrying it for her as they walked up the path to her house. Stephanie unlocked the door, and Kat joined her inside.

"You can set the suitcase there."

Kat set it by the couch and approached Stephanie, who shifted in place as if unsure of herself.

"Do you want anything to drink before you go? Or something to take with you on the drive? I don't like that you're driving back by yourself. I mean, you drove here by yourself. But still. It's a long drive and—"

Kat silenced Stephanie by claiming her mouth with a bruising kiss. She hated that she'd shut down on the drive home, hated that she'd made Stephanie feel any kind of uncertainty about where they were going with their fledgling relationship. She tried to reassure her with this kiss. She took her time exploring Stephanie's mouth, slipping her tongue inside and battling for dominance with Stephanie's. She slowed down to a simmer and eased out of the kiss.

Caressing Stephanie's cheek, she met her eyes for a long while before speaking again. "This might not have been the best weekend to start something." Stephanie opened her mouth to speak, but Kat stopped her by resting an index finger against Stephanie's lips. "You were with me during a time in my life when I was the most vulnerable. What that tells me is how much I trust you. How much I trust us. I want to take these feelings I have for you even further." She brushed lips with Stephanie again. "If you're willing."

"Yes," Stephanie whispered.

"I want to see you again… soon. I'll be visiting my mom in a couple of weeks. This time, I'll fly into Indianapolis, and we can rent a car. That is if you'd like to join me."

"I have a better idea. We can take my car."

"That sounds like a perfect plan."

Chapter 24

"How's the hammy feel?" Nick asked as they stretched out before the home game against the Mets. A little over two weeks had passed since the series in St. Louis, and Amy had just returned from a rehab assignment with the Reds Triple-A club, the Indianapolis Indians. Murphy told her she'd be in the lineup tonight. The Reds now led the Cardinals by three games in the Central Division.

"Feels great. No pain. No stiffness. I really tested it in Indy, too. Busted it going down the line a few times in the games."

As she did hurdle stretches in the grass near the stands, she could hear the kids screaming for her autograph. A chorus of "Amy! Amy! Over here!" and "Nick! Nick!" steadily streamed from a group of about twenty kids hanging over the padding by the Reds dugout.

She stood up. "Guess we'd better make some kids happy."

Nick sauntered over with her, and they signed autographs on the baseballs and programs thrust toward them. After signing the last baseball, Amy caught sight of a dark-haired beauty sitting four rows up behind the dugout. Stacy had standing tickets to any home game she wanted to attend, but that didn't mean Amy was happy about seeing her in the oppressive summer heat that Cincinnati was known for.

"Surprise," Stacy said as she stepped down to the railing. She gave Amy a quick kiss on the cheek. "I thought I'd make your first game back."

"Are you sure you should be out in the sun? It gets pretty hot out here and—"

Stacy stopped her. "Sweetheart, I'm pregnant. It doesn't mean I have to stay confined to the house for nine months."

Amy couldn't help it. Now that she had everything she'd ever dreamed of, including a career in major league baseball, a beautiful wife, and something she hadn't planned on—a baby—she didn't want anything wrong to happen to her precious world.

"Is that okay?" Stacy asked.

Amy had missed Stacy's earlier question.

"Is what okay?"

"Having Stephanie and Kat Benson over for dinner tomorrow night. I thought it'd be okay since you have a 1:10 day game. Stephanie said that Kat's in town to visit her mom. She asked if we could get together."

Amy wondered what had changed in the dynamics between mother and daughter where Kat would want to visit her. It wasn't her business, though.

"I'd love to have them over."

"I told them around 6:00 or 6:30. I figured that gave you enough time to decompress from the game."

Amy might not even be starting. Murphy had told her he would ease her back into full-time play. That probably meant she'd sit during a day game after a night game. She hadn't brought it up, though. She didn't want to give him any ideas.

"That's fine."

"I'd better let you go. I see Nick has started his crossovers. Love you, babe. Good luck tonight."

"Love you too, Stace."

Amy joined Nick in the outfield on his second set of crossovers. When they headed back in the other direction, they paused long enough to talk.

"Stacy looks great. How's she feeling?"

So far, Nick was the only one on the team or in management who knew Stacy was pregnant. Lisa and Frankie knew of course, plus family members. Other than that, they wanted to keep it to themselves awhile longer.

"Her morning sickness comes and goes. But her mood swings? Good Lord, Nick, she about bit my head off when I asked her to pass the salt at breakfast this morning. Then, later, when I was getting a shower, I heard her crying in the bedroom. I hurried and dried off to check on her. She was crying over an old episode of *Law and Order*."

"*Law and Order*? What's there to cry about on that show?"

"She tells me, 'Angie Harmon never should have left.' Then she starts bawling even more."

Nick laughed.

"Yeah, that was my reaction, too, which earned me a scathing look and a 'You don't even care about my feelings.' Now, over there in the stands, she's all happy again. I've read about the hormone shifts, and we had the talks with the doctor. But hearing about it and actually going through it are two completely different things."

"Hang in there, Mom. It'll get better. Thank God I don't have to deal with that with Ryan since we're adopting."

"Rub it in, why don't you."

They started back across the field.

"Oh, you love it, so don't give me that shit. You'll be a doting mommy once the baby's here. Putting up with Stacy's little mood swings isn't all that bad."

Amy grinned. "No, I guess not. And Stacy does have a point about Angie Harmon. The show wasn't the same without her."

"Hey, Collins. Long time, no see."

Lisa glanced up at Sarah. Her tan was darker, and she seemed well-rested. As Sarah sat down next to her and plugged in her laptop, Lisa said, "Don't take this the wrong way, but you look fantastic."

"Jesus Christ. What the hell has gotten into you? I look 'fantastic'?"

"Well, you do! How has it been, covering Kat Benson?"

"I've enjoyed it. It's fun seeing another female baseball player scratching her way up the ladder. It might take her a little longer than Amy, but that team is good for her. Marge does a damn fine job with the Bandits."

"She does. She still works with Amy when her hitting is a little off. It seems she's the one Amy can depend on the most to snap out of a slump." Lisa spotted a new addition to Sarah's left ring finger. "Whoa. You didn't go and get married and not tell me about it, did you?"

"What?" Sarah noticed what caught her attention. "No. Not yet."

"So you *are* thinking about marrying?"

"When the time is right, yeah, it might be something we'll do.

Right now, this is a commitment ring." Sarah nudged her shoulder. "What about you and Frankie?"

"We've talked about it."

"And?" Sarah made a circular motion with her finger.

"I think we might do it in the off-season. That'll give Amy a chance to take part in it."

"What? I'm not the best man for your wedding?" Sarah looked like she was trying to maintain a straight face, but then she laughed. "I'm kidding. I know how tight you both are."

"Quit bullshitting me like that, Sarah. I hope you know how much you mean to me, too."

"I have a pretty good idea." Sarah turned her attention to below where the Reds were taking the field. "How's Amy's hamstring? I kept up with her some in her rehab, although we both know it doesn't matter how you do playing, but rather how your healing injury holds up with the exertion."

"She told me she's ready to go. No lingering aftereffects."

Roberto Sanchez, who quickly became a top-of-the-rotation pitcher for the Reds, finished his warm-up tosses. He got into trouble by walking the first two Mets batters, but he settled in and got the next batter out on a double play. Eric Farrell, the Mets cleanup batter, hit the first pitch Sanchez threw him deep to left. Roberts, the Reds left fielder, caught the ball against the wall for the final out.

"Dodged some shit there," Sarah muttered as she tapped on her computer.

In the bottom of the inning, Tyler Denks, the Reds speedy center fielder, led off the inning with a single to right. Tim Rawls, who was also a fast runner, slapped a ball to the third baseman. He threw to second to get Denks, but the relay was too late.

Amy strode to the plate, checked Servace for the signs, and stepped into the box. She leveled her bat before the Mets pitcher fired a fastball that caught the outside part of the plate for a strike. If her body language was any indication, Amy didn't appear to agree with the call, but she didn't say anything to the umpire. The next pitch was a slow breaking ball that floated over the middle of the plate. She timed it and hit a line drive in the gap between left and center. Rawls easily scored, and Amy ended up on second with a stand-up double.

"Looked good running there," Lisa said. She was glad to see it. Sometimes hamstring injuries lingered. It appeared Amy's had healed.

Nick Sanders lumbered to the plate, which was usually how Lisa described him—as the lumbering third baseman. He gave Servace a cursory glance before stepping in. He let the first pitch go by for a strike and fouled the next one down the right field line where it landed in the first row of the stands. The next pitch was a fastball on the inner half of the plate, right in Sanders's wheelhouse. The crack of the bat could be heard all the way up to the press box. Lisa knew it was gone; it was only a matter of how far. The ball landed halfway up the second deck.

Sanders did his customary fast trot around the bases. The Mets pitcher picked up the rosin bag behind the mound, bounced it on his hand, and flung it into the dirt. The catcher approached him, using his mitt to cover his mouth while they talked. The pitcher nodded and faced the next batter. Roberts popped up, and Henderson grounded out for the last two outs of the inning.

The game remained 3-0 Reds until the top of the seventh when the Mets plated two after Sanchez retired the first two hitters. Murphy strolled slowly to the mound, already motioning for a right-hander in the bullpen to replace Sanchez. Sanchez handed the ball over. He kept his head down until he reached the Reds dugout. Then he tipped his hat to acknowledge the loud ovation from the crowd. The reliever got the next batter to line out to Rawls at second. The Reds didn't score in their half of the seventh, and both teams went hitless in the eighth. Danny Lopez, the Reds closer, came on in the top half of the ninth and struck out the side.

Lisa checked the Cardinals-Dodgers score before heading down on the elevator to the clubhouse. The Dodgers were pounding the Cardinals 8-1 going into the sixth inning on the West Coast. If that score held, the Reds would be four up on the Cardinals.

She first interviewed Sanders about his homerun in the first inning. It brought his total on the year to 30 and his RBI total to 112.

"There's talk about you being the frontrunner for the MVP this year. Any thoughts on that?" she asked him.

He shook his head. "I leave that up to you in the press to speculate on those kinds of things. I just play ball."

Lisa thanked him and approached Amy's locker where she was finishing up with the Mets beat reporter.

"How's the hamstring holding up?" she asked.

"Feels great. It really felt great in the first on that double."

"The Cards are losing 8-1 to the Dodgers. You might be up by four games in the Central. You have two more series with them later in September. How do you see the Reds doing against the other Central Division teams? I think you still have twenty or so games remaining against them."

"It's going to be tough. You and I know you can never count the Cardinals out. They've been winning too long for us to get complacent. The other teams in the Central will be gunning for us, too, even if they happen to be out of the race. Murph keeps telling us to focus on winning each series. I know it might sound like a cliché, but it's really as simple as that."

Lisa flipped her notebook shut. "Thanks, Aim. Good to see you back in the game."

"Great to be back and helping the team."

* * *

"What's the story with your sister and Kat?" Amy asked.

Stacy bent over the open stove door. She curled up the aluminum foil and, with a large fork, poked at the chicken baking inside. "They've been dating for a little over a month now. They met when Kat was playing in Indianapolis, and they saw each other again two weeks ago. Stephanie rode over with Kat when she was visiting her mother. She joined her this weekend for another visit."

"So is it serious?"

"I get the feeling it's in the early stages." Stacy slid the baking dish back inside the oven. "But from what Stephanie's told me, I think it can be serious."

Amy pictured Kat's mother in her inebriated state when they attended Kat's game. It surprised her that Kat was making so many visits, especially since she lived in Kansas City. Amy hoped nothing bad had happened.

Stacy cut into her thoughts. "How's the rice and broccoli?"

Amy lifted the lid off the rice heating on the stove top. "Nice and fluffy." She lifted the other lid. "The broccoli looks like broccoli." She made a face.

The doorbell rang. Stacy lightly backhanded Amy's stomach as she passed by to answer it. "You're such a kid. You don't have to eat the broccoli if you don't want to. Stephanie likes it." She opened the door and pulled her sister in for a hug.

"Good to see you, baby sis." Stacy motioned at Kat as she shut the door. "Come here. I don't do handshakes." Stacy embraced her and led them into the dining room. "I hope you're ready to eat because everything is pretty much done."

"What were you saying that I liked when we came in?" Stephanie said. "Hey, Amy." They hugged.

"Broccoli."

Amy caught Kat making a face. "See! Butches unite, Kat! Broccoli... blech!"

Kat and Amy shared a fist bump as Stephanie and Stacy glared at them. Stacy carried the chicken into the dining room, and Amy scooped the rice and broccoli into separate bowls. Soon, they were seated at the table.

They were quiet while they passed around the food. Kat started the conversation. "The Reds are sitting pretty, Amy, four, maybe five games up after winning again today. The Cards seem to be in a tailspin."

"Yeah, but like I was telling Lisa Collins, we all know how they're not dead in the water until they're completely eliminated. They've been at this for a while." Amy took the platter of chicken that Stacy handed to her and forked a piece onto her plate. She passed it on to Stephanie. "How are the Bandits doing this year? I hear from Dee on occasion and sometimes Marge, but it's hard to catch up during our season, especially when we travel."

"We're 22-3 and are first in our division. We've been winning quite a few of the exhibition games we've played against the men's teams around the area."

"How about you personally?"

Kat kept her head lowered. "I've been doing okay."

Stephanie spoke up. "Kat! You've been fantastic in the time

I've known you." She addressed Amy. "When we talk by phone, I always ask how she played that night. It's like pulling teeth, but eventually I get her to tell me. She's leading her league in hitting, stolen bases, and fielding percentage."

Amy hid her smile. Stephanie sounded every bit like Stacy when Stacy would brag on Amy's play.

"This is delicious, Stacy," Kat said as she took another bite of chicken.

"Thank you."

"If I can, I'll try to make another game, Kat," Amy told her. "It's getting tough with the season winding down, though."

"I don't expect you to make it to another one, Amy. You don't get that many off-days."

Amy wanted to tell Kat that she would be coming not only to see Kat play, but to critique the entire team… in the off chance she would be taking over as manager. Kat didn't need to know, because nothing was set in stone. Not until the season played out.

They chatted some more. Stacy shared how she'd been feeling, even admitting she'd been cranky and that poor Amy had taken the brunt of her anger on more than one occasion.

Amy took her hand. "It's all right, sweetheart. It's expected."

Stacy gave her a quick kiss. "You're too kind."

"I love you," Amy said. "I'll always be here for you." She glanced over at Stephanie and caught her and Kat sharing a heated stare. Yeah, there was definitely something serious going on. Amy thought back to a conversation she and Stacy had shared when Stacy said she hoped Stephanie would find someone and settle down soon. It seemed like that time was here.

Amy broke from her thoughts to hear Stephanie talk excitedly about a new local artist her gallery owner had discovered and that her paintings were selling well. Kat even opened up some about her visits with her mom. Amy thought she might be withholding something, but she wasn't going to press.

After dinner, they retired to the deck in the back. Amy regaled them with stories about life on the road for a professional baseball player. She could tell Kat was a little disappointed that it wasn't as glamorous as she might have thought it would be. But when Amy got into specifics about game situations, reading signs, rallying from two runs down in the ninth, Kat's brown eyes sparked with interest and enthusiasm. While they continued their baseball conversation, Stephanie and Stacy talked more about baby plans.

About nine, Amy was growing tired. Stacy must've noticed because she stood up and started collecting glasses from the drinks they'd carried out.

"Let me do that," Kat said. "You cooked and served us."

"I'll help," Stephanie chimed in.

Stacy tried to object, but they wouldn't listen. After carrying the dishes into the kitchen and filling the dishwasher, Kat and Stephanie headed to the door.

"Thank you so much for having us over," Kat said.

Stacy put her arm around Amy's waist as they stood in the open doorway. "We're glad you were in town and that the Reds schedule allowed for us to share dinner."

"Be sure and keep us all posted at home as to how you're doing, Stace," Stephanie told her. "You know how Mom is."

"God, yes. I remember Darlene calling me to say Mom was making her crazy with all her worrying when Darlene was pregnant."

"You both take care," Amy said. "Good luck with the rest of the season, Kat."

"Same to you."

After they left, Amy followed Stacy into the kitchen where she was putting away leftover food and cleaning off the stove. Amy took the pan of rice from her hands. "You go sit down. I've got this."

"Amy, you don't need to treat me with kid gloves."

Amy quickly set her straight. "It's not about you being pregnant. It's about you fixing the meal and me cleaning up." At Stacy's incredulous expression, Amy quickly added, "Okay. Maybe a little is about you being pregnant, because you do look tired. Go chill in the bedroom and catch up on that romance you were reading."

Stacy slipped behind her at the counter and ran her hand down Amy's abdomen. She cupped Amy's breasts. "How about we work on our own romance?"

Amy almost dropped the pan of rice. She set it down on the

counter and turned in Stacy's arms. "How about you go to the bedroom, let me finish this, and I'll meet you there in about ten…" Amy hissed when Stacy tweaked her nipples. "Make that five minutes."

Stacy gave her a cocky grin as she backed out of the room. "You got it, ace."

* * *

Kat and Stephanie again checked into the Hampton Inn. As Kat lifted her suitcase onto one of the queen-size beds, she nervously wondered about the sleeping arrangements. She hadn't been able to take her eyes off Stephanie tonight at dinner. She wondered if she'd been that obvious to Amy and Stacy. Stephanie met her gaze briefly.

"So… um… want to see what's on TV? Maybe we can find another classic." Stephanie picked up the remote and switched on the TV. She flipped quickly through the stations, finally settling on a movie. "Have you seen this one?"

Kat didn't see what was playing on the screen. Her focus was on the woman standing in front of her.

"I asked if—" Stephanie's words died on her lips as she turned to Kat.

Kat moved toward her, took the remote from her hand, and switched off the TV. She set the remote on the TV stand. She held Stephanie's hands and didn't miss the trembling of her fingers.

"You've been so patient with me, Stephanie. With us. Don't think I haven't noticed."

Stephanie withdrew her hands from Kat's grip, shifted closer, and lifted her fingertips to caress Kat's cheek. "I care about you so much. I didn't want to mess this up."

"You couldn't. M-mess it up, I mean," Kat stuttered.

Stephanie's hand dropped from Kat's cheek to her chest. They kissed. Kat was sure that Stephanie could feel her heartbeat pounding against her fingertips. It was as if Stephanie were holding her heart in the palm of her hand. When Stephanie teased the outside of Kat's breast, Kat gasped and tore her mouth away.

Stephanie stilled her hand. "Too much?"

"I… I…" Kat felt the flush of embarrassment work its way up

her neck.

"What is it, baby?"

"I've only done this a few times. It's never turned out very well."

Stephanie brushed her fingertips along Kat's jaw. "We can stop."

Kat grabbed her hand and held it to her cheek. "I'd like to make love. Before, my other experiences never amounted to anything. But this? I need this. I need you. It means something to me, Stephanie."

Stephanie's dark-brown eyes glistened with emotion. "Good. Because it does to me, too." She slowly unbuttoned her shirt. Kat followed each movement with rapt attention. Stephanie pulled out of the shirt. "Now you." She lifted Kat's T-shirt off.

Kat's nipples hardened at Stephanie's blatant stare, and she struggled not to self-consciously fold her arms in front of her chest. Then she noticed Stephanie's nipples were rigid peaks pressed against the white of her bra. Her next instinct was to remove that bra as quickly as possible.

"Your eyes tell me so much," Stephanie said in a ragged whisper.

Kat quit worrying if she was doing things right or wrong. She placed her hands around Stephanie's back. "May I?"

Stephanie bit her lip and nodded.

Kat unclasped the bra and stepped back as Stephanie let it fall to the floor. Kat's knees buckled, and she was suddenly very afraid she'd collapse. Stephanie's breasts were in perfect proportion to her body, the nipples high and tight. Kat reached for them with both hands, cupping them as if she were judging their weight. She lightly squeezed the nipples. Stephanie gasped.

"If you keep doing that, I'm going to come, and I don't want to until we're both naked and in bed."

With those words, Kat unclasped her own bra. Seeing the desire written on Stephanie's face, she didn't hesitate in easing the straps down and revealing her breasts.

"God, Kat." She mirrored Kat's move and cupped each breast in her hands. Then while rubbing her thumb against one nipple, she lowered her mouth to take the other between her lips.

Kat moaned and gripped Stephanie's head. A gush of wetness soaked her briefs. "Bed," she rasped out. "Please."

They moved to Stephanie's bed. She drew back the covers. Before she slid onto the mattress, she pulled off her panties. Kat felt like she was on fire as she took in Stephanie's toned and tan body.

"Now you." Stephanie hooked her thumbs in the waistband of Kat's briefs and tugged them to the floor. Stephanie's pupils had darkened even more with smoldering desire. "You're magnificent." She lay on her back on the bed and pulled Kat with her.

Stephanie's naked body flush against her own felt like thousands of tiny pinpricks against Kat's skin. She almost stopped breathing. "What do you like, Steph?" The nickname slipped out as if Kat had called her that a million times before. "I want to please you."

Stephanie brushed her thumb across Kat's lips. "You already are, baby. Do what comes naturally. Having you against me like this with nothing between us is making me so wet. Feel for yourself."

When Kat didn't make an immediate move, Stephanie grasped one of her hands and lowered it between her legs. Kat's own body answered with another gush of wetness. Stephanie guided Kat's fingers into her folds and began moving them. Kat opened her eyes and watched in wonder as Stephanie's face flushed in arousal.

"Like that," Stephanie whimpered. "Just like that." She released Kat's hand and twisted the sheets beside her hips with each pass of Kat's fingers. Kat drew closer to Stephanie's opening, and Stephanie thrust her hips higher. With the move, two of Kat's fingers slipped inside. She was immediately encased in quivering muscles. She kept up the rhythm, dipped her head, and sucked one of Stephanie's nipples into her mouth. Kat felt like she would climax herself when the muscles around her fingers jerked with spasms. "Oh God!" Stephanie cried out. One of her hands flew up and gripped Kat's hair almost painfully. Stephanie's body tensed, and Kat relished the feeling of Stephanie falling apart. Slowly, Stephanie released her hold on Kat's hair. Kat eased her fingers out, raised her head, and gave Stephanie a gentle kiss before falling to her side.

"If that was you not knowing how to please me, I'm in big trouble," Stephanie mumbled.

"So, it was good?" Kat knew it was, but she couldn't resist having her ego massaged even more.

"You're kidding, right? That was fucking amazing."

She said "fucking." I don't think she talks like that. Hot damn!

"Look at you." Stephanie moved onto her side and rubbed her thumb along Kat's jaw. "All proud of yourself."

"Well, yeah…" Before Kat could say another word, Stephanie pushed her onto her back and straddled her.

"God, you've got a great body." Stephanie trailed her fingers from Kat's shoulders, down her arms, and onto her chest. She brushed against her nipples and rubbed the muscles in Kat's stomach. Kat couldn't keep up with the sensations zapping through her body. Stephanie's fingertips seemed to contain little electrodes that knew where to touch her in all the right places.

Stephanie's mouth replaced her hands. She kissed her way down until she was between Kat's legs. "Is this okay?"

The gentleness in Stephanie's voice almost brought tears to Kat's eyes. "Yes," she whispered. The word had barely left her lips when she felt the first touch of Stephanie's mouth. She'd never let another woman do this before. It had always seemed so intimate, the ultimate giving of herself to her lover. She'd never felt that connection… until now.

Stephanie took her time tasting her, swiping her tongue through her folds, dipping into her opening. Then she took Kat's clit into her mouth and sucked.

"Oh, Steph!" Kat cried. She yanked Stephanie's hair and tugged her even tighter into her wetness. Kat's orgasm shot through her like a lightning bolt. Her hips rose off the bed, but Stephanie kept a firm grip on them as she coaxed every last ounce of pleasure from Kat's climax. Kat could take no more and feebly pushed Stephanie away. She felt Stephanie shift farther up the mattress. She tasted the remnants of her passion when Stephanie's lips met hers.

Stephanie wiped tears from Kat's cheeks. "I won't ask if I hurt you, because I know I didn't. But was this all right for you?"

Kat held her arm out for Stephanie to cuddle against her shoulder. "It was perfect. *You* were perfect."

Stephanie pulled the sheet over them. She settled again into Kat's arms. Before Kat succumbed to blessed sleep, she heard

Stephanie murmur, "I could get used to this." The words swirled around Kat's brain and nestled straight into her heart.

* * *

Kat sat in the small waiting area, trying her best not to be nervous. Her mind drifted to making love to Stephanie last night. It helped ease her anxiety as she waited for her mom. Kat had talked to her several times over the past couple of weeks. Sometimes she sounded upbeat. Sometimes she sounded wiped out and that the world was weighing heavy on her shoulders. Kat heard someone approach from behind. She stood up and tried her best to hold back a gasp, but one still escaped her lips.

Two weeks ago, Angela had appeared as good as Kat had seen her in quite some time. But today? Today she seemed like a new woman. Her dark hair hung loose on her shoulders. She was dressed casually in a pink T-shirt and worn jeans with frayed hems that draped over her sneakers.

Her eyes were clear and bright, as they were two weeks before. Something different reflected back at Kat, though. Angela wore a tranquil expression, the weary lines gone from her face.

"Kat, I'm so glad you came." Angela gripped both of Kat's hands in hers and kissed her on the cheek, then pulled her in for a long hug. "Can you visit for a while?"

"I planned on it."

They sat down side by side in matching lounge chairs.

"Mom, you look fantastic. I would ask how it's going in here, but I don't think I need to. You can see it on your face, in your eyes."

"Thank you for that. I've been doing a lot of soul-searching. I had some bad days the first week. You could probably tell when you called. Those were the days I was really craving a drink. Something happened this week, though. It's like it clicked over for me. I've been talking in therapy about why I started drinking in the first place. What we've focused on is that it didn't matter anymore. I wasn't thinking about your father as the years went by. I was simply thinking about my next drink. Then my next one and my next one." She waved her hand. "You get the picture."

She took Kat's hand. "We talked about my relationship with you, how much pressure I'd put on you over the years. How I cheated you out of your childhood."

"Mom, you don't—"

"No, let me finish, Kat." Angela scooted forward in her chair, closer to Kat. "You lost out on so much because of me and because of my addiction. Don't think I don't remember how many times you held me while I vomited the alcohol into the commode, how you cleaned me up, put me to bed, made sure there was always a glass of water and two Ibuprofen sitting on the nightstand." Her voice broke. "You saved me, Kat. Over and over. You saved me. I'll never be able to repay you or make it right. I'll never be able to give those years back to you." She caressed Kat's cheek that was wet with tears. "I can only say I'm sorry, that I'll do my damn best to stay sober, that I'll stay in therapy. I'll do anything not to screw this up." She wiped a stray tear away. "I love you, baby. So, so much." She started sobbing.

Kat couldn't take it anymore. She grabbed her mom and held her tight. She couldn't speak. She could only rock her mom in her arms, allowing her this chance to exorcise her demons. When she could finally talk around the tightness in her throat, Kat said the only words that needed to be said. "I love you, Mom."

On the drive back to Indianapolis, Kat sat with her head leaned back on the headrest, watching the blur of green from the trees beside the highway. Stephanie seemed to sense this was different from the last visit, and Kat wasn't shutting her out. She left Kat alone with her quiet reflection.

Which made Kat fall for her just a little more.

Chapter 25

With the end of the second week of September approaching, the Reds had taken control of the Central Division. They had a commanding eleven-game lead on the Cardinals who stayed ahead of the Pirates for second place. The Reds magic number to clinch the division shrank with each win.

Lisa arrived at the ballpark early Friday afternoon before the night game against Pittsburgh, a team the Reds could very well be facing in the playoffs. She was working on a feature of Nick Sanders for Major League.com. His 42 homeruns and 128 RBIs led the National League. He was third in average at .322. Unless Paul Terry of the Arizona Diamondbacks, his closest competition to the award, suddenly caught fire, in Lisa's opinion, Sanders was a shoo-in for the award. It was a classic case of going out on top for the retiring third baseman, something Lisa focused on in her piece.

She finished a paragraph and was about to start on the next when her cell rang.

"Hey, Frankie. This is a nice surprise."

"Lisa, have you checked your messages lately?"

The strain of Frankie's voice caused a cold fear to grip Lisa's insides.

"It's my dad, isn't it?"

"It is, but he's okay. They've admitted him to the hospital to reduce the fluid in his lungs. When you didn't call him back right away, he did a search for our home number and called me here."

Lisa was already saving her story and shutting down her laptop. She'd have to put a call into her editors about getting someone else to cover the game tonight and probably tomorrow night's game, too. They did have guest reporters on occasion. In fact, Sarah had written articles for a couple of the other teams that Major League.com picked up from *Baseball Weekly*. Maybe she could ask her.

"I'll drive you up there, Leese. You don't need to be behind the wheel."

Lisa was about to object but thought better of it. Frankie was right.

"I'll call New York and let them know." She spotted Sarah at the lower level of the press box. She waved to get her attention. "Listen, Frankie. I need to talk to Sarah. I'll be home as soon as I can."

Sarah made her way up the stairs to stand beside Lisa. "What's going on, Collins."

"I need to ask you for a big favor…"

* * *

"He's in ICU. There is limited visitation." The attendant behind the desk at the hospital checked the large clock on the wall. "You have a little time left this evening."

"Can you direct us where to go?" Lisa asked. They had driven straight up to Steubenville after Lisa made it home. Frankie had packed two days' worth of clothes for them, so they were able to leave as soon as Lisa got home.

"Third floor, to your left, and through the double doors. Someone will buzz you in."

As the elevator slowly lurched and jerked its way to the third floor, Lisa couldn't help but compare this to the hospitalization of Amy's mother last year. She'd been admitted for the same illness, and she didn't make it, dying after one night in the ICU.

"Don't put that thought in your head."

Lisa flinched at Frankie's voice. "I can't help it."

"Like I told you before, it's not the same as Amy's mom, Leese. The doctors have had your dad's heart failure under control with medication. Remember he told us he's had drainage a couple of times. It's a chronic condition, but I think he'll be okay."

Lisa knew Frankie wouldn't be saying something just to make her feel better.

The doors slid open to the third floor. The attendant at the desk beside the double doors checked for Ken's name and buzzed them in after cautioning them that they'd only have fifteen minutes.

Fifteen minutes didn't seem like enough time to say what Lisa needed to say. She'd been thinking about it on the drive up.

Her gait slowed as they approached his room, which had a large glass window that allowed the ICU nurses to see each patient. The light above his bed was out. It was hard to tell if the color of his face was ashen because of the lighting. He was resting. Lisa was thankful that he wasn't on a ventilator, but he did have oxygen tabs in his nose.

Frankie hung back as Lisa approached the bed. Lisa watched her dad's steady breathing for a few moments, his chest rising and falling with each breath. He must have sensed their presence; his eyes fluttered open. His pleased expression told Lisa she'd made the right decision in coming.

He reached out his hand. She moved to the side of the bed and grabbed it. It felt cold.

"You came."

"We did."

Ken coughed and struggled to catch his breath.

"Don't overexert yourself," Lisa said.

"Don't you worry about me." He squeezed her hand. "I didn't expect you to drive up, especially with no off-days for the Reds. I wanted you to know I was in the hospital. I figured you wouldn't be happy if I hadn't told you."

"You figured right." There was a long pause as she listened to the quiet hissing of the oxygen. "I wanted to talk to you." Before she said another word, Frankie interrupted her.

"Lisa, I'm going out to the waiting room. I'll be there when you're done."

She met Frankie's eyes that were full of understanding. "Thanks, Frankie."

Frankie left the room.

Ken started to speak, but a coughing jag hit.

Lisa filled the cup on the tray with water and held the straw while Ken took some sips.

"Better?" she asked.

He nodded.

She pulled over a chair and sat beside the bed. She kept her head down and ran her fingers over the blanket that covered him. "I've been doing a lot of thinking and not because of this." She motioned at the bed and the machines that surrounded him. "I've thought about the past, how you left mom, how you never contacted us… all the years between."

"Lisa, I—"

"No, let me finish. I've been angry at you for so long. I've held on to that anger to the point that it became a part of me, eating away at my chance to settle my feelings of abandonment." She gave a humorous laugh. "Believe me, I've had a lot of sessions with my therapist about this. But I'm tired now. I'm tired of holding the resentment in, tired of how it's consumed me. I've gotten to know you, too. I've heard your side of things. And I want the chance to get to know you better." She swiped at her damp cheeks. "I guess what I'm trying to say and doing a lousy job of it is I forgive you, Dad." Her voice cracked on the last word. "I love you, and I want us to have a chance with the years you have left on earth to smooth things out. Can we do that? Please?"

Tears were streaming down his face. Like her, he swiped them away. "Damn, Lisa. You've made your old man very happy. Happier than you'll ever know. Once I get out of here, we'll have the time to get to know each other even better. We'll make time. Life's too damn short. I love you, too. Now, give me a kiss and get out of here. Go back to Cincinnati and do your job."

Lisa bent over and kissed his cheek. He returned the kiss.

"I thought we'd stay through tomorrow. I already have someone to cover the team for these two games."

He seemed pleased at the news. "I won't argue then."

* * *

Dee flipped the ball to second. Kat knew she didn't have much time with the speedy runner flying down the first baseline. She barehanded the ball and fired a seed to the first baseman. A double play to end the game.

Kat filed in behind Dee and joined her teammates in slapping hands with their opponent, the Dragons, whose dour expressions gave away who won the game. The Dragons were ultra-competitive and resented always losing the league championship to the Bandits year in and year out. Some of the hand slaps were much harder than necessary.

Dee and Kat gathered up their bats and shoved them in the bat bag they shared.

"Wanna grab a bite to eat at O'Hara's?" Dee asked as they headed for the parking lot.

"Maybe you can drop me off. I'd better pack."

Dee shook her head. "Man, you two are going to run out of money with all this flying back and forth."

Kat was beginning to think the same thing but kept silent on the matter.

"How are you going to resolve living apart? Has she ever talked about moving to KC? 'Cuz there's no way in hell you're moving to Indianapolis. For one thing, Marge would go apeshit if you talked of leaving. For another, I wouldn't want you to go."

Kat and Stephanie had been flying back and forth to see each other for a few weeks. Kat had almost approached Stephanie about moving but was afraid to take the chance. She didn't know if she could bear to hear Stephanie say no.

"It might be something we talk about in the future."

Dee clapped her shoulder on the way to the car. "If I haven't said it lately, I'll say it again. I'm damn happy for you."

* * *

The plane started its descent to the Indianapolis International Airport. Kat gazed out the window, trying her best to spot Stephanie's car in the cell phone lot. After landing, she pulled out her cell to call her.

"I'll give you time to pick up your bag and be there in about fifteen minutes."

Kat had to smile at the excitement in Stephanie's voice. "I'll be waiting."

Kat held Stephanie in her arms, certain she was sleeping after hours of lovemaking. But she stirred and kissed Kat's bare shoulder.

"You've been pretty quiet tonight after getting here." Stephanie trailed her fingers between Kat's breasts while she spoke. "What are you thinking about?"

Here it is. Am I honest, or do I wait? She made the decision. She went with her heart.

"About how much I hate to leave you. This is all wonderful. Seeing you and being with you is wonderful, but leaving you cuts me to the core."

Stephanie leaned up on her elbow. Her dark hair fell onto her shoulders as she peered down at Kat. "I feel the same way."

Stephanie seemed to be struggling with what she'd say next. Without another thought, Kat blurted out, "I love you."

Stephanie didn't speak right away. Instead, her expression shifted from one of surprise to one of complete joy. Her eyes welled with tears. "I love you, too, Kat."

"Yeah?"

"Oh, yes." Stephanie leaned over to within a breath of Kat's lips. "Very, very, very much." She punctuated each word with another touch of her lips to Kat's until she thrust her tongue into Kat's mouth and claimed their love with a searing kiss.

Once Kat caught her breath, she plunged ahead. "Do you think you'd ever want to move to Kansas City?" It was probably the most tentative proposal in the history of love, but it was the best she could do.

A slow smile creased Stephanie's lips. "I thought you'd never ask."

Chapter 26

"You didn't have to treat me to dinner, not that I'm complaining." Sarah took a bite of her steak.

"I see you managed to order the most expensive steak on the menu." Lisa tried unsuccessfully to hide her smile.

"I distinctly remember you saying, and I quote, 'Order anything you want. It's on me.' Did you or did you not say that?"

"Yeah, but people say that shit and don't really mean it. Secretly, they're hoping you'll feel guilty and timid and order something in the mid-price range."

"Sorry to disappoint." Sarah smirked as she stabbed at another huge hunk of meat that she cut from her T-bone. She waved her fork at Lisa's plate. "Besides, you seem to have found your appetite again, too."

And Lisa had. She'd been anxious since their return from Steubenville, especially when either her cell phone or the landline rang. Her anxiety dissipated when they moved her dad into a regular room, and the next day, released him to go home. He reassured her he was feeling much stronger. He sounded stronger and only had a rare cough.

"Again, I was happy to fill in for you. I'm glad your father's much better."

"Me, too."

"Sounds like the two of you have gotten closer."

"We have. We had a heart-to-heart when he was in ICU."

"That doesn't surprise me. Some of the most heartfelt talks happen in ICU units."

Lisa wondered if Sarah was speaking from experience, but she quickly changed the subject. "The Reds might clinch the division tonight."

With a record of 90-63, the Reds had run away with the division, sweeping the Cardinals in St. Louis and in Cincinnati during the month of September. The Cardinals were playing the

Cubs in about an hour. The Reds would know the result by the start of their night game against the Brewers. A loss by the Cardinals, and the Reds would earn no less than a tie for the division championship. If the Cards lost and the Reds won, the Reds would claim it outright.

"Did you see this coming?" Sarah asked. She took a sip of water and swiped at her mouth with her napkin.

"I thought they'd have a good chance to win the division, but I sure as hell didn't expect them to run away with it."

"Maybe Sanders retiring has inspired them this year."

Lisa wondered about Amy's play, too. She'd been on fire since she returned from the disabled list. She was batting .283 for the season with 18 homeruns and 79 RBIs. In the weeks since she'd returned from her hamstring injury, though, she was batting .434 with 5 homeruns, 8 doubles, and 24 RBIs. Lisa had a feeling she could be looking at this as her last season. The decision might not be made yet, but it was as if Amy wasn't taking any chances and wanted to play her very best.

"Earth to Lisa."

"Huh?"

"I asked you what you thought."

"Yeah, you're probably right."

They finished their dinner, and Lisa picked up the bill. Regardless of the reasons for the Reds late season surge, it'd be fun to see them crowned Central Division champions tonight if everything fell into place.

* * *

"You won't mind me sitting in the stands tonight?" Stacy lounged in the bedroom, her back against the headboard, as Amy gathered up her gear for her drive to Great American Ball Park.

"The most important thing is how you're feeling." Amy studied her for any sign Stacy was holding back.

"I had a bit of morning sickness this week, but today I feel fine."

"Tired?"

"Did you think I was last night?"

Amy flushed. Last night had been amazing. Stacy was insatiable. It seemed pregnancy made her, well, horny. Amy couldn't think of a better word to describe her behavior... not that Amy was complaining. Nope. Not complaining at all.

Stacy got up and wrapped her arms around Amy. "I can't keep my hands off you these days. Hope that's okay."

"Okay? Damn, Stace. You've rocked my world. I mean, we've always had a passionate love life. But now? Damn," she repeated.

Stacy stood on her tiptoes to brush her lips against Amy's. "I can't help that I'm married to the sexiest woman alive."

Amy returned the kiss, only made it something much more by thrusting her tongue inside and grasping Stacy's hips to yank her closer.

When they pulled apart, they were both breathless.

"I need to go," Amy said in a raspy voice.

Stacy placed a quick peck on Amy's cheek. "I'll be sitting in my regular seat. Give them hell tonight, Perry.

Nick stood next to Amy as they changed out of their practice jerseys.

"I think I should get an award for my prediction at the end of last season."

"You should. The Nick Sanders Predicts We're Going to Kick Ass Next Year Award has a nice ring to it."

"That it does."

"We need to win this tonight. With the Cards losing, I don't want this to drag out to tomorrow's game." Amy tucked her jersey into her pants and buckled her belt. "I tell you what does have a nice ring. The National League Most Valuable Player Award."

Nick colored.

"Oh, my. I've embarrassed the unflappable Nick Sanders."

He shoved her. "Cut it out, Perry."

"Nick, you have the award all sewn up. Jesus, you're leading the universe in every hitting category there is. Hell, you could win it for all of major league baseball, if they gave that award out."

Nick grabbed his glove and batting gloves. "Enough. I'm heading out to the field." He started for the steps that led out to the dugout and the field.

"You know I love ya, right?"

"Get your ass out on the field," he shouted back.

In the on-deck circle, Amy had a sense of comfort knowing Stacy was four rows up behind the dugout. She kept her focus on rubbing the pine tar on her bat, afraid if she caught a glimpse of Stacy, she wouldn't concentrate in her at-bat.

She strode to the plate with two on in the bottom of the first. In past matchups, she'd had difficulties making contact against Heratio Inez, the Brewers pitcher, whose slowest pitch was a ninety-two-mile-per-hour slider. He steadily reached the high nineties on his fastball, which also had a lot of movement.

The first pitch was a slider that painted the black on the outside part of the plate for a strike. If he was going to be that pinpoint with his slider, Amy was screwed. Geared up for the heater, she swung through the next pitch, a breaking ball. Not having a clue as to what would come next, Amy guessed fastball. Her knees buckled as he dropped a curve over the heart of the plate.

Stalking back to the dugout, pissed off she hadn't come through for the team, Amy muttered, "Pick me up, Sandy," as she passed him. Unfortunately, he promptly hit into a double play to end the inning.

The game remained scoreless until the Brewers scored two runs with two outs in the top of the seventh. Murphy began his slow walk to the mound. He motioned for Coy Rivers, one of the young pitchers called up the first of the month. He got the next batter out on three straight pitches.

The Reds got a run in the bottom of the eighth. Entering the bottom of the ninth, they trailed 2-1. A pinch hitter came up for the pitcher's spot. He made it to first safely on an infield hit. Denks, the leadoff hitter, walked. Amy was warming up in the on-deck circle as Servace signaled Rawls to bunt the runners over. He laid down a perfect bunt that he deadened in the grass in front of the plate, almost beating it out for a hit.

"Bring 'em home, Amy!" Amy heard a familiar voice shout behind her as she walked to the plate. She snuck a peek over at Stacy who was standing with all the fans around her. She grinned at Amy and pumped her fists. Rather than make her nervous, seeing

Stacy centered Amy. Servace went through a series of signs, but Amy knew what her job was. Either a fly ball deep enough to score the runner from third, or better yet, a base hit to win the game. After a couple of practice swings, she took a deep breath and settled into the box.

The Brewers closer, one of the best in the majors, peered in for the sign. He checked the runners, reared back, and threw a fastball right by her.

Damn it. She stepped out of the box and took three vicious practice swings. Don't try to kill the ball, she thought. A simple base hit. A fly ball. That's all we need here. She dug in again and waited. A slider. I bet it'll be a slider, on the outside part of the plate. Amy guessed right. She was barely able to get her bat on the ball, but she got enough to nub it over the first baseman's head. It fell into no-man's land in right because the right fielder was playing off the line. Both the first baseman and right fielder hustled to the ball, but by the time the right fielder reached it, the runner from third had easily scored. Servace frantically waved Denks to the plate. Nick motioned for him to slide. The ball took an extra bounce, and Denks slid in safely.

We won. We won! As soon as the scrum finished mauling Denks at the plate, they rushed out en masse to greet Amy. She ducked her head as they pounded her back. In the melee, her helmet was knocked off, her shirt became untucked… and she didn't care. They were the Central Division Champions. After the heartbreak of last year, this was such an amazing feeling. Suddenly, someone lifted her up from behind. It could only be one person.

"Put me down, you big lug!" Amy had to shout to be heard over the roar of the crowd. Nick dropped her to her feet and spun her around to give her a huge hug.

"You did it, Perry!" He smacked her in the back a few more times.

She felt a hand on her shoulder. Murphy stood there, his face red, his hair mussed up. "Way to go, Perry. Way to go." He embraced her.

"Thanks, Skip."

Her teammates were donning championship T-shirts and hats. Amy put hers on when Servace handed them to her.

Nick draped his arm around her shoulders. "It's only the beginning. Don't forget that."

No, she definitely wasn't forgetting it. They'd find out who they would face in the playoffs after the Wild Card game between the Cards and Pirates. The only thing that mattered was they were moving on.

Let the fun begin.

Chapter 27

Stacy lay in Amy's arms. It was late. Amy should've been asleep hours ago. Too keyed up, she stared at the shadows dancing on the ceiling from the moonlight that streamed through the bedroom windows. Soft lips touched her shoulder.

"Can't sleep?" Stacy asked.

"No. Can't quit thinking about the game tomorrow." The St. Louis Cardinals had won the Wild Card game to earn a spot in the Divisional Playoffs, but the Reds had easily dispatched them from the postseason with a 3-0 series win. Next, they would face the Phillies, who'd swept the Giants. In the American League, the young, upstart Minnesota Twins, the Wild Card team, had won the first game of the League Championship Series against the Toronto Blue Jays.

"You're not worried about facing that jerk again, are you?" Tim Fairchild would start the first game for Philadelphia.

Amy chuckled. "He doesn't scare me."

"Good. I could still kick his ass for hitting you twice with a pitch. Fast balls, no less."

"You always have my back, don't you?"

Stacy snuggled closer. "Always."

Overcome again with the happiness she felt with the woman in her arms, Amy whispered, "Sometimes, it scares me, this life we share. I'm afraid if I blink, it'll all go away."

Stacy's breath hitched. "Amy, you're safe." She took Amy's hand and held it against her stomach. "We're safe."

"Oh, Stace." Amy pushed Stacy onto her back and kissed her, probing her mouth with her tongue. Their chests rose and fell as the kiss grew more passionate.

Stacy lowered her hand down Amy's abdomen and rested it between Amy's legs. "I think I can help you sleep."

Amy surrendered to the pleasure that only Stacy could give her. Soon, solace followed, and Amy drifted off to a peaceful sleep.

* * *

"Batting third and playing first base, number twenty-two, Amy Perry!"

The crowd roared as Amy trotted out to the first baseline to stand beside Rawls. "Pretty awesome, isn't it, Rawlsy?"

"Yeah." Tim Rawls gave every indication he was about to throw up.

"Deep breaths." Amy breathed in and out with him until he seemed to recover.

He gave her a weak smile. "Thanks."

"Batting fourth and playing third base, number eighteen, Nick Sanders!"

Again, the crowd roared. Then, a chant of "MVP! MVP!" started up and swelled to a tremendous crescendo.

Amy poked Nick in the arm. "See? *They* think you'll win the damn thing, too."

Nick tipped his hat. Out of the corner of his mouth, he muttered, "Shut the fuck up, Perry."

They stayed on the first baseline during the singing of the National Anthem. Afterward, when heading toward the dugout, Amy almost ran into a cameraman who was holding the camera low to the ground, filming her every move. She knew they liked to get up close and personal, but she hadn't experienced this before. She grabbed her glove.

"Jesus. I about tripped over that guy," she told Nick who was grabbing his own glove.

"Better get used to it. They love doing this shit in the playoffs and World Series. Makes it seem like it's 'in your living room.'"

Amy had helped Rawls with his nerves. He seemed to be fine. Unfortunately, she now felt like she could lose her lunch on the first base bag. She swallowed down her nerves and tossed the ball around the infield. It's just another game. It's just another game.

"Right," she said under her breath as she threw the ball on the infield toward Nick. "Keep saying it and maybe you'll believe it."

Josh Taylor, the Reds pitcher, easily retired the Phillies hitters in the top of the first. The first two Reds hitters struck out against

Tim Fairchild, the Phillies number one pitcher. Rawls swung at one in the dirt and was thrown out at first to complete the strikeout. The home plate umpire carried a new ball out to the mound. He came back to the plate and bent over to brush it off while Amy strode in from the on-deck circle.

A part of her wondered if Fairchild would carry over any crap from the regular season. Another part of her thought there was no way he'd jeopardize his standing in the playoffs or his team's chances of winning. He was more valuable on the mound than he was sitting at home with a suspension.

Still, she was ready for anything.

"Let's play ball tonight. None of the other shit," the umpire told her when she reached the plate.

"That's all I want to do, Terry. Tell him that."

"Just did when I carried out the new baseball."

We'll see, she thought and dug her right toe into the back of the box. Fairchild still glared at her over the webbing of his glove, but the first pitch was a breaking ball that caught the outside of the plate for a strike. The next pitch was a fastball on the inner half of the plate. Amy lined it into deep left. The crowd rose to their feet. The Phillies left fielder settled under it on the warning track for a loud out.

The Phillies scored three runs in the third inning. The game remained 3-0 until the sixth inning when the bottom of the Reds lineup strung together four hits to cut the Phillies lead to 3-2. The score remained 3-2 going into the bottom of the ninth.

Rawls led off the inning with a lineout to right field. Amy came to the plate hoping for any kind of hit. She was 0-3 and frustrated as hell. She swung wildly at the first two pitches from Doug Smith, the Phillies closer. She took a deep breath and tried to center herself before the next pitch. It was a slider down around her ankles. She barely got wood on the ball and was easily thrown out by the third baseman. When she entered the dugout, she stomped down to the bat rack and barely refrained from flinging her helmet to the cement floor. Instead, she set it in the slot, stripped off her gloves, and stood by the padding of the dugout, hoping Nick could pick up the team— like he had the entire season.

Like Amy, he fell behind early against Smith. He worked the

count full and fouled off four straight pitches. Amy could tell by his body language he was disgusted with himself for missing the last pitch that fell over the heart of the plate.

Smith made the mistake of trying to throw it by him again. Nick laid into the pitch and launched a rainbow to left center that kept going and going… and going. Amy held her breath when the center fielder leaped against the fence to catch the ball. It sailed two feet past his glove into the first row of the stands for a home run.

The Reds bench erupted in cheers and mobbed Nick when he came into the dugout.

Amy slapped his helmet. "MVP, Nick. You're the fucking MVP!"

Nick accepted the congratulations of all of his teammates lined up along the bench. He headed to the bat rack, peeled off his batting gloves, and placed his helmet in the slot.

"That shit doesn't count in the playoffs. New slate."

"Yeah, well, you're on your way to the MVP of the Championship Series if you keep this up." Amy had to shout over the crowd who wouldn't stop cheering until he took a curtain call.

He took two steps up the dugout stairs and waved.

Mark Roberts, the next batter, lined a double down in the right field gap. Now, they had the winning run at second. Again, the Reds players hung over the padding, anxiously watching while Todd Henderson, the right fielder, lined two balls hard down the right field line. When each ball landed foul, the crowd and the team groaned.

Henderson stepped out of the box, his lips moving—probably giving himself a little pep talk.

"Come on, Hendo," she whispered. "Drop one out there somewhere."

Smith reared back and fired a fastball clocked at ninety-eight on the scoreboard. Henderson hit a soft line drive into center. The centerfielder had been playing shallow and caught it on one bounce, but with two outs, Roberts, who had decent speed, was going on the pitch. Servace waved Roberts around third. The batter in the on-deck circle was motioning at Roberts to slide. Everyone in the dugout was shouting, "Slide! Slide!"

The ball arrived at the same time as Roberts. He slid to the back of the plate and avoided the tag of the Phillies catcher. He was safe.

The dugout exploded onto the field and greeted Roberts with hugs and backslaps. They ran out to Henderson and congratulated him while the crowd stayed on their feet long after the Phillies had walked off the field.

The team eventually made their way to the dugout.

"One down and three to go!" Amy shouted to Nick.

"You got that right!"

* * *

"Come back in here, Benson!" Dee yelled. "You're going to miss the last out!"

"Give me a minute! Gonna bring some brewskies in for us to celebrate." Kat hustled into the kitchen for three bottles of beer, juggling them in her hands as she carried them into the living room. Stephanie was visiting from Indianapolis. They'd decided they'd wait until the fall to search for a place together in Kansas City.

They were watching what they hoped would be the series-clinching win for the Reds. The team returned home to Cincinnati up 3-2. They were winning 4-1 going into the top of the ninth and had asked Danny Lopez, their closer, to get the last six outs. It would be his first two-inning save for the season.

Kat hurried in and handed out the beer with the hope they would be celebrating with the brew. She sat down next to Stephanie on the couch. Stephanie was literally on the edge of her seat. If Kat wasn't so invested in the outcome and pulling for Amy, she would've laughed at the intense expression Stephanie was sporting.

Lopez quickly got in front of the Phillies cleanup hitter. Down 1-2, he managed to foul off three pitches. On the next pitch, he popped up to Amy at first. She waved her arm wildly, mouthing, "I got it! I got it!"

They jumped up from their seats the second the ball fell into her glove. "Yes!" They shouted at the same time.

Stephanie and Kat embraced until Dee said, "They're showing Stacy in the stands."

Stephanie and Kat turned in time to see Stacy wiping away

tears. She hugged one of the players' wives seated next to her.

"We have a shot at seeing a game in the World Series," Dee said. "Remember? Amy promised Marge that if the Reds made it, she'd try to get some extra tickets. Not sure which game, but at this point, I really don't care."

"Me either." Kat kissed Stephanie on the cheek. "You'll be coming, too, right? Stacy would want you there."

"She already told me at least one game."

"Cool," Kat said.

The cameras caught the celebration in the clubhouse. All the players were wearing goggles and shaking champagne out of the bottles. Eventually, it settled down for the presentation of the League Championship trophy. Then, the National League President presented the Series MVP award. Nick Sanders stood next to Carl Pastini, the owner of the Reds. The FOX announcer shoved the microphone in Nick's face.

* * *

Nick, his hair soaked and his face dripping in champagne, accepted the trophy. "It's an honor, but I accept this on behalf of the team. We worked our butts off to get here, and none of us let up for 162 games."

The players cheered.

"You deserve it, Nick! Suck it up!" Amy shouted.

Everyone laughed.

"Seriously, this is very special to me, and I'm bringing it home to someone very special."

Amy held her breath, thinking Nick was about to out himself on national TV.

"Love you, babe," Nick choked out as his face reddened.

Eventually, Nick left the podium and joined Amy in the corner of the room for another long sip of champagne. He barely met her eyes. "I couldn't do it, Amy. I wanted to, but I couldn't. I was afraid that would become the story, and the team would lose focus. After the Series, I'll shout it from the rooftops. Well, if not the rooftops, at least into a microphone."

Amy put her arm around him and gave him a half hug. "Nick,

quit beating yourself up. For what it's worth, I think you did the right thing. Knowing the media, Lisa excluded of course, they would've eaten you alive. We need your head in the game." She held the champagne bottle over his head and grinned. "Put those goggles back on, big guy. Time for another bath."

He slipped the goggles over his eyes, and she whooped as she dumped the remnants of her champagne onto his head.

"This is a fucking awesome feeling, isn't it?" he yelled as he shook out his hair.

"Damn right!"

"We're not done, Perry. Remember that. We're not done. Gotta win four more games."

"I've got a good feeling, Sandy." Amy turned at the tap on her shoulder. "Lisa! Isn't this cool?"

Lisa wiped her face. "Would've been cooler if the press had been given goggles, too. Goddamn, this shit stings."

Amy reached behind her for the stack of towels. She tossed one to Lisa. "Here you go."

Lisa scrubbed the towel through her hair and over her face. When she pulled the towel away, she was grinning at Amy. "Feels pretty good, doesn't it, Aim?"

"You asking as a reporter or a friend?"

"Friend, right now."

"It's fanfuckingtastic!"

Lisa laughed and pulled her notebook out of her pocket. "Okay. Let's try it as a reporter."

Amy sobered. "Like Nick said, it feels great, but we're not done. Our goal since last year's loss in the one-game playoff has been to win the World Series. We've worked hard to get here. We hope we can pull it out."

"How did it feel hitting that double in the third off of Fairchild, given your history this season?"

Amy shook her head. "I was happy I could help the team and Nick knocked me in. Didn't matter who the pitcher was on the mound."

Lisa shut her notebook. "Let's try that answer as a friend. Off the record."

Amy leaned close and said into Lisa's ear. "I fucking loved it.

Couldn't have come against a better guy."

Lisa patted her on the back. "That's what I thought. Even told Sarah sitting next to me that it had to feel good for you."

Players had gathered around one of the TV monitors that showed the action on the field. The crowd hadn't left the stadium. Obviously, they were waiting for the Reds to enter the field again.

"Guess you better get back out there, huh?" Lisa said.

"Guess so. Hey, Phil. Got some extra championship T-shirts? Mr. Pastini said he would have extra ones for us to toss to the crowd."

Phil reached into a large cardboard box and lifted out a stack. "Here you go, everybody! Don't go out there empty-handed."

The players filed by and grabbed rolled-up T-shirts on their way back onto the field.

Amy grabbed a huge stack. "Have to head out." She tossed two T-shirts to Lisa. "Here's a couple for you and Frankie."

"We'll still be here when you all come back. Need some more quotes from everybody."

"No problem."

Amy fell in line behind Nick as the players streamed up the clubhouse steps into the dugout and out onto the field. When the crowd caught sight of them, the roar was deafening. Amy waved along with her teammates. Before she started running along the stands with the other players, she rushed over to the one person who mattered most to her.

Stacy was leaning over the railing.

Amy pulled her down for a kiss on the lips. She didn't care that she was probably being filmed and broadcast on national television. This was her wife, and Stacy deserved this moment as much as she did.

Stacy held Amy's face in her hands. "Do you know how much I love you?"

"Pretty sure I do." Amy put her hands over Stacy's. "Because I know how much I love you." Amy kissed her again. "There'll be more of this later."

Stacy giggled and playfully shoved her away. "Go! Go be with your teammates."

"See you soon!"

Voices cried out to Amy as she made her away around the stadium. She threw the rolled-up T-shirts to as many kids as she could. Time passed by in a blur. Soon, she was empty-handed. She smacked the outstretched hands, waving to the fans she couldn't touch.

God, I love this game, she thought. Can I give it up after this season?

Chapter 28

"Mom, this is Stephanie McGrady."

"Hello, Ms. Benson."

"Please, it's Angela." Kat's mom hugged Stephanie. "So, you're the beautiful young woman who's put such a bright smile on my little girl's face."

"Mom, I'm hardly a little girl anymore."

Angela playfully pinched Kat's cheek. "You'll always be my little girl." She welcomed them into the living room. "Can I get you any refreshments?"

Kat could tell her mom was nervous and tried to alleviate her anxiety. "We're here to visit. You don't need to serve us anything."

Kat and Stephanie took the couch, while Angela sat down in the nearby chair.

"How have you been doing?" Kat asked.

"Really well. I'm attending AA daily. They told me in the hospital to go as often as I felt I needed it, but that eventually, I'd know when to cut back once I felt stronger. I found a nice group down the street, and I've connected with the sponsor there."

Kat's throat tightened with emotion. She took a moment to respond. "I can't tell you again how proud I am of you. Well, I can. I'm very proud of you and the steps you've taken. I'm also glad we're talking once a week."

"Me, too, sweetheart. That means the world to me. And having you come in like you did today, that means the world to me, too. We lost touch too much these past few years. That's my fault—"

"We've already gone over some of this. You don't need to keep apologizing, Mom. Honest. Let's make this a fresh start, okay?"

Angela blew out a breath. "Okay."

"Ms. Ben… Angela, I love your house."

Kat had been so caught up in her mom meeting Stephanie for the first time that she hadn't noticed the changes made to the place.

Fresh flowers sat on the mantel. Some of the furnishings were new, the wood had been polished to a glossy sheen, the area carpets swept. It looked… homey.

"Thank you, Stephanie. I've tried to spruce it up some."

A photo on the mantel caught Kat's eye. She stood up and approached the framed picture. It was an action shot of her playing second base for the Bandits. She ran her fingers over the glass. "Where did you…"

Angela had moved behind her and placed her hand on Kat's shoulder. "I saw the photo in our local paper when you played here last. I made such a mess of things that day."

"Mom—"

"Let me finish, honey. I'm only stating facts. I made such a mess of things that I wanted something positive to remember that day. I contacted the paper and found out they sell some of their photos to the public. I bought this one. You say you're proud of me? I've always been very, very proud of you. More than you'll ever know."

Kat couldn't speak. She simply spun around and fell into her arms. It was so good to finally cry while in the comfort of her mother's embrace.

"Shh, baby," Angela whispered against her temple. She held Kat even tighter. When Kat's quiet cries dwindled to sniffles, she smoothed away the wetness on Kat's cheeks.

Kat heard Stephanie sniffle from the couch.

"Sorry." Stephanie wiped at her own cheeks. "I'm so happy for you both."

Angela took Kat's hand and led her back to the couch. "Don't you apologize, sweetheart. You're part of the family now."

"Oh, God, Mom. Don't get me started again," Kat choked out.

Angela held up her hands to ward off more tears. "How about a change in subject? You're here to attend the first game of the World Series?"

Excitement fluttered in Kat's stomach at the mere mention of the game. "Stacy made sure that Stephanie and I have tickets. If it goes to seven games, Amy has tickets for the entire Bandits team. I asked Marge to see if she could get you a ticket, too. Amy told her she'd try her best."

"You didn't have to do that. I can watch it on TV here."

"I want you there, Mom. Will you come if it goes to seven games? With the Reds having home field advantage against the Twins, if it came down to seven, they'd play it in Cincinnati."

"All right. If you want me there, I'd love to come. Thank you for thinking of me. Of course, I'd love to see them sweep."

Kat grinned. No matter what, her mom had stayed a Reds fan throughout the years.

"We hope they do, too, but Minnesota has excellent pitching. Should be a fun World Series."

* * *

"Nervous?" Frankie asked from behind the shower stall.

"I'm not nervous for me, but I am for Amy and the team—especially Amy." Lisa finished rinsing off and stepped out of the shower. Frankie handed her a towel.

"I think she'll handle it, don't you?"

"Yeah, but…"

"But?"

Lisa quickly toweled off and pulled on her underwear. Frankie followed her back into the bedroom. Before Lisa dressed, she sat down on the bed. Frankie settled in beside her.

"What's going on, Leese?"

"I've not brought it up again because it seemed like it wasn't real, yet here we are, the first game of the World Series. Maybe I was afraid I'd jinx it, but we could be witnessing the last games of Amy's career."

"I kind of forgot about that during the season."

"It'd be nice to see the Reds win the Series, and Amy and Nick could retire on top. That is if it's what Amy wants. I mean, what better way to leave the game? And remember Marge asked her to consider taking over the Bandits when she stepped down." Lisa pulled on her khakis.

"Damn, this has all kinds of subplots, hasn't it?"

"Yup. I'm keeping my mouth shut about it until she makes the announcement." Lisa finished with the last of the buttons on her denim shirt.

"On another note, are you excited about your dad coming in a couple of weeks?"

Lisa lit up at the prospect. "I tried to get him to come down for one of the games, but he said he wanted to spend time with me and knew I'd be busy working." She leaned over to lace up her sneakers.

"I'm happy for you, Leese."

Lisa never thought she'd feel this way, but she had to admit that it was freeing to let go of the anger and embrace the fact they'd finally connected.

* * *

Amy checked the bowl she usually tossed her keys into, but it was empty. "Damn it." She stomped around the living room, flipping up magazines and pushing her hand between cushions in her frantic search.

"Looking for these?" Stacy stood in the hallway that led into the living room with Amy's key ring dangling from her finger.

Amy sighed. "Thank God. I was about to come ask you to drive me to the ballpark." She took the keys from Stacy.

"I wouldn't mind doing that for you, sweetie, but you told me once you need that time during the drive to clear your head for the game."

"It doesn't mean I don't want you with me. You get that, right?"

"Yes. Quit worrying." She glanced at the clock. "It's time you hit the road."

Amy grabbed her gear and headed for the door. "I'll see you later?"

"Would I miss this? The first game of the World Series?"

Amy ducked her head and mumbled, "No."

Stacy came to her, tipped her chin up, and brushed her lips again with a soft kiss. "You're right. I wouldn't. Good luck out there tonight."

"Thanks, Stace. See you later at the park." She bent over and kissed Stacy's stomach. "See you later, too."

Stacy ran her fingers through Amy's hair. "I love it when you do that."

Amy straightened and cupped Stacy's cheek. "You two are my world."

Stacy placed her hand on top of Amy's and then kissed Amy's palm. "And you're ours. Kick some butt, babe."

Amy made it to the Equinox and tossed her bags into the back. On her drive to the park, thoughts flew through her mind—about the pitcher they'd be facing, about staying back on her swing, and ultimately, about the time ahead and the possibility her playing days might be numbered.

A few miles later, she parked in the players lot with her thoughts firmly on the night's game.

* * *

Amy chewed on her thumbnail at first base, a bad habit for tense situations. This was definitely one of those. The Reds were up 4-3 in the top of the eighth. The Twins had runners at first and second with one out. Murphy had dipped into the bullpen and called in his closer, Lopez, to get a five-out save. Again, it was something he rarely did during the season. But this was the postseason, and team convention changed, sometimes from out to out.

The Twins left-handed power hitter, Bill Stroman, was in the batter's box and ahead 3-1 in the count. Amy stayed on her toes as Lopez went to the plate. A fastball on the inner half. Before Amy could barely react, Stroman lined the pitch down the first baseline. She dove, stretched her body to the limit, and snagged it in her glove. The runner on first was halfway to second. Amy scrambled to her feet and sprinted to the base, easily doubling up the runner.

"Woo hoo!" Nick shouted and held up his glove for her to tap on the way to the dugout. "Way to snag it, Perry!"

She couldn't keep the grin off her face as they trotted into the dugout. Lopez met her at the top of the steps and smacked hands with her.

"Thanks for saving my ass," he said.

"You had it nailed down, Danny. Go out there and get the last three outs."

The Reds went down quietly in the bottom of the eighth. In the top of the ninth, the Twins again got two on, but Lopez induced a double play. A pinch hitter was the Twins last hope. Lopez jumped ahead 1-2 and retired him on a nasty slider down and in.

Amy wanted to toss her glove in the air with joy, like she used to do as a kid when the pitcher recorded the last out of a win. She played it cool, though, and congratulated Lopez. She lined up behind her teammates as they smacked hands.

Nick jogged beside her, whipped off her hat, and ruffled her hair. "One down, three to go."

"Give me my hat, doofus."

"Big baby. Here." He set it on her head with the bill in the back.

"So not cool."

"Damn, Perry, you'd have thought we lost the game. Cheer up!"

"I will after three more wins."

"Don't tighten up on me, okay?"

Amy realized how ridiculous she sounded. He was right. They'd won the first game of the World Series. Why was she stressing?

"You're right, Nick. Don't know where my head is."

"Oh, I think I know where some of it is." He nodded toward the stands where Stacy stood and waved. "You have quite a bit on your mind."

Amy waved back at her. "I'll see you at home," she yelled.

"Love you, babe. Great game!"

Amy did have a good game, going 2-4 with two runs scored. Nick had again been the real hero, knocking in three on a bases-clearing double in the fifth.

For payback, she snatched Nick's hat off his head, and played "keep away" until they got to the top of the dugout steps. A TV reporter stood there, waiting.

"Nick, could we get you on camera?"

"Guess you better look good for your close-up." Amy plopped the hat back on his head. "Smile for the cameras, big guy."

"Oh, shut the f—"

She shook her finger at him. "Ah, ah, ah."

He glared at her as she blew him kisses and headed into the clubhouse.

Chapter 29

"Sweetheart," Angela said, "I didn't expect you to get a ticket for me tonight, too. Tomorrow night would've been enough."

Rick Fowler, the Reds starter, finished his warm-ups. They were seated a row behind Stacy and the players' wives. The Reds had left town with a 2-0 lead in the Series. They lost the next three games in Minneapolis, all one-run losses.

"We don't even know if there'll be a seventh game, Mom."

Angela slapped Kat lightly on the arm. "Oh, now don't you go talking like that."

Stephanie must've overheard her, too. "You're mom's right, Kat. Where's the faith?"

Kat took in her mom's and Stephanie's attire. Angela was decked out in a Reds sweatshirt and Reds hat, a hat that had seen better days. She told Kat it was her lucky one and there was no way she wasn't wearing it to the game. Stephanie, like her sister, was wearing an authentic Amy Perry jersey. She'd put her hair in a ponytail and pulled it through the opening in the back of her cap.

Kat was a little more conservative. She wore her old Reds jacket but hadn't donned a hat. "I have faith. I'm a little nervous, okay?"

Stephanie put her arm around Kat's waist. "We are, too, aren't we, Angela?"

"God, yes."

"But we have faith in Amy and Nick and the boys."

Kat simply nodded as the butterflies soared in her stomach with the first pitch.

* * *

Amy sat next to Nick in the dugout as the bottom of the order came to the plate.

"Pick us up here, Lonnie!" she shouted, clapping her hands.

Lonnie Bell, the shortstop, slapped a ball down the third baseline. He hustled down to first with an infield single.

"That's it! Way to go!"

"Still pissed off at myself in the last inning," Nick muttered. He'd struck out with the bases loaded. The score in the sixth was tied 3-3.

Amy slapped his leg. "Quit being so hard on yourself. You'll have some more chances."

"Yeah, but it would've been nice to come through for the team."

The next batter hit into a six-four-three double play.

"It's okay, Tony. You'll get 'em next time." Amy smacked the catcher on the butt as he walked by.

The pinch hitter for the pitcher came up to bat and popped out to the first baseman. Amy grabbed her glove and headed out to her position.

* * *

"Knock him in, Aim." Lisa was sitting on the edge of her seat, not even trying to hide the fact she was rooting for Amy to come through here in the bottom of the eighth.

"Would be nice to see them go to seven, wouldn't it?" Sarah said.

The score was still tied 3-3, each team without a hit since the sixth. The Reds had a runner at third with one out. Amy stepped out of the batter's box, unsnapping and snapping her batting gloves as she read the signs from the third base coach.

"Definitely would be nice," Lisa said.

Amy fouled off two straight breaking balls from the Twins reliever. He circled behind the mound, picked up the rosin bag, and bounced it on his throwing hand.

"What do you think? Fastball or another breaking ball," Sarah asked.

They played this game throughout the season, each one challenging the other to what came next. A wager was usually involved.

"Fastball, outside corner."

As the Twins pitcher toed the rubber, Sarah said, "Breaking ball, inside."

"For a beer?"

"Do we ever wager anything else?"

The next pitch was a ninety-seven-mile-an-hour fastball on the outside black of the plate. Amy lunged for the ball, putting enough wood on it to poke it over the second baseman's head for a single, easily scoring the runner from third.

Lisa jumped up. "Good going, Aim!" Sarah cheered, too.

"Michelob at Tim's Place?" Lisa shouted over the roar of the crowd.

"Oh shut up, Collins."

Jeffries, the first base coach, smacked Amy hard on the back. "Way to stay with it, Perry." He held his hand loosely on her shoulder. "You got one out. Run down hard on a ground ball in the infield. Keep your head up on anything else."

Amy took a short lead off first. Nick jumped all over the first pitch. He hit it square, but the Twins shortstop made a great stop. He flipped the ball to the second baseman. Amy slid hard but the second baseman easily tapped the bag and threw the ball to first for an inning-ending double play.

Amy handed her helmet and batting gloves to Jeffries. Rawls carried her glove out to her.

"Way to go, Perry. Let's get these last three."

Lopez ran in from the bullpen for the save situation. Amy tossed the ball around the infield. She could tell Nick was beating himself up for the double play from the way he was firing the ball to first.

"Shake it off, Nick," she said under her breath.

He literally did shake his head as if he heard her. He gave her a slight smile as he threw the next ball much softer.

Lopez struck out the first two batters. Again, their power hitter, Stroman, strode to the plate. He had 45 homeruns during the season. For the postseason, he hit a phenomenal 8 homeruns, including 3 in the first five games of the Series. He launched the first pitch from Lopez deep down the left field line. Amy held her breath as the ball cut through the night and released it when the ball curved left of the foul pole.

Lopez took some time behind the mound rubbing up the ball. He toed the rubber and peered in for the sign.

Another fastball on the outer part of the plate. Stroman went the other way again and smacked the ball on two hops down the third baseline. Nick dove, snatched the ball in his glove, and from his knees, fired a seed to Amy for the last out of the game.

Amy pumped her fist. "Yeah! Yeah, big man!"

Lonnie Bell hopped on Nick's back. He laughed. "Get off of me, Lonnie."

Lopez hugged him, as did Rawls.

Amy came over to him and hugged him, too. "How'd that feel? What a play!"

"It felt great after hitting into that double play."

"Damn right. Never put your head down, Sandy. You mean too much to the team."

"One more, Perry. One more!"

* * *

Lisa took a sip of her Michelob.

"There she is." Sarah pointed her beer bottle toward the door.

Frankie was making her way into the bar. Lisa stood up from her stool and motioned her over.

Frankie waved to Sarah, gave Lisa a quick kiss on the cheek, and sat down on the empty stool next to her. "Do you think you could've picked a quieter place?" Frankie said over the din of the celebrating crowd.

"I don't think it would matter where we went tonight in the city, Frankie. Everyplace would be like this one."

"It was Lisa's idea," Sarah said.

"I won the bet, so get over it, Swift."

"You two." Frankie shook her head when the bartender took her order. "You're always going at it."

"Not drinking, hon?" Lisa asked her.

"No. I'm saving it for tomorrow night's game."

"Amen to that." Lisa held up her bottle and clinked it with Sarah's.

"How do you think Josh Taylor will be tomorrow night on three days' rest?" Sarah asked Lisa.

"I think he's going to be so pumped, he should be fine. That's what he's getting paid for."

"Yeah, but sometimes it doesn't work out that way," Sarah said as she took another sip of her Budweiser.

"I have a good feeling about this one." Lisa downed the rest of her beer.

Frankie put her arm around Lisa. "Here's hoping you're right, Leese."

* * *

"Can I get anyone anything?" Angela shouted from the kitchen.

Kat and Stephanie were curled up together on the couch. Stephanie had been rubbing the back of Kat's neck for the past ten minutes, and she was slowly putting Kat to sleep.

"No thanks, Angela," Stephanie answered. "I think we're about to go to bed."

Kat struggled to sit up. She yawned. "I'm thinking that's a good idea."

Angela walked in from the kitchen, sipping out of a bottle of water. She grinned at Kat. "You look knackered, as the Brits say."

Kat stood up and stretched her back. She pulled Stephanie to her feet. "That's because I am, Mom. You've been like the Energy Bunny tonight."

"I'm pumped for tomorrow night's game. I can't believe I'll be at the seventh game of the World Series. But the best part?" She gave Kat a hug. "The best part is I get to share it with my daughter and her beautiful partner."

"Oh, Angela. Don't make me cry." Stephanie hugged her, too.

"Let's not forget about Marge Tompkins and the rest of the team. They'll all be there tomorrow night."

"Should be a lot of fun. She knows..." Angela let her voice trail off.

Kat patted her shoulder. "She knows you're sober."

Angela's face reddened. "I wasn't having one of my better days last time I saw her. Hell, I was falling down drunk."

Kat hugged her again. "But you're better now," she whispered in her ear. "She'll be happy for you."

Angela gave her another quick squeeze before letting go. "All right. you two, off to bed. I'll fix you a nice breakfast in the morning."

Kat and Stephanie headed down the hall to the larger of the spare bedrooms. Kat shut the door behind her. Stephanie was already stripping down. "I'm going to take a quick shower." Her butt swayed as she passed by.

"Is that an invitation?"

Stephanie winked at her. "I'll let you figure it out."

Kat quickly shed her clothes on her way to joining Stephanie. "Remember, we need to be quiet."

Stephanie yanked her into the shower stall. "Shouldn't be an issue."

* * *

Amy closed her eyes again in an effort to get to sleep, but it was an impossible task—especially after having a dream about her mom. Unlike last year on the night before their final regular season game, this one wasn't a nightmare. Yes, it had been a dream, but seeing her mom healthy and smiling had comforted her, though it left her mind racing. When it became clear she wasn't going to drift off anytime soon, she quietly slipped out from under the covers. She hesitated at the door when Stacy stirred. Thankfully, she rolled over and didn't wake. Amy made her way into the kitchen for a bottle of water.

She listened to the second hand tick on the wall clock and thought of the dream. She was on a ball diamond. The sky was the bluest she'd ever seen, the grass so green, it almost hurt her eyes. Joy filled her very being as she stood at the plate waiting on pitches from her mom, Thelma. It harkened back to a time when her mother would take her to the local Little League park to help Amy hone her swing.

Of course, her mother didn't throw hard, but it didn't matter. In the dream, Thelma shouted out, "Don't drop that right shoulder!" Those words were so much an echo of what she'd told Amy throughout her childhood playing days. Then she heard her father's gentle laughter. Amy saw him sitting in the stands.

The door to the bedroom creaked open, and footsteps drew nearer.

Stacy dropped her arms around Amy from behind and kissed her ear. "Couldn't sleep?"

"No."

Stacy rounded the couch and sat down beside her. Amy set her water bottle on the coffee table and pulled her close. Stacy rested her head on Amy's shoulder and draped her arm around Amy's stomach.

"You didn't have a bad dream, did you?"

"No. Actually, it was a good dream. My mom was pitching balls to me like when I was a kid."

"She's watching over you. Your dad is, too."

"Yeah, he was there in the stands."

Stacy patted her stomach. "See? They're with you, Amy. They never leave you."

Amy kissed the top of Stacy's head. "It feels good. It got me to thinking about everything I've been through to get here."

Stacy peered up at her. "Are you still thinking of quitting the game if you win?"

Amy nodded.

"But you'll wait until some time passes after the season, won't you? I don't want you to make a sudden decision that you'll regret," Stacy said. Amy started to speak, but Stacy silenced her with a quick kiss. "Listen to me for a minute and have an open mind, okay?" She waited for Amy to acknowledge her with another nod. "I know how much this baby means to you, means to us. I think we need to keep in mind, though, how hard you worked to get here, what all you had to go through. I've been thinking, too, that you could be just as much help if you kept playing than if you quit to coach. I remember how much Kat looked up to you when she was here for dinner."

Amy thought back to Kat's insightful questions about the game, how excited she was as Amy talked about certain pitchers and how it felt to hit against them. She reluctantly had to agree with what Stacy was telling her.

"You might be right," she murmured.

Stacy rubbed her thumb lightly over Amy's forehead. "Lose the frown line and don't worry. I'm only telling you this so we can have a really meaningful discussion when the season is over. You won't simply go through the motions and announce your retirement anyway. Okay?" She gave Amy a penetrating stare.

"Dear God, I know I'm beat when you give me that look. All right. We'll wait." Amy leaned in and kissed her. "Besides, let's not get ahead of ourselves. We need to win the game first. Then, we'll go from there." She stood and grabbed Stacy's hand. "For now, let's go back to bed."

When they reached the bedroom, Stacy cuddled up next to Amy. "No matter what happens, know how proud I am of you, Amy, and how very much I love you."

Amy pressed her lips to Stacy's. "I love you, Stacy. I can't imagine my life without you in it."

"That's good, babe. Because you don't have to."

Chapter 30

"Well, this is it, Collins. Not only the last game of the Series, it's the last game of the season." Sarah plugged in her laptop in the space next to Lisa.

"Always the master of stating the obvious, Swift."

Sarah clapped her on the back. "You're only grumpy because you'll miss me in the off-season."

"We can always remedy that. How about you and Mary getting together with us this winter? Maybe Frankie and I can leave the frigid cold and fly out to Seattle to visit."

"That sounds like a plan. Mary would like the chance to get to know you both." Sarah nodded down at the field. "Still feeling like Taylor can handle the short rest?"

"He's done it twice during the season and had a 2.45 ERA for those two games."

"Listen to you. Why does it not surprise me you'd spout off this statistic?"

"Because I'm a stats geek and I keep up on this shit?"

"Yeah. That'd be it." Sarah motioned toward the stands behind the Reds dugout. "I think the entire Bandits team made it in for this one."

Lisa looked down to where she motioned. "It's pretty cool." Stacy was in her regular spot with the Bandits team seated behind her. Her sister and Kat Benson sat next to her. It also appeared Kat's mother had made the game. Lisa had learned from Amy, who heard it from Stacy, that Kat's mom was sober now. That was really good to hear.

"I see Frankie made it."

Lisa had bought the ticket before the Series started and was glad she could actually give it to Frankie for the game.

"She was pretty pumped this afternoon."

Taylor had finished his last warm-up toss. The game was on.

* * *

The Twins went down one-two-three in the top of the first. With one out, Rawls slapped a single to right. Amy stood next to the batter's box and checked out Servace's signs. Nothing but hit away, at least the first pitch. She fouled off a fastball from the Twins' ace. She waited for Servace's next sign. A hit and run, which made sense with the speedy Rawls at first. No matter what, Amy needed to make contact. The next throw was way off the outside part of the plate, but thankfully, it was a breaking pitch. Amy had time to lunge and hit it over the first baseman, who'd been holding Rawls at first. Rawls never broke stride and easily ended up on third. With only one out, Sanders could get the first run on the board with either a hit or a fly ball.

He walked up to the plate and gave a cursory glance at Servace. He swung at the first pitch, hit it deep to left for a sacrifice fly, and Rawls scored. Roberts grounded out to the third baseman for the last out.

Amy stripped off her gloves, threw them in her helmet, and handed everything to Jeffries. Lonnie, the shortstop, carried her cap, glove, and ball to her. She felt more relaxed now with the first inning done. Only twenty-four outs to go.

* * *

In the bottom of the fourth, with the Twins leading 2-1, Amy took her lead off second. She'd doubled with two outs. Nick had worked the count full after being behind 0-2.

Come on. Just a base hit.

Nick answered her plea and lined the ball into right center. Servace pinwheeled his arm as he waved her around third. Roberts threw his hands down for her to slide. She arrived at the plate before the ball and easily avoided the catcher's tag.

Tie game.

Top of the seventh, and the Reds faced a dire situation. The Twins had loaded the bases with only one out. The score was still tied 2-2, but the Twins could blow it open here.

Amy glanced in the dugout. Murphy made the circular motion with his hand: stall the game to give the reliever more time to warm up. She and the catcher trotted slowly to the mound. She picked up the rosin bag, squeezed it a couple of times, then joined in on the tail end of the conversation. As the catcher headed back to the plate, Amy decided to lighten it up a bit in hopes of easing Taylor's nerves.

"How's that new daughter of yours?" she asked.

He seemed surprised. "Ashley?"

"Yeah. Are she and your wife doing well?"

A smile tugged at his lips, and his face brightened at the question. "They're doing great."

"Good. That's good to hear." She backpedaled to her position. "Let's get these outs, Josh."

His expression transformed from joy to determination. He took his place on the mound, went back to work, and quickly got ahead of the Twins third-place hitter. The noise from the crowd began to swell with each pitch. The next pitch was a hard slider in on the hands. The hitter lined the ball on one hop to the shortstop. He quickly underhanded it to Rawls who leaped out of the way of the charging Twins runner and threw it to Amy. She stretched for the errant throw and caught in on a short hop in time for an inning-ending double play.

Amy heard Rawls's whoop over the cheers of the crowd.

"Way to pick it, Perry!" He patted Amy on the back with his glove on his way to the dugout.

Now, if they could grind out at least one run, she thought.

* * *

"God, I don't know how much more of this I can take." Stacy held her face in her hands.

"Here's hoping they end it here and take us out of our misery," Stephanie told her. "Get this inning going, Amy!"

It was the bottom of the ninth, and the score was still 2-2. The Twins closer, Enrique Suarez, was on the mound.

"Doesn't this guy throw over 100?" Kat asked Stacy.

"Yeah. One of the top closers in the game."

"I have a good feeling," Angela said, giving Kat a quick hug. "Amy will catch up with one of those one-hundred-mile-per-hour fastballs and get on base."

"I hope you're right, Mom."

* * *

Amy rubbed down her bat with pine tar. Nick stood next to her as Suarez warmed up.

"Jesus," she muttered as the catcher's mitt popped with each fastball.

"Don't try to do too much, Perry. Let his fastball do the work. Poke your bat at it, and it should fly."

Amy laughed without humor. "If I can see it, I'll do my best."

"Get on, and I'll move you around."

She nodded as she headed to the plate. Again, this was one of those times when Servace didn't have a sign. He simply smacked his hands together in encouragement. She took a couple of practice swings, sucked in a deep breath, and settled into the box.

The first pitch zipped by her before she could even blink. She couldn't help glancing up on the scoreboard to see how fast it was: 101 miles per hour. Goddamn.

The next pitch was a slider down and in. She didn't understand why Suarez was even messing around with a pitch other than his fastball, but he had her guessing. She adjusted her gloves and dug back in.

Slider, she thought. She went with her gut instinct and geared up for the pitch. Another slider on the outside half of the plate. She caught the ball square and lined it deep into the right-center gap.

"Go! Go! Go!" Jeffries yelled at her even before her toe touched first.

Out of the corner of her eye, she saw the right fielder field the ball and hit the cutoff man, the second baseman. She slid headfirst, and her fingers curled around the bag as the shortstop smacked his glove on her back. The second base umpire called her safe. She raised her hand to call for time, stood up, and brushed off her uniform.

Nick practically stomped to the plate with his jaw set. Amy

could bet money that no matter what, he would hit the ball to the right side to move her to third and give her an opportunity to score with only one out.

He needs to catch up with Suarez's fastball, Amy thought. I suspect that's all he'll be throwing to Nick.

Nick seemed to be of the same mindset. He didn't wait to get behind in the count. He swung at the first pitch, a one-hundred-and-two-mile-per-hour fastball, and nubbed it off the end of his bat to the second baseman. Amy hustled over to third as the second baseman threw Nick out at first.

The roar of the crowd, which she'd thought was already deafening, seemed to ratchet up several more decibels.

As Roberts approached the plate, Servace put his arm around Amy who stood on the bag. He whispered, "jackrabbit" in her ear.

Holy shit. With one out in the bottom of the ninth and the World Series on the line, Murphy was calling for a suicide squeeze. But Roberts was the best bunter on the team. She focused on home plate. At that moment, it seemed so much farther than ninety feet away. She checked the outfielders who had moved in even closer. The infield was playing in, too. The only run that mattered was hers, and the Twins would do anything possible to cut her down.

Amy took her lead off third but did nothing to give away what had been called from the bench. One of the advantages she had was Suarez's big leg kick. She'd need all the help she could get. He gave her one last look before he turned his attention to the plate. He kicked his leg, brought his hands above his head, and fired the ball to home.

Amy broke toward the plate the instant his leg moved toward home. A slider, much easier to bunt than a one-hundred-mile-per-hour fastball. Roberts stuck out his bat and deadened the ball.

With each step from third to home, images from Amy's life flashed through her mind like a movie reel.

Her mom arguing with the manager to allow her to play on the boys baseball team.

Seventy feet to home.

Marge Tompkins talking to her about joining the Bandits.

Sixty feet.

Her first interview with Lisa Collins.

Forty feet.
Her first game as a Cincinnati Red.
Twenty feet.
Falling in love with Stacy.
Ten feet.
A baby on the way.
Slide!
Suarez pounced on the ball. From his knees, he flipped it toward home.

Amy slid her foot toward the back of the plate. The catcher slapped her ankle with his mitt. Bang-bang. The umpire's face hovered inches over the play. Her chest heaving for air, Amy waited for the call.

"Safe!"

The jubilant Reds team stormed onto the field to pummel her. She ducked to meet the onslaught and relished each thump. Was this the end of her career as the first woman player in major league baseball? Or would she return next season?

Amy grinned as Nick swallowed her in a bear hug. She shook off her inner turmoil and allowed herself to revel in the triumphant moment. This moment... right here, right now.

The Champs.

Photo credit: Patty Schramm

Author Chris Paynter with her father on September 11, 2010.

About the Author

Chris Paynter is the author of seven novels, including the *Playing for First* baseball series. Her *Survived by Her Longtime Companion* was a 2013 Lambda Literary Award Finalist and winner of the 2013 Ann Bannon Popular Choice Award. Her short stories have appeared in two anthologies: Regal Crest's *Women in Uniform: Medics and Soldiers and Cops, Oh My!* (2010) and Cleis Press's *Love Burns Bright: A Lifetime of Lesbian Romance* (2013). After earning a Bachelor's degree in journalism, Chris worked as a general assignment reporter and sportswriter until accepting her current position as the editorial specialist to a law journal. A sports junkie, you can find her screaming at the TV during a Colts game or living vicariously through her Cincinnati Reds. She resides in Indianapolis with her wife, Phyllis, and their beagle, Buddy the Wonder Dog, also fondly known as "He who must be obeyed." When not writing or editing books, Chris loves to get lost in a good romance.

Visit her website: www.ckpaynter.com
Email her at: ckpaynter@ckpaynter.com
Visit her Author Page on Facebook:
www.facebook.com/ChrisPaynterAuthor
Find her on Twitter: @ckpaynter

Make sure to check out these other Companion Publication titles by Chris Paynter:

To Love Free	978-1-942204-00-8
And a Time to Dance	978-1-942204-09-1
Survived by Her Longtime Companion	978-1-942204-07-7
Two for the Show	978-1-942204-05-3
Come Back to Me	978-1-942204-03-9
Playing for First	978-1-942204-01-5